Alphas

Printed in the United States of America: First Printing, 2022.
ISBN 978-1-7378376-4-0 (eBook)
ISBN 978-1-7378376-5-7 (paperback)

www.huckleberryrahrauthor.wordpress.com

Copy/Line Editor: Wes Imrisek
Developmental Editor: Angela Grimes
Cover Art: Getcovers.com
Formatting: R. L. Davennor

CHAPTER 1

"Ms. Stone, you're better than this!" The gruff, disappointed voice cut across the gym over the shouts of hundreds of students.

A ball flew over my head, barely missing my nose. Once my eyes uncrossed, I focused on the rafters above me and counted four balls stuck up there. I squinted. *Is that Owen's name on one of the balls? Ugh! I can't get away from him.*

Mr. Nelson's voice rang out again. "On your feet, Ms. Stone, if you don't want to go to jail!"

Shutting my eyes, I shook my head. My voice barely above a whisper, I said, "I think I'm better off staying down here." Apparently, it had been loud enough.

"Maybe, but you're a tripping hazard," Mr. Nelson snapped back.

Isn't he on the other side of the gymnasium?

I hadn't flopped on my back in gym since last March. Well, I *had*, but not nearly as much. And *this* time it was in front of the entire student body. Why some administrator had decided we should welcome winter break with a full school dodgeball game was beyond me. Upper classes versus lower classes. At least my side was winning. Probably not because of me.

Why does everyone love dodgeball?

Most of the students were having fun. I could smell their excitement. Some of them had perverse glee at being able to wallop fellow schoolmates with balls. Then, there was the general anticipation of the holidays and kids hyped up on sugar.

A pair of hands waved in my face. I lifted my arms and two of my best friends pulled me up, both laughing. Bevin handed me a yellow ball; he held in his laughter better than Sarah. "Come on champ, you can do this."

We stood in the back of the upper class field. Behind us was the jail with the underclass students who had gotten tagged out. We felt safe from getting hit, standing this far back. Leaning against Bevin, I checked out the rest of the area. Sarah, already back at it, danced across our side, scooping up balls and pegging underclass folk. She was amazing.

Sarah had been a star athlete her whole life. She excelled at these games. While I understood the classroom and how to be studious, she was the captain of multiple school teams. Her challenge as a werepanther lay in not being too fantastic. She tried to avoid being recruited onto more teams.

In many ways, Bevin shone in the classroom, like me. While Sarah and I were werepanthers, Bevin was still a norm. That being said, he was holding his own on this field of battle. Unlike me, he had a good arm. He had pegged a few kids. I had thrown some balls. Some had even made it across the line.

Piper, my girlfriend, sat in "jail." She'd been pegged less than a minute into the game. When I looked over at her, her arms were wrapped around her middle as she laughed at me.

I accepted the yellow ball Bevin handed me and took aim at the mobs of freshmen and sophomores. I threw it with all my skill and miraculously struck someone. I don't know who was more shocked. A ball came whizzing towards me and I leapt out of the way. I tried to do it human fast, not wereanimal fast. I didn't want to be too obvious.

I had two wereanimals in me: a wolf, and a panther. They gave me superhuman abilities. So long as I paid some attention, I shouldn't get hit with a ball. I was fast, I could jump, and in animal form I was sleek. What I wasn't in any form was athletic. I couldn't catch or throw a ball. I checked for incoming balls as I scooped up a green one by my foot. Surveying the underclass students, I took aim, and threw…and it hit the ground well before reaching their side of the gym.

Someone's laughter cut through the noise of the squeals, shrieks, and sneaker squeaks of the other players.

Three balls came whizzing towards me. Duck, turn, spin, and jump. I trotted over and picked up two balls, a blue one and a green one. I threw the blue one. It made it across the line and…nothing. I squinted, took aim at a thick group of students, and threw the green ball.

The ball whizzed into the throng of students; it was about to hit one of them in the head. At the last second, a hand whipped out and Estrella, a freshman girl I knew, caught the ball. My jaw dropped as my body nearly flopped double in disbelief.

"You're out, Jade! Get your butt in jail!" she yelled, as she flipped her perfect ponytail. Estrella's older brother, José, was a werewolf. Last year, he was one of the members of my clique. I missed having him around, but knew he was killing it in college.

Sarah passed me with a chuckle. "Don't worry, I'll get her for you. Panther pride, sister."

Laughing, I headed to the edge of the field of play and inched along the perimeter of the gymnasium—the only room big enough to house this many students throwing balls—and slowly shuffled to the back. As I went, I watched the game. Just because I was out didn't mean a ball wouldn't come flying out of nowhere and knock me back on my butt.

Halfway to the back of the gym I realized I had chosen my path poorly. Mr. Nelson stood between me and jail. I had been avoiding him since my sophomore year when he had been my gym teacher. He and I had never seen eye to eye. He *loved* my brother and his star athletic qualities and seemed to be habitually disappointed in my lack of similar capabilities.

This year, instead of Mr. Nelson, Ms. Coff had the pleasure of daily gym punishment. Fresh from college, she oozed enthusiasm to get everyone excited for fitness. Since Owen had left for college before she arrived, she didn't know him, and treated me as she did any other student.

I stared at Mr. Nelson and thought about turning around to circumnavigate the gym. He focused on the action and probably wouldn't notice. Shifting my weight to my back foot, I prepared to change direction when he rumbled, "Hurry up, Ms. Stone, get into jail."

Pausing, I dropped my chin to my chest in defeat. Now I would have to walk past him no matter what. My only decision was whether to cross in front of him, and catch his notice again, or sneak behind him and crawl over all the ball bags. I chose the former. He grabbed my arm to stop me.

Frozen in place, I missed what he said. The panther in me, who loved finding other wereanimals, screamed at me.

As an epsilon werewolf, I had a unique relationship with my animals, which included being able to communicate with them directly. Recently, I learned one of my abilities included classifying wereanimals by touch. To my animals, especially my panther who loved games, determining wereanimals in others excited them. And right now, they were telling me loud and clear that Mr. Nelson was a wereanimal.

Dad had convinced me to hone the ability to sense wereanimals in others only a few of months earlier because I couldn't always trust my nose to tell me when there were other wereanimals around. I tried to determine what type of animal Mr. Nelson had. My panther couldn't place him; it wasn't a panther, or a wolf. I took a sniff. I couldn't smell any animal. *What is he?*

"What are you?" I mumbled.

No! Did I say that out loud?

Mr. Nelson froze, and his grip on my arm became like iron. "What did you ask me?"

My mind went blank. I looked up at him, my breath ragged. "Can I be excused to the bathroom?"

His eyes grew steely, and his voice was low, almost a whisper. "Ms. Stone, I asked you to repeat yourself. What did you ask me?" If I wasn't a wereanimal, I wouldn't have been able to hear him. His grip squeezed tight enough it felt like he hit bone. I could pull away if I were willing to make a scene, but I wasn't.

Taking a breath, I tried to slow my system to find my

center. This was difficult with his hand squeezing my arm so tightly. Another one of my epsilon wolf tricks was my ability to calm other wereanimals. I needed to find my center, if I didn't have it, I couldn't share it, spread it to him. With a gasp, his grip loosened. It was enough.

I broke free and ran.

CHAPTER 2

I sat down next to Piper to watch the end of the game. About half the players sat in jail, and those remaining were out there to win.

Though both sides boasted good players, the star overall was Sarah. She gracefully navigated our side, evading attacks and targeting the other side with precision and grace. No ball could touch her and every ball she threw hit its mark. A group of seven or eight underclassmen grouped together to take her out. Two seniors created a wall in sacrifice to save her. It was spectacular.

"What did Mr. Nelson say to you?"

Sarah bowed her body in a C shape to avoid a ball and then grabbed two balls to throw back at her assailant. Bevin and a few other seniors scooped up balls just as fast and targeted students across the field.

"Huh?"

"Mr. Nelson, when you were coming over here. What did he say to you? I saw him grab your arm."

I started to turn to Piper, but then Bevin yelled, "Now!" I snapped around to watch the action.

Suddenly, a group of fifteen upper class students all whipped balls down the line together. They'd each taken up two or three balls and did a rapid-fire attack, depleting the balls on their side to almost nothing. Thirty to forty balls took out over half the underclass students. It was a devastating campaign—and Bevin had been the leader, of course! He excelled at that sort of thing; people always listened to him and followed him.

I shot Piper a quick glance before the drama overtook my concentration again. "Right, Mr. Nelson." Dread tensed my gut. I wasn't ready to share. "He just expects more from me. You know, the usual." The room vibrated with the screams and jeers of the students. However, it wasn't the right time or place to discuss wereanimals.

The freshmen and sophomores in front were disorganized and I smirked at the chaos Bevin's plans had wrought on the younger students. They just grabbed and threw balls at will. Estrella, popular and structured, tried to get something together, but she wasn't Bevin. As a senior, Bevin had an air of confidence that made people want to follow his lead. Estrella, a mere freshman, had potential, but it wasn't enough.

I saw the gleam of Bevin's smile as he circled his side of the room again.

Tapping Piper's arm, I bounced. "Piper, he's doing it again. Bevin's going to do it again!"

Sarah ran across the field with an armload of balls, picking off key students. All the underclass students watched her. They started to take aim.

At a key moment, Bevin boomed, "Now!"

The balls pelted down on the freshmen and sophomores like rain. I held my breath. One of the balls hit Estrella. I leapt up and hooted. She whipped around and tried to bean me with the ball she was holding. I veered out of the way just in time. However, the jail was too packed with students, and I lost my footing, landing on Piper. I laughed; I laughed so hard I couldn't stop.

Piper stared down at me, smiling. She gave me a quick kiss before I could control my mirth enough to straighten up and get back to the game.

After the two brilliant, organized attacks, the triumph of the upper class came fast. After their victory, Sarah disappeared in a group, overrun with half the juniors and seniors. I ran over to Bevin. "That was amazing. *You* were amazing!" I gave him a big hug.

Laughing, he hugged me back. "Thanks."

"Look, I know we were going to head out together, but can we just meet at the meeting? I'll explain later." His disappointment bubbled from him. I held his hands as he gazed at me.

I could smell his confusion and frustration. He didn't like going to these meetings alone. He used to go with José, but now that wasn't an option, with José in college. "Sure. But you'll tell me later what's up." It wasn't a question.

I started for the back door when I heard, "Ms. Stone, to my office."

Bevin's hand shot out to stop me. "Do you even have Mr. Nelson for class this year?"

I shook my head. "No, and that's who I was trying to avoid."

"Well, looks like you fail in gym class twice today."

I punched him in the arm. "You are not helping."

He gave me a big smile and waggled his eyebrows. "Who said I was trying?"

"Ms. Stone. Now!"

Sighing, I headed for the gym office, grabbing my coat and bag as I passed them. I threw my bag over my shoulder. Mr. Nelson led the way out of the gym through the hallway entrance, the door via the gym was too crowded with celebrating students. The hallway was empty by the offices the last hour of the day before winter break.

I entered his office. The tiny room held two desks. Both

were old, green metal beasts that had probably been around since the dawn of time. His was messy, covered with papers, charts, and clipboards. Though cluttered, I felt that there was a strange organization to Ms. Coff's desk.

He pointed to a chair, and I sat.

He took the seat opposite me, put his elbows on his desk, chin on his fists, and just stared at me. I stared back. After a few minutes, I started to survey the room, uncomfortable with his scrutiny.

His voice pulled me out of my investigation. "What are you, Ms. Stone?"

My brows rose and I smiled at him. My heart leapt into my throat, and I stopped breathing for a moment, scrambling for an answer. I tried to take a calming breath, but my pulse wouldn't listen. "Excuse me?"

"You heard me. What are you?"

I shook my head slightly. "I don't think I understand the question, Mr. Nelson."

"Oh, you understand it. You understood it when you asked it of me, and you understand it now when I ask it of you. So, tell me. What are you?" He smelled dangerous. It was the first scent I'd been able to pull from him, and it shocked me.

I pursed my lips and shook my head again. "You first."

He lifted his head and sneered at me with a half-smile. "You know, you and your brother have always smelled off. But you more so than Owen. I've always wondered about you. Your brother is a wolf. He doesn't try to hide it. Sarah, she isn't a wolf. A cat maybe? Which is odd in Wisconsin; but I noticed her smell change after spring break, so I'm guessing she went somewhere else. But then there's you."

He dropped his hands and leaned back in his chair. "I don't know what you are, Ms. Stone."

"That makes two of us, Mr. Nelson. And how come you don't smell like anything? You obviously can smell us."

At that, his stern demeanor finally broke, and he laughed. "Sarah was brilliant out there today, wasn't she? You should be like her. Why do you always end up falling on your butt in class? You are a werecreature. I don't know which one yet, but you should be lithe and limber, not clumsy and awkward."

My head fell back, and I shut my eyes, searching inwardly for inspiration. "I've never been athletic, Mr. Nelson." I rubbed my face in frustration. "And when I was in your class, I was just a normal girl who you terrorized… up until spring break, that is."

"You never smelled normal. Always something of the forest with you."

I looked at him and shrugged. "Well, I was what I was. Now I can run. I can jump. I can even leap pretty far. But I can't throw a ball. I'm better at some things, but I'm still no athlete. We'll leave the athletics to my superiors, like Owen and Sarah, and just about any norm out there."

"Well, ain't that the truth."

I snorted. "But that doesn't answer my question from the gym; what are you?"

He gave me a half-smile. "You can't tell?"

"Nope. I know you aren't a wolf or a panther. That's all I can tell."

He nodded, eyes narrowing as if letting the puzzle pieces fall into place. "Panther…. How did you know I was anything at all?"

I sighed. "Have you heard of an epsilon wolf?"

His eyes widened. "Yeah. But only as a myth."

I extended my arms out to the sides and bowed my head. "Well, now you've met the myth."

"Is that why you've always smelled so…weird?"

I harrumphed. "That's part of it. That's why I could calm you down enough to get away. The weird is also because I have two animals: wolf and panther. So, now you know my secrets, Mr. Nelson. Your turn."

A weird expression took over Mr. Nelson's face, it took me a few second to realize it was a smile. "Wolf and panther. Epsilon wolf. Fair trade. Nice to meet you, Ms. Stone. I'm a werebear."

CHAPTER 3

I left Mr. Nelson's office about an hour later. Before I shared more information, we had called my parents in a conference call to determine a path forward. Outside the gym office, I ran into Sarah. I spun a circle in the hall checking to see who else was around. "What are you doing here?" I asked her.

She just stared. "Really? You disappear with your least favorite teacher after an epic win, and you think I'm just going to head off for winter break?"

I checked out Mr. Nelson's office but didn't hear anything. When I left, he had been packing up to leave as well. I sniffed and didn't smell him around.

Sarah's eyebrow went up. "Talk." It was a demand. I felt the pull of my alpha.

I grabbed her arm and dragged her down the hall. Just because I couldn't smell him didn't mean much. Apparently, the bears had tricks of their own, and masking scents was one of them. When I got to the women's bathroom, I pushed her in.

Sarah shook her head as she gave me a placating look. "Paranoid much?"

"If you only knew," I mumbled.

"Exactly, if I only knew. Now, what do I need to know?"

I walked down the aisle, opening doors to make sure we were really alone. I turned and saw Sarah tapping her nose. "I know it stinks in here, but we have ways that are a bit quicker."

I scooted to the counter and bounced up, so I sat on it, back to the mirror. "Well, alpha mine, Mr. Nelson knows you're a cat."

Sarah's heart rate sped up. I could sense her forcing it to slow. "What?"

"Yep, he smelled it on you last spring. It's why he gave you the paperwork for track but then didn't follow through with the track team pitch. He saw your brilliance, but then smelled your change. He knew it would be too much for you."

"Too much for me? Jerk! I could've done it. I just didn't *want* to do it."

I snorted. "Last spring? No, you couldn't've. There was *way* too much going on. You probably could this year if you wanted to."

"Would you do it with me?"

My mirth fled and my face muscles slacken. "Wha…?" My mind went blank.

Fingers snapped in front of my face. "Earth to Jade, this isn't a big thing. Join track with me."

"But I'm not athletic."

Her eyes got distant. "But you can run and jump. You could be amazing." She started bouncing on her toes and then switched to pacing the length of the bathroom. "Think of it. You need to add something non-academic to your transcript for college applications. This would be perfect."

I groaned as my shoulders drooped. "But sports. Sarah, that sounds awful."

She whipped around. "No, it sounds great." She started tapping her fingers in the air as she thought about it. "Mr. Nelson is a were—were-what exactly?"

I'd almost forgotten what had started this conversation. "Bear."

"No way. Really? That's…I don't know what that is. Do your parents know?"

"Yeah, we called them as soon as we started to talk. I figured they would have to know before I said too much. We couldn't say much over the phone, but I got the go-ahead to talk to Mr. Nelson. They now know something is going on. Mr. Nelson will probably come over this weekend to talk to them."

Sarah laughed. "I bet he's pissed. He kept his secret for how long? Then you come along and out him. This is gold. Anyway, he's the coach. He can work with us. We can win, but not by too much."

I groaned. Sarah eyed me suspiciously. "What?"

"You do know this means we'll have *two* training programs going on at the same time, don't you?"

She froze for just a second before continuing her pacing. "Well, hell."

My dad started all new wereanimals on a physical training program after the change. He did it to help us stay safe. After my initial transformation into a panther, I was attacked by a pack werewolf and didn't know how to protect myself. Dad found the situation unacceptable and immediately began a second career as my personal trainer. Within a few days there were clipboards, whiteboards, and expectations. They sucked, but we were all safer for them.

Sarah stopped her pacing as her face lit up. "Did you just agree to join the track team?"

I groaned knowing a losing battle when I was in one.

A few minutes later, Sarah walked with me to find Bevin at the GSA meeting where I agreed to not leave him alone. We ran into Piper along the way.

I gave her a hug. "I thought you'd've left by now."

"Mom's picking me up in a minute." She slung her bag

on her back and secured her locker.

"Have fun with the grandparents," I said.

She groaned. "I will, but I'll miss you. I can't believe I'm going away for two weeks." Pausing, she smiled. "It's good, though. Going away and coming back, that's new… it's good."

We hugged once more. I gave her a quick kiss before she ran off.

I turned to Sarah. "Don't you have to leave, too? Your flight is tonight, isn't it?"

She checked her watch. "Yeah. I was hoping to say bye to Bevin, but you're right, I'm going to be late. Hawaii waits for no one." She gave me a tight squeeze. "See you next year!"

I finally made it to the meeting. Bevin sat alone at a table, pouting. "Where have you been? You're late!"

School was out, winter break officially had started. The 'meeting' was more of a social event. Along the back wall stood a long table with food and drinks. Decorations covered everything and everyone in rainbows and inclusive signs. I liked it.

I threw my bag on the table and plopped down next to him. I checked out the other students in the room; there were about a dozen of them. "What gives? There are plenty of people here. You don't need me here. And you know where I was…"

He sighed. "I know, it's just been hard since I don't have

José to come to these meetings with me. Not to mention, since you're now out, why aren't you a regular? It *is* the gay/straight alliance. You should've been coming all along."

"I know. I'm an awful friend. I just knew it was your thing; yours and José's. I'm here now. I really don't know anyone here, do you?"

"Yeah, a few. But not well."

"How was your meeting with Mr. Nelson?"

"You wouldn't believe me if I told you."

Bevin raised an eyebrow. "Oh?"

I leaned in close and whispered. "He's a wereanimal."

Bevin's eyes widened and his mouth opened into an 'O.' He lowered his voice, too. "Really? Like a werewolf? How come you didn't figure this out earlier?"

I huffed. "He has a way to mask his scent. It's a bodywash that neutralizes smells. He said he would tell my parents about it when he meets them over break."

"He's going to meet them?"

"Well, he doesn't have a choice now, does he? I know about him, so they know."

Bevin's face blossomed into a huge smile. "I bet that chaps his hide. Bet he's been hiding in plain sight all these years, and then you come into the picture and *bam*! His hiding is done. It was when he grabbed your arm, wasn't it?"

I nodded, once again impressed by Bevin's observation skills. "Yeah, my panther went wild because he isn't a wolf or a panther. She didn't know how to classify him."

"Serves him right. He should've left you alone. Well, then, what is he?"

I waggled my eyebrows, my smile widening. "Are you ready for this? Do you want to guess? Think about him, what would your first guess be?"

Bevin's sapphire blue eyes, stunning on most days, began to dance. "No way! He isn't! A…bear?"

"Right in one."

We both laughed. This had been our ongoing joke for years. Others in the room stared at us.

Once I got myself under control I asked, "Want a drink?"

Bevin nodded. I got up to gather each of us a soda. At the table, a kid, a guy I barely recognized, laid his hand on my arm. "Hey, you're Jade, right?"

I stared at him, scrunching up my face in concentration. I knew him. I glanced at the ceiling for inspiration and then back down to him. "Yeah, that's me. You're…Phillip, right?"

His whole body changed. He had been holding back, blending into the background, but when I named him, his smile lit up our corner of the room. His gray eyes took on a bit of the blue from his shirt and he seemed to stand taller. "You know me!"

"Aren't you in my math class?"

"I am. AP bio and physics as well. You may not have noticed because you and Bevin are always distracting each other." He laughed quietly.

I snorted, then slapped my hands over my mouth. I

nodded, laughing softly at myself as I dropped my hands. "That's true. So, what's up?"

He blushed, face warming to a red to match the room's festive decor. "Well, I was wondering…umm, well, I…phew, this is harder than I thought."

I eyed him suspiciously. "Now, you know I like girls. I think everyone here knows that by now. So, you aren't trying to ask me out, so this shouldn't be that hard." I leaned in close, then shot my focus over my shoulder at Bevin, returning it to Phillip. "Bevin?"

Phillip's face burned a deeper red. He backed away and started to leave.

"Wait. Don't go."

He paused and looked back. "I just…this was a mistake."

"Do you want to talk with Bevin? Maybe ask *him* out?"

Phillip froze. I would have been worried if I couldn't hear his heart beating and see the slight movement of his shirt as he breathed. The smell of his interest flowed out of him like a flower bouquet.

Gathering the two cans of sodas, I went around the table and took his hand. I dragged him over to where Bevin was waiting for me. Bevin gave me a questioning look, brows coming together.

Placing the sodas on the table, I asked, "You know Phillip?"

"Well, he's in our bio class. He was in our science class last year as well. He's hard to miss. Almost as smart as you, smarty-pants."

Rolling my eyes, I dropped down onto the bench across from Bevin. Of course he knew Phillip. As Bevin showed he knew who Phillip was, I could feel the new kid relax. His breathing slowed, and I saw his muscles loosen. I let go of his hand and opened up my soda.

Phillip smiled at Bevin. "That was awesome what you did today during dodgeball. I can't believe you got everyone organized like that. You are such an amazing leader!"

Bevin chuckled. "Sarah—you know, the flashy one— she and I discussed it over lunch today. If we could get everyone together, we knew we could win."

My jaw dropped. "Wait. What? Where was I? Why wasn't I part of the plan?"

"Oh, you were. We knew we had to wait until you were in dodgeball jail. There was no way you could be part of the offense." He waited for my huff of indignation. "Your attack would just mess everyone up. That was actually our signal as to when to start the plan."

Oh, I wanted to knock that smile off his face!

Phillip laughed and sat down next to us.

I watched how comfortable he was sitting next to Bevin. His breathing slowed and his smile grew. "So, you two have many classes together?" I asked.

Phillip nodded. "Several. I'm a senior, like Bevin. We've had classes together for years. We were partnered up in science a lot in middle school." He shot a look at Bevin then back to me. "Actually, until *you* showed up, we were usually partnered up and given challenge problems."

Bevin chuckled. "He's not wrong. Phillip and I were given the problems that you and I are now blessed with."

Bevin's finger tapped on the table as he counted back. He was obviously thinking about all the projects they had done together. "Phillip, do you remember in seventh grade when we had to make that volcano and we put too much food coloring in it? Your mom wanted to kill us when we dyed her kitchen green!"

They both laughed.

Phillip stared off into space, a smile on his face. He slowly moved one of his hands, so it just touched Bevin's. "Mom still reminds me of that. She'll ask for the green cutting board…it was white when we first got it."

I laughed with them about the story. Bevin glanced down and his eyes widened when he noticed his and Phillip's hands were touching.

Phillip got quiet for a second and gazed down at his hands. He looked up at Bevin and took a huge breath. "Bevin, I have…I was wondering…I…" He looked at me. I wasn't sure if he wanted me to help or to leave.

"Should I go? I could go get us some cookies."

Phillip paled and the scent of his fear peppered the area, but he nodded.

I got up and patted Bevin on his shoulder. He just gave me a dumbfounded gaze. He was completely lost.

I walked over to the cookie table, which was far enough

for human privacy, but, as a werepanther, I could still hear them. I turned to the side, giving the illusion of privacy. *Bad Jade!*

"What's up Phillip, everything okay?" Bevin sounded concerned. I noticed their fingers were still touching.

"Yeah. I just…I was…well…" Phillip took a deep breath and spoke the next few words at top speed. "I was wondering if you'd like to go out with me, maybe to a movie?"

I peeked over and saw him drop his gaze to his lap then force himself to look back up at Bevin. Bevin, for his part, seemed stunned. I wasn't even sure if he was breathing.

Phillip saw the expression and misinterpreted it. He snatched his hand back. "Oh, well, never mind." He started to get up.

Bevin reached for Phillip's hand. "Wait, no, don't go. I mean, yes. I would like that."

Smiling, I gathered some cookies. I turned to see them talking quietly together, hands still clasped. "Is it safe to come back?"

Their heads popped up like prairie dogs and they nodded. I chuckled and returned to the table with the treats.

CHAPTER 4

I grabbed a slice of meaty pizza and took a huge bite, moaning in pleasure. Pebble giggled next to me as she finished off her first slice. Hers had pineapple and ham. Controversial, but good.

Before I could take another bite, the front door crashed open. "I'm home! Did'ja miss me?" There was a dragging sound and thump before Owen skipped into the dining room, plopping down across from me.

Closing his eyes, he took a deep breath, then snatched three slices of pie. He held them up for a moment before realizing he had nowhere to put them. Mom, Dad, and I just stared, unmoved. Pebble, on the other hand, smiled, hopped down, and found him a plate.

He dropped his food trove and gave her a quick kiss atop her head. "At least someone cares."

I snorted and continued to eat.

Mom put down her glass of wine. "So, he has no scent at all?"

I shook my head and tried to swallow my last big bite. "None. Even sitting in his office for an hour—torture by the way…nothing."

Dad cocked his head. "Bet you're glad of your training now." He took a drink from his beer. "Did he tell you how he managed it?"

"He said it's a bear secret." At my parents' looks of disgust I raised my hands. "Don't worry, I didn't leave it there. You know me, I pushed."

Owen snorted. I glared at him and half-stuck out my tongue.

"Anyway, he said there was a body soap and deodorant someone in his sleuth manufactures that deadens scent. He also said he'd come over this weekend to discuss more with you."

Owen's eyes narrowed. "Sleuth? Like a detective?"

We all ignored him.

Mom finished off her pizza and leaned back, crossing her legs. "Did he say why he's never stopped by before?"

"Yeah, he said he was trying to stay hidden."

Owen finally had too much. He'd eaten two slices and finished off a cup of soda. "Okay, what are y'all talking about? Who's coming over this weekend? And who's the sleuth?"

All our heads swung to him. Then I faced Mom. "He knew exactly when both Owen and I had turned. I don't know that his nose is as good as ours, but it's at least *that* good."

Owen banged his fists against the table. "Who? Who are you talking about?"

Dad stared at him then let out a breath. "Your old gym teacher. Apparently, he's been hiding in plain sight. He grabbed Jade's arm today, and, well, the cat's out of the bag."

Owen's eyes grew. "Mr. Nelson's a werepanther?"

I snorted. "No. Think about the man; what animal does he look like?"

Owen's face scrunched up in concentration. I swore I could see smoke billowing from his ears. I was afraid he would hurt himself.

I sighed. "He's a werebear. A group of bears is called a sleuth. Wow; you okay over there? Did ya hurt yourself?"

"Bear? There are werebears?" Owen's head snapped to Mom. "What other creatures are out there? What have you been hiding from us?"

Mom massaged her temples, letting her head rest on the back of her chair. "I don't know. When I was a kid there were stories of all types of animals. But they were just that, stories. No one knew anything for certain."

I turned to Owen. "Mr. Nelson seemed to know more.

He knew what an epsilon wolf was. He thought it was a myth, but the concept wasn't new to him."

"But he didn't know that you could out him with just a touch?"

A smile spread across my face. "Nope."

I turned to Pebble. "Want more pizza?"

"No. Can I go watch TV?"

Dad looked at his watch. "You can watch for forty-five minutes, then it's time to brush your teeth and go to bed, pipsqueak."

She jumped down, gathered her plate and glass, and took them to the kitchen. She was down in the basement watching her favorite cartoon in no time flat.

I smiled at Owen. I hadn't seen him since Thanksgiving. "Did you pass all your classes?"

He groaned. "Finals suck."

My eyes narrowed. "What does that mean?"

"It means I think I did, but final grades don't come out until next Tuesday. I'll tell you then."

Mom gave him a warm smile. "What was the best thing about college?"

"The people. Except…everyone kept coming up to me and telling me their issues. I mean, I tried to help, and I think I did in a few cases, but it was weird."

My brows came together, and I gaped at him. He looked like my brother, he smelled like my brother, but helping random people? That didn't sound like Owen.

Mom and Dad leaned forward. Dad broke the silence. "Was it just people you knew from the dorms and classes?"

Owen shook his head. "It started off that way, but then people would approach me during meals, people I barely knew. They'd just join me and halfway through the meal they'd be telling me their deepest secrets."

He put down his soda and looked at me. "You know, I've seen people do this to you, but I never thought it would happen to me."

I snorted. "Welcome to my world. Did you mind helping? Did the intrusions bother you?"

Owen paused and looked up into the corner of the dining room in thought. After a bit, he grabbed another slice of pizza, but before he took a bite, he answered. "You know, it didn't. When I could find an answer, it felt good. When I couldn't, I usually figured out a place to direct them for help, which also felt good."

Mom smiled. "You know, Owen, you're undecided right now. I know you were thinking about going into some sort of training, maybe education, but did you ever think about psychology?"

He froze and looked at her with a desperate look, eyes wide, heart rate up. "No. Why?"

Saturday morning, I was up before anyone else, the pack gym all to myself. I stood there readying myself for the day. With a mental push, I was off. After a fifteen-minute warmup run, I gazed at the whiteboard trying to determine my next move. Today's torture was cardio. I debated between running some more or attempting a guided exercise program. Knowing my limits, I tended to avoid organized exercise but a switch in routine could be fun.

I went over to one of the side rooms and switched on the TV. Selecting YouTube, I found a forty-five-minute HIIT routine that combined weights and movement. I thought about skipping the fifteen-minute warm-up, but it was winter break and I had nothing better to do. No one was around to witness me flailing around and my eventual failures, so what could it hurt?

I started up the routine. The warm-up went well; basic motions, marching and squats, nothing too complicated. Then the main workout began. At a few spots I had to stop, lean forward, and really watch to figure out what the leader was doing. Cocking my head to the side, I pondered whether her movements were possible.

At times I stopped, rewound, and had to start a part over because I had spent the time learning and not doing. In the middle of a routine, we had to kick, chain-step, roll our arms, and…*what is she doing?* Then I kicked my supporting leg out from under me. *Ouch!*

And…I landed on my back.

"That's great, one more time…" she said with her super hyper appeal.

I groaned, noticing we didn't have support beams with balls caught in them in *our* ceiling, like at school. Maybe I should get Pebble to do some artwork, so I had something to look at when I fell.

I was about to get up when the door opened. "Ms. Stone, I did not expect to see you in the same position here as at school."

I flopped my arm over my eyes and let out a whine. *Why is he here?*

"Great job, everyone, time for the cool down," the excited voice in the video continued.

I wanted to cry.

"Looks like you're already cooling down," Mr. Nelson remarked.

I let out the breath I was holding, counted to ten, and then sat up. "Hi, Mr. Nelson. To what do I owe this unexpected surprise?" Dad stood behind him trying not to laugh.

I glared at him and huffed as I got to my feet and turned off the TV. As I moved around the room, I realized I could smell bear. I spun to Mr. Nelson and stared at him. "Bear?"

"I figured since I was coming here today, there was no reason to waste good product on people who knew. Yes, this is what my animal smells like."

"Huh. Can I shake your hand?"

His brows dipped for a second in confusion, but then his face cleared with comprehension. He reached out and let me shake his hand. Panther poked her nose out and sniffed. The handshake only lasted a few seconds, but it was long enough for her to read him. I let go. "Thanks."

I turned to Dad. "I wish I knew he was coming this early, I'd've chosen to run. Anyway, I think I'll go shower."

Mr. Nelson clasped my arm in his hand. "Wait. I have to see. How fast can *you* run?"

In response, I snickered. I was tired, but this was something I could do. Mr. Nelson had seen a lot of my failures. It may be nice to show off a bit. I shrugged. "Fast enough."

Dad's mouth twitched a few times as we made our way into the main gym area. "Jade has shown improvement over the last few months." His voice was flat as he gave his assessment.

I headed to the track, but before I started, Owen appeared from the stairway, eyes glued to his phone.

I smirked. "I'll run, but he runs with me."

Owen's head popped up. He saw the three of us standing here. He smiled widely; he always loved gym class. "Hi, Mr. Nelson. Did I hear something about a run? Wait until you see Jade, she can smoke even me…. Is that bear I smell?"

Dad seemed satisfied. "Perfect. Ten minutes. Can you get three miles?"

Mr. Nelson's eyes got a calculating look. His face took on an expression somewhere between challenge and disbelief.

My jaw started to drop and then I narrowed my eyes. "Nope. But I can get close."

Owen laughed. The two of us took off, not holding back. Mr. Nelson watched, the look of pride on his face matching Dad's.

Ugh, the idea of having two trainers made my skin itch.

CHAPTER 5

A few days before New Year's Eve, Owen decided he wanted to learn how to shift between animals. I had been practicing. I decided to focus on going from wolf to panther. Panther was my easier form, so the shift didn't end in me passing out. I had managed the shift three times now, and the third time I hadn't fallen over when I was done.

Owen wanted to go the same way. Panther wasn't as easy for him, but in panther form he ran faster and jumped higher. All in all, it was a better escape form.

José was visiting, hanging out, and avoiding his sister who had a group of her friends over. A house full of freshmen girls would be too much for anyone.

We headed out to the backyard. Owen and I shifted to our wolves and took a quick run out into the woods to stretch our muscles. When we returned, Dad had a few steaks ready and a bucket of water. *Ugh, dead meat.*

Dad took out his clipboard. "Okay, Jade, you made the transition in just under five minutes last time. You *are* getting quicker. I would like you to transition and try to make it out to the river for a drink. If you can find your panther in under four minutes, I think this would be viable in the field."

I yipped my understanding. Spreading out my feet for stability, I focused on my paw, a trick I used to find my wolf. I imagined my petite wolf paw becoming my larger, more lethal panther paw. With my next exhale, I released my panther. The extra pain of going from wolf to panther never disappointed. I breathed through the bones moving and the fur retreating and regrowing. My face shifted. Muscles reformed. My body grew as I transformed from wolf to panther.

I trembled as I became the panther. I took a few steps, wobbly and uncertain. *Do. Not. Fall.*

"Chica. You look like a drunken sailor!" José snorted.

I shone my predator eyes on him and roared.

He laughed. "Very impressive. You gonna flop over now? Here kitty, kitty. You drunk on catnip?"

I chuffed, whipped my tail at him, and bounded off

towards the woods. My first landing was a bit wobbly, but I didn't fall. My heart pounded faster with my audacity at trying to leap, but I continued until I reached the water and drank from the icy river. The cold woke my senses. On my trot back, I felt stronger and steadier.

I stopped at the edge of the yard. Owen struggled to transform between wolf and panther. It looked rough. I watched the horror show named Owen in my backyard. *Goodness, is that what I look like during this transition? It's awful. No wonder Owen joked that the change alone would scare enemies away.* The fur retreated and grew. Bones cracked and reformed. His snout morphed. And it all happened in slow motion.

The time ticked away. His morphing didn't end. I sat and whined. Dad, who took notes, turned his head in my direction and nodded at me. He returned to writing things down while consulting the stopwatch.

Transfixed by my brother, I didn't notice José until he spoke, almost starling another roar from me. "Did your first attempt take this long?"

I nodded.

Squatting next to me, he put a hand on my back. The connection settled me. "This is terrifying. I know Owen has seen every one of your attempts. Why is he doing this to himself?"

I whined softly.

José patted my head. "I know, no fair; you can't answer.

It just won't end."

We couldn't tear our eyes away.

Eventually a dark brown panther lay on his side, panting, whining, and not moving. Dad called out, "Thirteen minutes, fifty-three seconds."

José and I made our way across the yard. I nosed Owen and he growled low in his chest. He raised his head an inch before flopping down and passing out.

I couldn't hide my pleasure. Finally, someone else was passing out. Dad and José sniffed.

José narrowed his eyes. "Chica, that's just low, even for you. Enjoying your brother's pain? Wow! I mean…wow!"

I bumped him with my shoulder in amusement.

Dad eyed me. "Can you get back to wolf?"

I stared at him intently. *No!*

His eyebrow raised as if he could hear me. There was no way he could, but he smiled hopefully.

I shook my head.

He shrugged. "Okay, well, back to human. We need to get Owen out of the cold…at least to the porch."

I chuffed out a sigh and moved to where my clothes were piled neatly. Soon my humanity flowed over me, and the cool air became very apparent. The shift took a bit longer than usual; I was tired from wearing each and every one of my skins. By the time I was done and dressed, Owen was nicely situated on the porch.

The three of us headed in for hot chocolate.

Dad looked over his notes. "I think you should practice a couple more times before school starts. Then I'll put this on a once-a-week rotation. Every third week I want you to go panther to wolf. I'm not exactly sure of when this will be useful, but we may as well cover our bases."

"Will it be on Aunt Allison days, when we're training with others from the pack?"

"Not a bad idea."

I nodded. I knew where fighting Dad on his ideas got me. "What about Owen?"

"I'll have him practicing every other day until he heads back to campus as well. Hopefully he'll get his time into the single digits."

"And not pass out like the college student he is," José mumbled into his mug.

I snorted and Dad sighed.

I jumped up and searched the freezer for some frozen burritos. Finding them, I took two, placed them on a plate and took them out to the microwave. José asked, "How many of those are for me?"

I rolled my eyes and held up the entire box until he held up three fingers. Knowing what would happen next, I shifted my gaze to Dad. He cracked a smile and held up four. I took out seven more burritos. I put the first two in the microwave.

As if the smell were a summons, Owen stumbled in. "Food, want." And he threw himself on the bench seat of the kitchen table next to José.

Grumbling, I checked under the flap and counted five more in the box. There was no way the microwave could handle all those at once. I gave up and turned on the oven. While the burritos were baking, I brought out salsa and sour cream. I smiled at José. "I'm guessing this will not be up to your normal Mexican culinary standards."

Laughing, he said, "Chica, my Dad's burritos would make you cry in the pure delight of bean and cheese pleasure. And then you'd never be able to eat another freezer burrito again."

My mouth watered just thinking about it. "Dad, when is Alejandro next cooking for the pack?"

The oven timer beeped before he could answer. I brought out a pyramid of burrito goodness. Dad had gathered plates and forks. The four of us demolished the stack faster than it took Owen to shift from wolf to panther.

CHAPTER 6

Full moon night came in the middle of winter break while Sarah vacationed in Hawaii and Piper visited her grandma up north.

I finished up my morning run. José and Owen had joined me near the end. Their runs were not as long as mine, but they had more weight-training in their playbook. In a fight, my game-plan was to figure out how to disengage and run away. I had a few attacks I could implement, but running was my best strategy, which suited me fine.

Owen watched me over his shoulder. "What, no strength training?"

"Shower. Food. See you after you're done with this." I waved my hand at all the weights and drills written down for them.

Owen smiled and José groaned. José picked up two dumbbells and started doing bicep curls and squats in combination. Owen gave him a critical once over, nodding in approval, before grabbing his own weights.

I left before I got roped into doing more.

After my shower, I headed to the kitchen where I prepared coffee and waffles. While I mixed the batter, Dad joined me and cooked sausages. Slowly the kitchen filled with hungry werewolves, er, family members.

I sat on a counter stool since the table seats had been taken by José, Owen, Pebble, and my parents. I could've joined them, but it felt more peaceful where I sat.

I shut my eyes and let the sweet joy of real maple syrup take over for a few minutes. I'd added some fruit to the plate to show I could be healthy, but my fork kept hitting the waffle. Huh?

Finally, with my belly full of sweet goodness, I focused on the room at large. "Who's watching the kiddos tonight? Is anyone else besides Piper out of town?"

Dad consulted his phone. "Dillan, Bevin, and Estrella. Annie may be available. She's in for the holidays. Tyler took Lilly to visit her grandparents. He said he would be able to sneak off for a night run and we shouldn't worry."

After Tyler and his family had been attacked by the

rogue wolf, Tyler thought he'd have to give up his regular family. Once Dad understood his misconception, it was nice for Lilly to be able to spend the holidays being spoiled.

I nodded at that. "Sarah should be good. Panthers aren't actually called by the moon after the first few months. It came as a surprise to her after the first few moons called her to change, but then suddenly she realized it wasn't a necessity, but a choice. She just runs with us because it's exciting. I mean, at first the pull was there, but now she thinks she can skip the change."

Half the table had stopped eating and just stared at me in different levels of shock. Mom's eyes narrowed. Dad's fork stopped halfway to his mouth. José's mouth dropped open, and his hands went slack on the table. Only Owen and Pebble seemed unphased, munching away at their stacks of waffles.

Pebble had figured out that the less she reacted, the more she learned. She had become my secret sister-spy, gathering all sorts of intel for me. Owen probably already knew all about the werepanther-moon thing. He and Sarah were dating.

Dad cocked his head. "Do *you* need to shift?"

I closed my eyes to think about the question. My animals were there the help me gauge my need to shift. After my internal survey, I opened my eyes and nodded. "I think so. The wolf is strong enough that her needs must be met."

Dad nodded back at me, and everyone continued their meal.

I shifted my eyes to Pebble. "Hey, squirt, do you want to head out after breakfast and take a run?"

Her head shot up and a smile broke out across her face. "Can we?"

José reached out to take my hand and asked softly, "Can I join you?"

Owen smirked. "Of course, the four of us will take a joy run."

I shook my head and snorted. It wasn't the playful run I had imagined, but it would still be fun.

With four of us along, we could let Pebble take a longer run than normal. She went out at least once a month, but only with me. I usually had homework and chores, so we needed to cut the run short. Today was part of winter break—no requirement, no chores, a mini-pack around me—we could stretch our legs and go.

I stopped the boys after breakfast before they disappeared to Owen's room. "I think we should head down south along the bike path."

Owen's nose scrunched. I could smell his disgust at the idea. "People bike in this weather. Hell, they bike when it's snowing. The bike path isn't safe."

I threw up my hands, palms facing him. "No, that isn't what I meant. Not *on* the path, but there's a trail that runs alongside the bike path. It's through the woods, about ten to fifteen feet in, depending on where you are."

José's eyes narrowed. "Why do you know of this path?"

I knew the moment Owen figured it out. His mirth rolled off him. "It was the geese, wasn't it? That's how you got away."

A few months ago, I had been running in human form when a gaggle of geese attacked me. The only way to get away was to shift into panther form and leap into a tree above them. From there, I found the path and made my escape home. I didn't think I'd ever live that down. Since the incident, I'd been given a stuffed goose, geese pajamas, and new geese-print bedding. I was pretty sure my family was planning on plastering my room in geese.

Narrowing my eyes, I refused to confirm his suspicion. "It's a good path. We can run about forty to forty-five minutes south before turning back. Pebble hasn't had a good run since before school started. And you," I poked José in the chest, "haven't ever run during the day for fun." I smiled. "This will be great."

After a minute, they both nodded, and I could smell their pleasure at the plan. Pebble, who poked her head around the corner at the end of the hall, said, "Can we go yet?"

It didn't take long for us to get to the backyard and let our wolves out. José and I took the longest. José because he was relatively new, and me because I still had to focus to not become my panther. Once done, José's red wolf stood tall and proud, the most dominant of the four of us. Owen and Pebble were a matched gray set. And my black wolf meant we probably would look intimidating as we ran, though we'd stay out of sight.

The bike path was only a short trot away. From there, we found the game path and headed south.

About forty minutes later, we neared our turn-around point. The snow drifts on either side of the path reached six to eight inches high, but deer had already broken a trail making it easy to traverse. We smelled prey, but Pebble felt bad when we hurt the cute furry animals, so we had agreed beforehand not to hurt any of the small game.

We approached a bend in the path, and we let Pebble race ahead of us. She yipped in delight, stretching her legs, and leaping with joy. The wind at our back pushed us even faster. My elation turned to cold dread when I heard Pebble's happy yips turn to growls.

A human shrieked. "Is that a wolf?" Recognizing the voice, a low growl started deep in my chest. I dashed after Pebble.

"Oh, my God, Alyssa, don't move! Are there more of them? It looks so tiny. Is it a baby?"

I bounded around the corner and came to an abrupt stop. Three bundled up young women blocked the path, their phones pointed at Pebble. I knew all of them.

"Did you get it?" One of them started hitting another's arm.

"Look at that one, it's all black." The growl moved from

my chest to my throat. My lip peeled away from my teeth. Their phones all swung up and pointed at me as their eyes widened in fear. I glared up into the face of Brooke, Owen's ex-girlfriend. I thought she had moved out of state for college. But winter break brought people home.

My entire body vibrated as a snarl escaped me. Feet spread wide, I lowered my head and tensed, preparing for battle.

One of them, Tiffany, spoke in a shaky voice. "Brooke, Alyssa, don't move. I don't want to be attacked. I've read that if you run from wild animals, they chase you. They *are* wild animals." Since when was Tiffany the smart one? Her fear smelled almost sweet, like candy. No wonder animals attacked people who were afraid.

My growl grew louder.

Brooke rolled her eyes. Her fear scented the air, but she tried to act cool. "It's a small wolf and its mom or dad. There are three of us." Despite her bravado, I could see her hands shaking.

Before I could move, Owen and José stepped in front of me. All three girls lowered their phones and shuffled backward.

Tiffany let out another yelp. "Alyssa, there are two more. Look, that one is gray like the little one; maybe it's the mother. Can we be leave now?" Tiffany took another slow step back. Her fear blanketing the air smelled as lovely as hot chocolate in the morning.

I snorted laughter. In wolf form it sounded like a

sneeze. I could smell the amusement coming from José and the annoyance emanating from Owen.

Alyssa turned her head a bit but didn't stop watching us. "Tiffany, did you get pictures of all four? This will be a great addition to the school paper."

Tiffany, hands shaking, held up her phone once again. Her focus darted down for a second then back to us. "Can we go now? The paper's article is set."

Brooke huffed and tapped a foot. She crossed her arms over her chest. *Gods, I do not miss that.* When she'd graduated, I'd been happy to see her go. "Alyssa, I don't go to your school anymore. *I'm* in college. What do I care about your silly school paper?" Her scent was more peppery than sweet—fear and annoyance.

José managed to get between the girls and Pebble. He nudged her until she broke out of her immobilizing shock. She darted back up the trail, and we followed. The trio was lucky we were werewolves and not an actual wolf family protecting their young. Wild wolves probably would've attacked.

During our run home I was more cautious, but with the wind blowing into our noses, there were no more surprise encounters.

Once home, we leapt up into the treehouse so Pebble could rest. After her nap she would run and play with other pack members and their kids. Full moon day tended to be fun for her. We were trying to make sure she stayed innocent despite her early transition to werewolf. We hoped that if she stayed sheltered, maybe she could both survive and grow up to become a healthy adult. So far, being turned at five seemed to result in a closer merging between her and her wolf.

Last summer, Mom gave me a book on werewolf lore. As I read through the book, I learned more about the natural abilities of intuition and premonition that the wolf side of werewolves possessed. Pebble seemed to be developing these traits while in human form, as well.

The treehouse had two parts: an open patio and a closed structure. We brought her into the latter for warmth. Last summer, Pebble and I had built a permanent fort with pillows and blankets. Dad helped us wire the treehouse so we could add a space heater to the little house as well. It wasn't perfect, but at least Pebble wouldn't freeze in the winter.

Once Pebble was settled, Owen, José, and I shifted, dressed, and went inside to find my parents.

Dad sat in the living room watching the news. It was one of his sources for weird happenings around the area.

I plopped down next to him. "We ran into people. They were photographing nature…"

His eyes slid to me and the boys as he muted the TV. "And?"

"They have cute photos of a baby gray wolf and her mommy for the school paper. I don't know how they'll explain me and José."

Dad sighed and rubbed his face with this hand. "Well, I

guess wolves in nature isn't the worst. Wild animals are all over the area. How close were you to the house?"

I looked at the others then did some quick calculations. "Maybe fifteen to twenty miles south of here. We were running but Pebble has short legs."

Dad nodded. "Okay, that isn't the worst, then. We shouldn't have people with pitchforks at our backdoor just yet."

My phone dinged. I looked down and saw a picture of the group of us. It was from Bevin. It was a text with the message, "Look what's making the rounds on social media."

I opened the photo. It was our picture with the words, "Danger, wild wolves found near bike path" splashed across the top. There was a full article. I sighed and handed my phone to Dad.

Dad scanned the article and shook his head. "Well, no more running on that path. I have a feeling that game trail will be destroyed for whichever animals used it."

The next day the local paper ran an article speculating about the possibility that the pictured wolves had killed the local kids last fall. The photograph attached to the article was a close-up of my wolf in attack posture. I guess a black wolf makes for a great villain. *Should I feel annoyed or amused at the assumption that fur color ups the danger of the animal?*

CHAPTER 7

It was the last weekend of winter break. Owen, José, Bevin, and I sat in the basement, in denial about classes resuming on Monday. Well, Bevin and I tried to ignore the impending doom of school; José and Owen had a couple more weeks.

We clustered around a large gaming table playing Settlers of Catan. We'd just started and the fight over who got to play blue had been fierce.

I rolled a three. No one got resources. "I can't believe we have to go back to school on Monday. It was just New Year's. So not fair. And you two get until the end of the month." I punched José in the arm.

José quirked a smile. "Chica, you didn't have a week of grueling finals. I know you think you have finals coming up, but college finals are no joke."

Bevin took the dice and rolled. "At least you get time off from dorm living." He patted my head. "I don't know how you'll survive, Jade."

I rolled my eyes. "I'm getting better."

He rolled a nine. I hooted and grabbed several resources.

Bevin shook his head. "No, you're not. You just think you are."

Owen snickered. "You have see-leck-tive memory, sis. Don't you remember shopping for Christmas gifts? You swooned into my arms like a damsel in distress."

"What?! I did not," I groused. "The mall was full of really stressed people. It hurt. We shopped. Don't exaggerate. Not to mention, you're not that much better than me, panther-boy."

Owen placed his cards down in front of himself and leaned back. "You swooned."

I assumed a haughty air. "I requested ice cream."

José face broke out in a huge smile. "That tracks."

I grinned back. "Speaking of, anyone want any?" I leapt up and headed to the kitchenette.

After hearing a chorus of agreements, I found four bowls in the cupboard and then gathered the rest of the goodies. Not that I was surprised in a basement full of teenage boys.

By the time I'd filled the bowls with ice cream and toppings, they'd moved from the table. Owen sat in one recliner. José and Bevin shared one of the couches. Game on hold. A game made of cardboard didn't mix well with ice cream. It took two trips to hand out the giant bowls, and when I was done, I flopped down in the other recliner.

After a few bites, Owen looked over at Bevin. "How are you after the whole Cody ordeal?"

Cody had been Bevin's first boyfriend. Deep down, Cody had cared for Bevin, but that probably didn't matter much. He'd ended up being a psychopathic man-eating rogue werewolf who'd killed and devoured several kids we knew.

Cody had been taken care of just before Thanksgiving. Him being a rogue werewolf in our area, the responsibility to handle him had fallen on our pack. Normally the thought of killing and death made my stomach turn, but he had been a horrible person. *No, a horrible monster.*

It had only been about six weeks, though, so the feelings were still raw for Bevin. For all of us, really. I didn't think Owen was trying to bring up painful memories. He asked in earnest, but Bevin's face paled, and his heart rate quickened. He faced this at school every day. Being on winter break, Bevin probably wanted just that, a break.

"Probably not the best topic, bro," I said softly.

Owen shrugged, hands flying out to the sides. "Look, it isn't his fault that Cody ended up being a bad first boyfriend, but, in the end, we've all had bad relationships.

We have them, and then we move on. I figure, we're family, we can help." He gave Bevin a supportive smile. "Are there other guys at the school, or is it too soon?" Somehow Owen was trying to make things easier, I thought.

Bevin tipped his head back. "It isn't that it's too soon, it's that I'm wrong."

Owen's brows furrowed in confusion.

Bevin straightened and took a bite of ice cream. At Owen's baffled look, Bevin continued. "Look, I like guys, always have, but to someone like you," he pointed at Owen, "I'm a guy, and you like girls, and for someone like him," this time he pointed at José, "I'm not a guy or maybe not enough of one. Until I have my surgery, I feel uncomfortable in this body and…I dunno, it sucks." José flinched at Bevin's words, but his concern was palpable.

Owen nodded, narrowing his eyes as he appeared to be focusing hard to follow along. He seemed genuinely perplexed. "But you're clearly a guy. Doesn't the gay community accept you?" This last was aimed at José.

When Bevin started his transition, Owen was one of the first to stop messing up his pronouns. I guess to Owen, a person was who a person was. Interesting.

José watched Bevin with a contemplative look. "When you were young, you knew in your heart you were a guy, right?"

Bevin nodded.

José continued. "So, does that mean when you were a kid, you felt like I do? Did you grow up feeling like a gay guy?"

José looked like he was at the crossroads of complete confusion and an epiphany.

"I guess," murmured Bevin. "I guess I've never really thought about it. I've always felt like I was a guy, and I've always liked guys, so, yeah, I guess."

José shut his eyes and massaged his forehead. "Being gay has been a fight my whole life. I've dreamed about my sexuality not being controversial. You know I love you, Bev; we talk almost every night, I really wish you didn't have to fight this fight." He stared down at his feet. "Can I ask you a question?"

Bevin rotated so fully face José. "Sure, what?"

José sighed. "I don't know how to ask." He shot me and then Owen a quick look, shook his head, and then took Bevin's hands. I could hear his heart rate increase, his nerves increasing.

One more breath and then he stared right into Bevin's eyes. "Please don't take this the wrong way, just hear my words, but…Wouldn't it be easier if you never came out? Then you could date guys and not have to worry."

This would've been more offensive if José didn't sound so lost. Growing up gay was still a hard thing. It was becoming more accepted, but it was still controversial. The idea of being mainstream must have seemed attractive to him.

Owen gave José a confused look. "Dude, but he's a he. I wouldn't want to wear dresses."

At first, Bevin froze and tried to pull away, but José

held tight. Then he sighed. "I did think about it some. It *would* be so much easier to just wear jeans and a t-shirt. This binder sucks." He waved his hands vaguely at his body. "But when I present as a girl, I feel gross. Wrong. I feel like I'm lying."

He shot me a quick glance. "Sorry, Jade. Women are kind of icky."

I shrugged and giggled. "No offense taken; you be you, bro. How much longer are you in that contraption anyway?" I added.

"I turn eighteen on May eighth, so as close to then as possible. Right after AP exams, if I keep my grades up and can skip finals."

José whispered the birthday we all knew but blurred the date so it sounded more like "mate" than May eighth.

Bevin's shoulders dropped. "Anyway, I just don't feel like myself that way. It *would* be easier in some ways if I never came out, but then I wouldn't be me. I wouldn't have been comfortable in my own skin. I know one day soon I'll be comfortable in my skin, and I look forward to that day. I wish you understood better. You really are one of my closest friends, José." Bevin ended a little sadly. He finally pulled his hand away from José. He grabbed his ice cream and took a bite.

"I do get it, mostly, it just seems like you've taken such a hard path in life." José pulled Bevin into a hug. "You know I love you, Bev, that's why I want your life to be easier."

He pulled back and mirrored Bevin's sad expression; shoulders drooped, eyes downcast.

Though he was saying the right words, I could smell the turmoil of his emotions as he struggled with everything.

I pointed my ice-cream-covered spoon at Bevin. "No more moping about. You have a date coming up."

Both Owen and José rotated in their seats and gaped.

Bevin, for his part, burned a nice shade of red. "Jade, what the hell?"

"You asked for it. You were getting too down. I know you're sad about the past, but you have something coming up that's exciting. Have you been talking on the phone at all with Phillip?"

Bevin's blush traveled higher, and he nodded. "A little. With the holidays it's been hard. We're thinking about going to a movie next weekend."

As Bevin's heart rate increased with excitement, José seemed to get depressed. I wasn't sure why, but I knew this wasn't the time or place to ask him. His smell was weird as well, confused.

Bevin didn't seem to notice that José was acting weird. Just then, a pillow flew through the air and hit José in the head. Luckily his bowl of ice cream, empty by now, was on the table.

"What the hell, Owen?" José complained.

"What?" Owen grinned. "You were getting maudlin. You needed something to shake you up."

We all gaped at him.

Bevin was the first to be able to speak. "Did you just say 'maudlin'?"

"Dude. I'm in college. Duh."

I couldn't help it, I laughed. And ate more ice cream. It had marshmallows. My cure for most things. Too bad it hadn't cured whatever ailed José.

José gazed at the ceiling as if trying to find patience. "Okay, Mr. Maudlin, back to the game."

I gathered the bowls and tossed them in the sink. It was Owen's turn to roll the dice.

Once we were done with the game, we started a movie. It was late, and it didn't take long for the boys to fall asleep.

My mind was spinning too fast for sleep. This happened to me once in a while. I just had to get up and move. I rose and started walking around the house. I ended up in the upstairs living room, sitting on one of the couches with a small lamp for light.

I picked up a book and tried to read, but I couldn't focus. José worried me—something was wrong with him, I could feel it. But I didn't know what it was. I didn't bring it up in front of everyone because I was pretty sure it was personal. I wasn't sure he would even tell me.

I got up and went into the kitchen to grab a slice of cold pizza and put a mug of water in the microwave for tea. When the microwave beeped, I selected a bag of peppermint and chamomile tea. Spinning on my heel, I let out a yelp as I gaped at José standing behind me. My hand hit my chest as my heart rate doubled.

"Sorry." He bit the inside of his lips to keep from laughing.

I held onto the counter, slowing down my breathing. After dropping a tea bag in the mug, I went to the kitchen table with my tea and slice of pizza.

Watching me, he grabbed his own pizza and a soda, and then joined me.

After a few bites of pizza and a sip of soda, he asked, "You better?"

"Yeah. I just didn't hear you come up from the basement. I thought you were asleep."

His mouth twitched. "I didn't mean to scare you. I heard you come up. I wasn't sure if you wanted to be alone."

"Nah. You okay?"

"Me? I'm great."

I stared him down using my imitation of Mom's teacher look. It wasn't very powerful yet, but I had been practicing on Pebble.

He threw his hands up in defeat. "Fine, okay, whatever… you win. I've been on edge lately."

I paused before taking a bite of pizza. "But why?"

"I don't know. Ever since my wolf came out…" José's looked up at me, eyes desperate. "Jade, he wants something."

I leaned forward and took his hands. "What does he want?"

"I'm not sure. Could you do your epsilon thing? Could you ask him?"

Leaning back, I considered him. I hadn't expected this. "Are you sure?"

"Please Jade, I need to know. Something is happening inside me…. Help me."

He sounded desperate and he smelled scared. I closed my eyes. Panther started forward. *No. Wolf.*

Taking José's hand, Wolf crept forward and entered José. José was so dominant that my wolf paused for a few heartbeats, almost as if asking permission to enter.

José's wolf came forward and tapped noses with us. Permission granted.

Hello, brother, what is the problem?

My mate is out there, and no one will listen.

I shook my head. *Your what?*

My mate, my perfect match. I've smelled him. I can't get to him. I can't reach him. No one will listen.

My wolf nosed José's red wolf in sympathy. Somehow, she understood what I couldn't.

I reached out. *Can we help?*

José's wolf howled in agony, *No!*

CHAPTER 8

Monday morning came despite my wishes. Winter break was never long enough. My only glimmer of excitement lay in seeing Sarah and Piper, but that was a small gift compared to the soft warmth of my bed.

Beep! Beep!

I snapped awake and hit my alarm. My brain groggy, I sat up, dragged myself out of bed, and slipped on clean clothes. Normally, I was a morning person. I wasn't sure what was wrong with me.

Oddly tired, I trudged to the kitchen and found Mom holding out a mug of coffee and making me some eggs and toast. I took the coffee and lowered myself into a kitchen chair.

She felt my forehead. "You feel fine. You don't look fine. Everything okay?"

"Just tired, I guess. I've been sleeping bad thinking about my friends. I'll be okay. Thanks for this." I held up the coffee.

She set a plate of food in front of me, and I tucked in. "Are you worried about that article?"

I shook my head. "Not really. Dad's right. We won't run that path again and we should be safe."

Mom just looked at me thoughtfully.

I shrugged and then gave her a big smile. "Or we could go back up north…that was fun."

She chuckled as she sat down with her food.

After breakfast, I suited up for the cold and headed out to meet Sarah. She was in our normal meeting spot looking tan and miserable. She cupped her hands near her mouth, and she tried to blow warmth into them.

I saw her cheeks crinkle in a smile as I approached. "So freezing. Hawaii awesome. Walk now?"

We quickly hugged before making our way to school. Bevin caught up with us as we entered the building. We navigated the maze of students to the lockers where we found Piper. Divesting myself of coat, mittens, scarf, and extra books, I found a dry place and sat next to her.

She'd watched us all unload our outdoor wear. "We have about ten minutes until class. Not enough time to catch up from two weeks of winter break. Anything big to keep us excited until lunch?" Her hopeful gaze swept over each of us.

I snorted. "Was your grandparents' place that boring?"

Her head banged the locker behind her. "You have no idea."

Bevin swung his bag onto his shoulder and held his hand out to pull me up. He gave Piper a mischievous grin. "Well, I have a date on Friday, and we are all invited to a party on Saturday. How about that?" With that, he spun on his heel and walked away.

Grabbing my bag, I gave Piper a quick hug.

Her eyes went wide. "He what? And we were what?"

"Well, you got your teaser." I kissed her on the cheek and left to follow Bevin. I caught up to him about halfway to class. "That was mean, and you know it."

He hooked his arm in mine but didn't slow down. "I know, but this will get most of the shock out without me having to deal with it. I'm sure I'll get texts throughout the morning. They're easier to deal with."

I knocked my head against his arm. "Heh, smart. Who knew?"

He laughed. "It happens on occasion."

We got to class and found Phillip sitting at our normal table. There weren't assigned seats, just tables and open seating. Most people sat with their friends, though some sat alone. I guess we had a third.

I sat down with a seat between me and Phillip for Bevin to take. "Heya, Phillip, have a good break?"

Bevin sat and we both got our stuff out as Phillip answered. "Yeah. Lots of the sugars and sleeping in. What more could a guy ask for?"

As I opened my mouth to ask another question, class started, and I had to focus on taking notes.

Phillip and I walked together from science to math class. Now that I knew we had our first two classes together, I didn't have to go it alone. He didn't, however, join us for lunch. It was too soon for that.

I arrived at the lunchroom first and headed for a corner table. Phillip sat on the other side of the large room with a group from the GSA. Sarah found me first, dropping her tray of fries and a chicken sandwich. Stealing one of her fries, I pointed at her with it. "Okay, Hawaii was fun?"

"Yes! It was so relaxing. Beaches, volcanoes, the surf…" Her eyes got a far-off, relaxed look.

With a sigh, I ate the fry. "I just wish I wasn't banned from going on trips with your family after what happened in Florida. I think a beach would have been nice last week."

Sarah froze, vision snapping into focus as she zoomed in on me. "What? No. You weren't banned."

I tried to hold a stricken face, eyes wide, brows held high. I even added a sniff for extra effect. That was probably what put it over the top.

She narrowed her eyes at me, suddenly realizing I was

messing with her, and threw a fry at me. I caught it and ate it, laughing.

Bevin slid in next to Sarah and Piper plopped down next to me.

I ate a few more bites before asking Sarah, "Are you *sure* I'm not banned? I mean, last time we went off together, your life changed pretty drastically."

Sarah just shook her head at me. "You know, I can tell you're only half-joking. I can read you…You aren't excommunicated from my family…at least, not anymore. Maybe at first, but my mom likes you again."

I smiled. There was definitely a time when Sarah's parents, especially her mom, treated me like a pariah. They had even warned me to stay away from her.

Piper bumped my shoulder. "Enough." She turned to Bevin. "Now, about this date and party. Give me the deets."

"It's a gathering for the GSA; everyone's invited. It's at Phillip's house from eight to midnight. His parents will be going out to dinner and a movie. Apparently, they trust the group." He shrugged.

The more he spoke, the bigger our smiles got. Except for Sarah. "If I'm straight, can I still go?"

Bevin just looked at her with no emotion. "Nope. Not at all." Rotating to us with a smile, he said, "It'll be amazing."

I rolled my eyes and Piper chuckled.

Bevin shot Sarah a disbelieving look over his shoulder. "It's the gay/*straight* alliance, doofus. Why wouldn't you be able to come?"

Sarah ducked her head. "Oh, yeah, that makes sense. Cool. Are Owen or José coming?"

Bevin paused to think about it. "Sure. They're in town for another week. I'll mention it to José," he pointed at me, "if *you* can mention it to Owen."

"Sounds good to me."

Sarah shoulder-bumped Bevin. "So, who's the boy, and what about the date?"

Bevin grabbed his sandwich and took a bite. He then waved at his mouth animatedly and shrugged.

Sarah rolled her eyes, shaking her head in amusement. She stared at me. "Have you thought about joining track with me?"

The other two stopped their playing and slowly turned to face me. My shoulders dropped, and my chin jutted out towards Sarah in disbelief. I whined, "Not this again."

"Why not?"

My hands flew up. "I'm not athletic, that's why. You do the sports stuff; I do the AP stuff. It's worked for years. Why ruin a good thing?"

Sarah huffed. "Are you saying the English class we share isn't AP?"

My head fell to my arms on the table and Piper laughed at me.

Bevin had finally swallowed his bite. "Wait, what? Track?"

My head popped up. "No."

Piper gently rested her hand on mine. "Why not? I mean, I know why not last year, but why not this year? You could do the running events; even the jumping ones." She gazed off into space, imagining my future meets. "It could be amazing."

I groaned.

Sarah laughed in triumph.

Bevin nodded, seeming to piece it all together.

"Can't we go back to harassing Bevin? If you don't talk about…"

Bevin's hands shot up in a double stop. "Fine, fine, just stop." He looked at Sarah and Piper. "His name is Phillip. He's a senior, like me. We've been in classes together for years. We've even been on projects together since…" He dropped his gaze to his tray, and I could hear his heart rate start to speed up. Finally, he met my eyes. "Since before, you know. Middle school. He knows. He's okay with it."

My smile grew as I faced the others. "One of the first stories the two of them reminisced about was a science project from middle school. It was cute."

As the three of us continued to discuss Bevin and Phillip, a wave of dizziness overtook me. I put my head back down on my crossed arms.

Bevin kneaded my back. "You okay?"

"Yeah, give me a sec."

I closed my eyes and found my panther. *Everything okay?*

My panther perked up. *Yes. Helping friends.*

What?

I tried to lift my head, but the wave of dizziness intensified. My head started to throb.

Sarah spoke to the table at large. "She needs more calories."

The scent of chocolate brought me back to life. Yummy. Piper held a piece near my mouth. I ate it. Then another bite. I pushed myself up. I took the bar and finished it.

Sarah watched me critically. "You're not better. Can you make it to class? The bell's about to ring."

I nodded slowly. "Yeah. I'll be fine." I waved the wrapper. "Thanks for this. It helped."

Piper searched her bag. "Do you need another one?"

"I'll grab some chips from the machine on the way out, and a soda. I should be fine."

Bevin still rubbed my back. "What happened?"

I shook my head. "Your guess is as good as mine."

CHAPTER 9

Curled under my warm blankets Saturday morning, I didn't want to get up. Usually, I was the first in the gym. I had a few minutes to cuddle in the warmth of my covers before anyone noticed my absence.

A knock at my door jerked me awake. *Who the heck is up?* Taking a sniff, I got my groggy brain working. *Dad? He can't be up. He's always the last one awake.*

My door creaked open, and his steps approached my bed. My heart rate kicked up. There had to be an emergency. *Are my medical skills needed? Did Aunt Allison call?* What else could get him up this early in the morning? Even worried, I couldn't seem to get myself moving.

He sat on the side of my bed and stroked my back. "Jade, honey, it's time to get up." He pulled my covers down enough to uncover my face. I saw my clock: ten forty-two. What? How could it be so late?

"Am I sick?"

"I don't think so. Your mom said you've been struggling to wake up every morning this week. Anything I should know about?"

Groaning, I finally pulled myself up to a sitting position. My head spun and I collapsed back against the wall. Another headache. My voice low and pitiful, I asked, "Coffee?"

Dad nodded and left to get me caffeine. When he returned, he had liquid ambrosia and a breakfast sandwich. I ate and drank. The combination was magic.

Rubbing my leg, he asked, "Feeling better?"

I nodded as I finished the last of my much-needed calories.

He nodded, satisfied. "Go take a shower, get dressed, and we'll talk over lunch."

I eyed him skeptically. "What about my training for the day?"

"Even I can see that something's up."

My hands fell to the bed in disbelief. "What?"

His smile widened as he continued. "We'll just double the workload to get you caught up once we figure out what's wrong with you."

I moaned and fell back down onto the bed.

Dad made Mongolian beef for lunch while I showered and dressed. I put on cozy sweats, figuring I had no plans before the party. The meal was one of my dad's specialties that I loved. I could eat all of it. I dug in.

Mom sat with a bowl of hot and sour soup. "Did this start during break?"

I shook my head, unwilling to stop stuffing my face.

"I wonder if it's something at school," she said.

I shrugged.

"All of your classes are the same. Anything more stressful?"

I just glared.

Mom gave me a deadpan look. "I know finals are this week, but they've never been this stressful for you. Anything else?"

I shook my head.

She looked to Dad. "Thoughts?"

"Yeah. Have you ever seen her eat this much this fast? Whatever it is, it's taking a lot out of her."

Looking down, I realized I had finished off a third bowl and my stomach growled for more. That said, I felt loads better.

I smiled up at Dad. "This is the best I've felt in a week. Just keep cooking this meal and I'll be right as rain."

He smiled back and shook his head. "Nope."

I sighed in defeat. "It was worth a shot."

José came over later in the afternoon to hang out before the party. We were in the basement playing Exploding Kittens with Owen.

Dealing out cards, I asked, "One more week and you both have to head back to campus?"

They both groaned. José picked up his cards and narrowed his eyes at me. "Please don't mention it, chica. Being home, away from the smells of my roommate, has been blissful."

Owen played a card and José played a 'nope,' card on it.

"Denied," I said, laughing at his look of disappointment.

Owen smirked. "Shouldn't you be studying for all *your* finals?"

I drooped, collapsing my cards, and sneering at him. "Probably, but this is my last weekend day with the two of you, so I thought I'd let that take priority." I started to stand up. "I could leave if you'd prefer."

He reached out and clasped my arm. "No, I was just goofing. It's your turn."

I huffed out a laugh and laid a card down.

We continued to play for an hour, then I decided it was time to get ready. I went off to change. I put on a pair of black jeans, a black undershirt, and a nice silk shirt. Sarah had bought it for me. It was a bit fancy; a deep emerald green that swooped over each shoulder around to my back.

Once dressed, I found José sitting alone in the living room.

I plopped down next to him. "You okay?"

"Sure am."

I tapped my nose. "Werepanther. Remember? Wanna try that one again?"

He let out a puff of air. "You are annoying."

"Fact. Now, you okay?"

Picking up a pillow, he hugged it to his chest. "You know I'm not. You never explained what my wolf told you."

Resting my head on his shoulder, I placed a hand on his leg. We both needed the extra contact. "That's because it didn't make sense."

"Try me."

"He said he was looking for your mate."

José froze next to me. "My…what's that, now?"

Sitting up, I stared at him directly. "Exactly. That's why I didn't say it before. It didn't sound like what Mom and Dad have. I've been meaning to do some research, but this has been a crazy week. I'll talk to them tomorrow, hopefully. If that doesn't work, I'll check the book." Last summer Mom had given me an encyclopedia of all facts werewolf. It was mostly folklore, but if you knew what you were looking for, you could find out a lot of things.

"Okay, fine. That's weird. You're right. That makes no sense."

I shook my head. "Nope."

"Maybe you misunderstood. Maybe you can try again?"

"Maybe. But not right now."

His head dropped back against the back of the couch. "Fine, be that way."

I knocked my shoulder against his. "I will."

Owen chose that moment to pop out of the hallway and join us. "If we leave now, we can swing over and pick up Sarah, then Piper, then Bevin."

I thought about it: six of us in the car. "I think Bevin is driving himself; he mentioned helping set up. Piper's dad is paranoid; he's driving her there and back. We just need to get Sarah."

Owen smiled. "Perfect."

We headed out to his car and arrived at the party fashionably late. The main hall had a door leading to the left that opened to the formal dining room where everyone was storing their outer wear. We dumped our coats. My head started to pound, and I slumped against the wall. Sarah and Owen were already off and didn't see me waver, but José quickly slid an arm around my waist.

"You okay, chica?"

I shook my head then leaned on him. I closed my eyes and took strength from our pack connection. "I don't know why this keeps happening." I took a few deep breaths while José stroked my back and the pain receded.

I pulled back and gave him a half smile. "Thanks, I think I'm good." Once I felt steadier, we were off to find the others.

Sarah, Owen, and Piper were dancing in a cleared-out room I assumed was the living room. Piper loved to dance, and I stopped to watch her for a minute. Her movements and grace were intoxicating. The room was full of dancers, but she was all I saw. Shaking myself, I joined them. I wasn't going to let my headache ruin the night. José wasn't too far behind me. The music was loud, the beat was fast, and we were knocking it out hard.

After a few songs, I pointed to the kitchen and mimed getting a drink. I found bottles of water and soda on the counter and went for the water. My head spun. I thought I just took a sip, but when I put the bottle down, it was empty.

Sarah, who had followed me in, just stared at me, concerned. "Jade, are you okay?"

"I wish people would stop asking me that."

"Who all's been asking?"

I kicked myself for bringing it up and grabbed a soda. "It's nothing. I've just been tired. I'll be fine."

I spun to watch our friends dancing. José and Piper were oddly good together, and Owen was a goof, as usual. "Where's Bevin?"

Sarah pointed to a corner where he and Phillip sat talking. Their heads were practically touching, they sat so close.

Smiling, a warmth blossomed in me at how happy Bevin looked. "Cute."

Sarah leaned forward to hear me over the music. "What?"

Snorting, I tried again louder. "I said 'cute'!"

She nodded.

José chose that moment to join us. "What's cute? Mine and Piper's brilliant dance moves? That girl can definitely cut up a dance floor. She's a keeper, chica."

"Well, yeah, that, but also that." I pointed.

José spun in place, snatching up a water bottle as he pirouetted. His gaze followed my finger, and he spotted the couple in the corner. He froze and I could smell his confusion. His heart rate increased, and a sense of dread overtook me.

Sarah looked between José and me with a puzzled expression.

I didn't know what was happening, either. I tried to lift my hand, but my energy was gone. My words barely a whisper, I protested, "José, don't."

He didn't hear me. In jerking motions, he made his way to Bevin. I could feel his confusion and dread battling it out.

I tried again. "Sarah, stop him."

She was watching José, focused on him, and didn't hear me.

José got to Bevin and said, loudly enough for me to hear over the music, "You're making a mistake."

Bevin, who had been caught up in his moment with Phillip and hadn't seen José's approach, jerked his head up at this. "José, when did you get here?"

"Bevin, you're making a mistake!"

Bevin's head dipped and his eyebrows met over his

eyes, which sparkled in the light. "What? What are you talking about?"

Phillip stared up at José. "José, long time no see. But what gives, man?"

José's confusion deepened. The more he tried to figure it out, the harder it was for me to follow. His focus towards Bevin intensified. "A mistake, amigo…"

Owen made it to them, clasped José by the shoulders, and spun him around. "José, I'm not sure what's up, but can we talk?"

José's eyes started to glow as if lit from within. It could be blamed on the lights if you didn't know what was happening, but he shot Owen a look, and Owen dropped to his knees in submission. José looked down at Owen and said loudly, "No."

I felt a pull, saw Sarah run to help Owen, and then my knees hit the floor. And then I felt nothing.

CHAPTER 10

I forced my eyes open and found myself in bed. *How did I get here? When did I get here? What day is it?* My attempt to roll over failed and I groaned with the effort. I had no energy.

Pebble's tiny voice flowed over me. "Mom, Dad, she's up."

She must have been waiting for me to regain consciousness. I tried to open my eyes, but even that felt like too much effort. Footsteps pounded closer and a door opened. I could smell my parents and food. My stomach grumbled in appreciation.

Mom sat on the edge of the bed. "You awake?"

Nodding, I wasn't sure if I could do much else. She

covered my hand with her own. "Can you take some of my energy? Enough to be able to eat?"

I could take energy from other wereanimals because I was an epsilon wolf. I didn't know of any others who could do it. This had saved me on other occasions, and if I could take some from Mom now, it would help me to get moving faster.

I focused on my animals, and they seemed as out of it as I was. Mentally poking them, Panther moved to where Mom's hand lay on mine and she gathered a small trickle of energy for us. I nearly cried in relief as I could finally breathe. It wasn't much, but it was enough to let me open my eyes.

Mom shook her hand and rubbed her head. She looked over to Dad. "Next time you get to take one for the team."

The two of them helped me up to a sitting position and I started in on breakfast. After a few bites I asked, "How did I get here? What day is it? What happened?"

Dad sat down at my desk and finally met my eyes. "According to Piper, José started to act weird. The stranger he acted, the weaker you got. Then you passed out and no one could wake you up. They finally brought you home."

I tried to remember. "José…" I nodded, and something clicked. "My wolf said she was helping a friend this week. Could she have left part of herself—myself—gah! Whatever! Could some magical—" I waved my hands about, "—mumbo jumbo have been left connecting me and José?"

Mom shrugged. "I have no idea. At this point, you are the expert. You do new things every time we talk. You'll have to go in and ask your animals."

Dad stood and started to pace. "And if you did, what does this mean? Could it have included communication or was it only a way for him to siphon energy?"

"Well, are we still connected?"

They both just stared at me. *Right…I'm the expert…*

I grabbed my coffee and started drinking. I smiled down at Pebble who was playing on the floor. "Lunch, dessert, lots of calories, shower, then we'll figure it out."

Mom nodded; Dad snorted. "I feel like I have two sons at this point. We sent Owen out for Thai food. He should be back soon. He's worried about having to carry you out of a party, and a dry party at that."

Making my way to the kitchen, I dug in the fridge for some soda and heard a car pull into the driveway. I sat at the table, excited for lunch.

Owen came in with bags full of food. I wasn't sure how many people he was planning on feeding, but I was ready to start. The others joined me, and we all focused on eating instead of talking. By the time I was done, I wasn't sure I could move, but I felt full and almost human.

Owen checked me out. "Well, you have color again, that's an improvement."

I made a face at him.

He smiled and lightly punched my shoulder. "You don't get it. José was acting weird. I went to stop him. Then you collapsed, which did a better job of stopping him than anything I could've done. That pretty much ended the party. Phillip wanted to call an ambulance, but Sarah and I convinced him that you would be fine."

He shot my parents a half-smile. "We should get her one of those medical bracelets."

I snarled.

His arms flew up as he shrugged. "What, passing seems to be your new favorite pastime. It was only a matter of time before it happened in front of norms. Anyway, Sarah could feel that you were fine, so José and I carried you out. Bevin stayed behind to smooth things over."

Well, at least that answered some of the questions I had.

Mom added, "I spoke with the parents this morning and told them you were in good health. I explained that you had exercised this morning and hadn't eaten enough."

Owen snorted at the story, and I chuckled. "Oh, sure, the one morning I don't exercise and that's the excuse!"

Dad started clearing the plates and storing the leftovers. He mussed Pebble's hair. "Hey, pipsqueak, why don't you suit up and play in the backyard? It's warm enough. Maybe Owen can build a snowman with you."

Owen started to whine, but then shrugged. "Yeah, I guess there won't be much to see." He poked me in the chest. "But you'll tell me everything afterwards." It wasn't a question.

Once the two of them were outside, Mom looked at me. "Can we do anything to help?"

I shrugged. "I have no idea. I may need your wolf to

help mine to stop the connection. I mean, I may be able to as well, I just don't know what I'll find."

Mom clasped my hands and pulled. "Let's try this on the couch. That way if you lose consciousness, at least you'll be somewhere comfortable."

Trudging to the couch, I grumbled about passing out all the time. "Why is it I faint so much? This sucks."

Mom patted me on the back. "Luck of the draw, dear one, luck of the draw."

I flopped down on the couch and hugged a pillow to my chest. I relaxed my muscles, closed my eyes, and focused on my animals.

Panther was up. A sleek black cat, beautiful, fierce, and confident in her place in the world. I went deeper. At first, I couldn't find my wolf, which scared me. Panther rubbed her head against my side, scent-marking me, trying to make me feel better.

Where is Wolf?

Panther gazed up at me then tilted her head as if confused by a silly question. She took off and I followed.

Wolf was in a cave, deep in the shadows, her black fur making her almost impossible to find. She looked wan and thin.

What's wrong?

I am helping our friend.

How?

He needs a connection to pack, I have given it to him.

What have you done?

We are connected.

It is too much; I can't maintain it. You can't maintain it. It has to stop.

Then stop it.

What?

I am you and you are me. End the connection.

With a huff, I sat there and thought about what Wolf had said. We were one. I closed my eyes and focused on the connections. When I opened them, I saw my links to the pack and my packmates. Each member had what looked like a string from my beast to theirs. The string to my alphas were thicker, almost like double helixes.

Curious, I faced Panther. She had the bonds, too.

My senses were on overload as I walked over to Wolf and touched one of the double helix strands. I heard Mom gasp. I found the connection to Dad and touched it and heard something crash in the kitchen. Then there was talking. I didn't want to leave this place, so I tried not to focus on what they were saying. One of the connections glowed, almost pulsating.

My animals sat on either side of me as I tried to figure out what I was experiencing. The aggravated connection had to lead to José. I focused on it. *José, can you hear me?*

I could almost feel him freeze. If I focused hard enough, I could almost see him in his living room at his parents' place. *What the hell, Jade, is that you? Am I hearing voices in my head?* He sounded freaked out.

I guess that made sense. *No, just the next stage in the evolution of my weirdness. I've been feeding you my energy this week. Don't know why my wolf thought it was needed. Long story short, when I figure out how to stop it, it may be jarring.*

Well, hell, no wonder I've been Superman this week. Thanks for the heads up, but you can talk through this connection, too?

Apparently.

Love ya, chica, but, wow, your weirdness is evolving. I could almost see him shaking his head in disbelief.

I cocked my head and thought, *End.*

Nothing happened.

Wolf's tongue lolled out. She was laughing at me. I closed my eyes to become her and thought, *End!*

I heard a snap and opened my eyes. The pulsing connection was gone. I took a deep breath. Suddenly, I had more energy than I'd had in days.

I touched José's connection. It was still there, it just wasn't on.

Are you okay?

Yes…no, chica! I may sleep for a week. If you hadn't warned me, I may have thought I was dying. How did you survive with me taking so much of your energy?

I'm just amazing like that.

How did you even figure this out?

I'm omniscient, didn't you know?

His amusement and incredulity flowed back to me.

Curiously, I touched Owen's string and said, *Boo!* I could feel him jump before I dropped the string and opened my actual eyes.

Mom was still sitting next to me. She held a plate of food. My stomach growled. I selected a cupcake and took a big bite.

"Everything figured out?"

"Not even close, but I closed the connection to José."

The door to the back slammed open and then shut as Owen ran in.

"Jade, what the hell was that?"

Eyes wide, I blinked up at him. "What are you talking about?"

CHAPTER 11

I survived a week of finals. Without José in my brain, my energy levels were higher, but I still got daily headaches. *What am I missing?*

While I prepared my coffee after my Saturday morning run, I found a note attached to the cupboard with the mugs. *Jade, training at ten. Living room. Love M&D.*

Training? I just did my training. With finals over, I had the weekend slated for reading and lollygagging. Owen popped out of nowhere and tackled me in a hug.

Coffee splashed on me before I could drop the mug on the counter. "What's up?"

"I head back to Whitewater today, Dad will drive me. Gonna miss you."

"Dork."

"Probably, but it's true. Being at college, I have to hide half of who I am. It's been nice being home."

We sat and drank coffee. After a few minutes of silence, my belly grumbled, and I sighed. "Is this what life has always been like for you? Controlled by your stomach?"

Owen snorted. "Pretty much."

He got up and grabbed two bowls, a box of cereal, and the milk. I filled the bowls as he went back for spoons. Though I was hungry enough to eat anything, I really wanted protein.

"Is José back in the dorms?"

Owen shrugged. "Not sure, but probably. Classes start on Tuesday. After MLK."

After I dug into the cereal, my stomach stopped cramping. "It's nice you have until after Martin Luther King Jr.'s remembrance. That was a long break, unlike us who barely had more than a week. But you go for, what, four days, then you'll be back for the full moon." I sighed dramatically. "Then I can really get rid of you both."

Mom came in then, followed by Pebble. "What have you two eaten?"

I held up the box of cereal and shook it as Pebble scooted in next to me.

She frowned. "Not enough protein." She went to the

fridge and took out the eggs, cheese, and some left-over sausage. She started frying up a meaty egg scramble. I found some bread and toasted it, adding butter. Owen grabbed a few apples and oranges and sliced them to add to the table's offerings. Once done, the four of us tucked in.

Dad came in and saw there was enough of everything for him to eat and he smiled a tired smile. "So, Jade, ready to train?"

My brows dipped. "I already followed what was in my book. What more, exactly, am I training this morning?"

He waggled his brows. "That weird connection thing you did last weekend. I want to see what you can do with it. We'll start with the three of us, but I did warn Tanner you may try to reach out to him."

Selecting some fruit, I scrunched up my face. "I'm surprised you haven't called a pack meeting yet."

Owen snorted.

Mom patted my hand. "Not until you've figured it out. It's still too new."

Well, that was something.

Mom and I moved to the living room while Dad, Owen, and Pebble cleaned up. Once the cleaning was done, Pebble would go to the basement to play, and Dad and Owen would join us in the living room.

Mom sat next to me and held my hand. "What do you need?"

I shrugged. "No idea." I sat back and crossed my legs. I

snatched a pillow and closed my eyes.

Panther? Wolf?

They were both there, as they always were. I imagined sitting down. Figuring I'd be there awhile, I thought about my mental mindscape and created a camp scene with a fire, logs to sit on, and a small cabin. Much better. I sat on a log, and Panther and Wolf came around between me and the fire.

Are the connections that were there last time still there?

Wolf cocked her head to the side. *Of course.*

How can I access them?

Why do you ask that which you know?

I dropped my face into my hands. This wasn't working. Focusing on Wolf, I thought, *Connections.*

When I searched, I didn't see anything. I stood and paced or did whatever it was you did when having an internal crisis. I went back to Wolf and put my hand on her head and thought, *Mom.*

Again, nothing happened. I was getting frustrated.

Can you make the connections visible? I asked again in desperation.

Yes, no, of course. I am you, and you are me. We can do it.

But how?

Cocking her head, Wolf gazed at me with her deep, knowing eyes…my eyes. *By doing it.*

I rubbed my forehead. My headache was getting worse. I turned to Panther.

Do you have any ideas?

Panther just stared at me, eyes glowing bright and green. No help there.

After a few more minutes I opened my eyes. I clenched my fists in frustration before releasing the tension and shaking my hands out.

Mom massaged my shoulder. "Anything?"

"No. I don't know how to get the connections up again. My wolf says it's possible, I just don't know how."

"Well, it's something you can keep trying. It doesn't seem to drain your energy."

"Not really. My head hurts, but it's been hurting for a few days."

Mom's brow knit. "That's odd."

"Yeah, I know. We'll figure it out."

It took a few weeks to get into the groove of the second semester. By the time I did, it was February and the weather sucked. Cold, windy, and miserable. The one bright spot was, I had taken my driving test and passed. I could now legally drive! Downside? I didn't have a car.

Two weeks into the semester, I entered the lunchroom and got into the food line. My head was pounding. For some reason the scents were overwhelming today. It was like everyone was testing out new body sprays and perfumes. Maybe it was for Valentine's Day. A blizzard raged outside, which meant I couldn't escape to the great outdoors. Miserable and in pain, I focused inward and didn't pay attention to the people around me.

I felt a tap on my shoulder. I squeezed my eyes shut before opening them and checking over my shoulder. Standing there was a vision of perfection.

Everything about her was flawless. Perfect button nose, ideal hair in a sleek ponytail. On-trend outfit…well, I assumed that last. I actually had no idea. I tended to wear jeans and whatever top was clean. Fashion wasn't my thing, but she looked put together, and she was popular, so I imagined it was ideal. "Hi, Estrella, how is everything?"

"Can I talk to you about Bevin?"

My face scrunched and my forehead wrinkled in that way all the magazines said I should avoid. "Bevin? What about him?"

"He hasn't been taking any of José's calls and it's ruining *my* calls with *mi hermano*. I don't know what's going on, but can you fix it?"

I stepped backwards as the line slowly moved. "Have you thought about talking to Bevin yourself? You two are together once a month. You know *him* as well as you know *me*."

She dramatically raised and dropped her shoulders as she took a huge breath. "You are so much better at this. I just don't know what to do. Puh-leeeze…"

My eyes narrowed. We slowly inched towards the food. I just wanted to get away from this request. I thought about saying no when she clasped my hand and squeezed. "You have to say yes, Jade, you just have to."

Oh, my gods, she isn't a werewolf! She doesn't have a seed in her. As an epsilon wolf, I could determine either the wereanimal of a person or their potential with just a touch. I did not want to deal with this right now. My free hand kneaded my skull. The pounding got worse.

"What'll you have? You're holding up the line."

I snatched my hand back and spun to the lunch lady. "Fries, burger, pizza…please."

She looked me up and down. "You can't order for more people than yourself. One entrée."

I felt my mouth bunch into a sneer. My stomach grumbled. "It's all for me."

Again, she gave me a once over. "Right." She sneered.

Before I could answer, Estrella put a hand on my arm. "She'll have pizza and fries. I'll have a burger and fries."

The lunch lady eyed us both, but then started dishing out two trays. We got to the end of the line and paid. Estrella followed me to the table with my friends where she dumped her tray of food on mine.

A brow flew up as I looked at her. "I brought my lunch today. I just needed to talk to you. Remember my request." She twirled and headed off to her side of the lunchroom.

Why did I feel like I'd made a deal with the devil?

Sitting down, I rested my head on Bevin's arm. He was taller than me and his arm was at the perfect level to be a pillow. I selected food at random off my tray to eat.

Everyone was watching me. Bevin stroked my back. "What did *she* want?"

"You."

His hand stopped moving, and I whimpered. He snorted and started rubbing again.

"What exactly does that mean?"

"Why have you stopped your nightly phone calls with José?"

This time his hand dropped away, and he moved enough that I had to sit up. I moaned with the pain of the movement but sat up so I could continue to eat.

"Not that it's any of your business, but I've just been trying to figure out what happened during the party, that's all."

"I think he has, too."

Bevin sighed. "Look, Phillip and I have just started dating. It's nice."

Sarah's nose scrunched up. "Nice?"

Bevin's head dropped. "I know, not the best word. This is all new to me."

I looked at the tray. Where had my pizza gone? I checked out my friends' trays. None of them had pizza in front of them. Huh?

Piper must have seen my confusion. "You ate the pizza and most of the fries. If you want, I have another chocolate bar."

"Huh?" I perked up. "Yeah, I'd like that." I turned to Bevin. "Are you happy with Phillip?"

He shrugged. "I am, it's just…I'm happy. It's new and weird. I'm getting used to having a…" he lowered his voice, "…a boyfriend. I think José was reacting to my confusion. It's like he's my alpha before I'm a werewolf. I'm not ready for that. I just want my friend back."

I let out a breath I didn't know I was holding. "You know what, that makes sense. Your wolf is close to coming out. His wolf is really dominant. If he's planning on being your alpha, maybe he was just in extra protective mode. He needed my energy to get to you, and somehow figured out how to do it to help."

Everyone at the table was nodding. Sarah finished her sandwich. "That makes the most sense so far. I'm just glad you figured out how to stop it." She looked at me with concern…alpha concern, *gulp*. "We're going to have to figure out how to mainline calories into you soon."

I snorted at the truth of that statement.

Bevin seemed to brace himself before facing me and Piper. "Would you two want to do a double-date thingy with me and Phillip? Maybe dinner, or games, or something?"

I looked at Piper, who shrugged. Smiling, I slid my hand over Bevin's and gave it a squeeze. "Sure."

After school, Sarah dragged me to the first informational meeting for track and field. I sat in the back and tried to stay out of sight. My head still hurt, and I didn't want to be there.

The current track members stood in the front of the room talking about why we should join. They were so…peppy. Sarah sat next to me; excitement poured off her in waves.

"And then, after each meet, we come back here and head to get ice cream to celebrate. Team-building, you know?"

I perked up at that. Sarah saw my interest and laughed. "Is that all I had to do to get you here, mention the ice cream?"

I glared at her, but my interest had just gone up.

After the meeting, everyone started packing up to head home. I moved fast, trying to be the first one out. So far, I had gone unnoticed, and I wanted to continue being a ghost.

I had made it to the door when I heard, "Ms. Stone, Ms. Baller, please stay after." Mr. Nelson's voice rang out over the crowd.

Snarling, I turned back to the room. Sarah let out a huff of laughter as she swung her arm around my shoulder. We made our way to the front where he sat behind a desk. I stood there bouncing, wanting to leave. I knew he would wait until the room emptied to say anything to us.

I gazed at my watch as the last students left.

Mr. Nelson slowly closed the magazine he'd been reading. "In a hurry, Ms. Stone?"

"Not really…just debating if coming to this meeting was a good idea or not, sir."

He finally looked up and stared at us. "I don't know either. Having you two on the team means we'll win. The question is, can you two hold back to win by reasonable amounts?"

Sarah growled low in her throat.

Mr. Nelson's eyebrow raised. "None of that, Ms. Baller; we want to be seen as normal. Hissing and growling are too animalistic, don't you think?"

I had to bite my cheek to stop from responding.

He stared at us for a good minute before continuing. "I'll admit, I want you both on the team. The idea makes me...pleased." He didn't sound pleased. "But, if this is going to work, we'll have to set up extra training. We'll also have to be strategic about events. You two can't compete against each other..."

He took a long gulp of his coffee. His eyes closed for a minute like the coffee was a lifeline. I totally got that. "Who's faster?" I raised my hand. His brows hit his non-existent hair line. "Really?"

Sarah barked out a laugh. "I know, right? Here I am, the athletic one, but yeah, she can run faster and longer than me. She can also jump really well. I would put her on distance and jumping. I'm good for sprinting and passing things, like the baton. If you put a baton in her hand, the team will lose. First, she'll drop it, then she'll probably fall down and trip everyone."

I rolled my eyes at that but couldn't disagree. I turned to her. "How much have you thought about this? I hadn't even decided if I would come until today."

Sarah gave me a half-smile. "Oh, I would have carried you here if I had to. I had decided and I was going to try any pull I had, even the alpha one."

Mr. Nelson started to choke. After coughing for a few minutes, he looked up. "You're her alpha?"

Sarah's eyes danced. "I know, it's crazy. We were bitten at the same time, but pow! I got all this extra info about her. She has her own tricks, but I'm alpha. She has a wolf alpha too…. She's just extra lucky that way."

I huffed. "So, back to track. Regular practice, plus more? We already have Dad's set up, how much more are you expecting?"

He picked up two books and tapped them against the heel of his hand. "I've been coordinating with your dad." He handed each of us a book. "This will be your secondary schedule."

My face contorted in confusion. "I didn't even know I was coming until today. How is it you have these booklets ready for us?"

He gave a smug shrug. "I have my ways."

I paged through the book. There were dates and expectations. Some were for the home gym; some were for after practice with him here at the school.

I glared at Sarah as I paged through the calendar of doom.

She waved at it, pointing at the cover. "Look, ice cream cones!"

CHAPTER 12

When I got up for school on Monday morning, our house was full of people. Usually the first to wake up, I was shocked to run into people on the way to the gym. I made a beeline to the kitchen where I found Fred and Janet coordinating with my parents. Someone had made coffee so I poured a cup, hoping the caffeine would help with the start of my new regular morning headaches.

During the last week of February, Chris and Andy, two of our submissive wolves, decided to take a winter camping trip with their ten-year-old daughter Chloe. Chloe begged for her best friend Hannah, Bevin's youngest sister, to be invited along. They planned on leaving on Friday, an Inservice day with the school, and then returning on Monday morning. No one had heard from them Monday morning before school. Chris or Andy should have called in by six, but they hadn't.

Mom and Dad organized a search and rescue team. Our best trackers—Tanner, Clair, and Greg—were assembling. I wanted to go along, but I had school. I was surprised Bevin wasn't around, but he was at home getting himself and Heather, his middle sister, ready for school. Janet felt school would be a better distraction than tromping around a cold mountain.

As everyone moved around planning the day, I threw a bunch of ingredients in a pan to make a quick egg scramble. I searched and found a tortilla to convert mine into a breakfast wrap. I ran to my room to change into school clothes and then left. I met up with Sarah and Bevin a block from school. Bevin didn't look good. His eyes were red, and he kept wiping them.

I ran up to him and gave him a big hug. "I'm sure she'll be fine. Andy and Chris are good wolves. They'll keep both girls safe."

Bevin nodded quickly. "It's just that Hannah doesn't really like the outdoors, and it's cold. Oh, gods, this is horrible." He fell back into my arms and started to sob.

We stood like that for a few minutes. Sarah joined us in the hug.

Finally, Bevin pulled back. "Okay, I'll be fine. We have to get to school before we freeze."

I squeezed his hand. "They brought in the A-Team to track them down. It's good."

We made it into the school and up to the lockers. Piper took one look at us, and her eyes bugged out. "What did I miss?"

Sarah quickly filled her in, and she put her arms around Bevin, adding her support to ours.

On the way to AP bio, Bevin slipped into a bathroom to wash his face. By the time we got to class you could hardly tell he was upset. Phillip had arrived before us again, which wasn't surprising since we barely got to our seats before the bell rang. Bevin threw himself into taking notes and ignoring the greater world around him. Neither Phillip nor I could distract him from class.

Afterward, he packed up and dashed out before I could say anything to him. As we walked to math Phillip asked, "Is Bevin okay?"

I shrugged. "I think he had a rough night." My head continued to pound so I rubbed at my temples, hoping the day wouldn't continue to be so stressful, but knowing my hopes were fruitless.

Phillip just nodded and dropped the subject.

When I got to lunch, I barely had time to sit before I received a text message from Dad.

I called the school, you have an

appointment. Outside, now.

Piper and I were the only ones there, so I showed her the text before gathering my stuff and standing to leave. After getting to my locker and suiting up, I left the school and found Aunt Allison waiting for me.

"So, I'm sick? What's wrong with me?"

She shot out of the parking a lot faster than I'd ever seen her drive. Instead of navigating out of town, she headed towards downtown Madison. "We can't pick up their trail. We all discussed our options and realized that we need the two best noses we can think of."

"Two best noses?" Gazing out the window watching the cold tundra of February in Wisconsin fly by me it hit me. "José? Are we heading to pick him up, too?"

"Right in one, hon. We need the two of you to find the trail."

Aunt Allison turned onto the beltline, a mix of highways, and hit the top speed. We flew past a few exits before she got off and headed for the university. José sat waiting for us outside Union South, one of the many university buildings. He slipped into the backseat, and we were off.

I spun as far as my belt would allow. "How much do you know about what's going on?"

"Not much. I just got a text saying I was getting picked up and that I was needed. What's up?"

I filled him in as Aunt Allison's vehicle flew down I90.

"How's Bevin dealing with all of this?"

I shrugged. "Not good. He's freaking out but really doesn't want anyone to know. He's closing down into himself, pushing people away."

José sighed, shoulders drooped, staring at his hands. "Ever wish you could erase a minute of your life?"

I huffed out a laugh.

We continued in silence until we reached a parking lot with familiar cars.

"Okay, kiddos, put your fur on."

José and I got out of the car and found a place to shift. Once we were furry, we sniffed out my aunt and parents who showed us where Chris and Andy had parked. Sniffing, I found the trail that they must have taken last Friday. I trotted down the trail and José followed my lead. When I checked over my shoulder, I realized Tanner and Greg followed as well. I wasn't sure where Clare, Fred, or Janet were.

The trail went straight up the mountain, well, a Wisconsin mountain…. Eventually, it branched out. I started to the left, but José whined and hopped towards the right branch. I shook my head and bounced to the left. He snarled low in his throat and gave me an alpha stare. I rolled my eyes as Tanner and Greg lowered themselves in submission.

This wasn't getting us anywhere.

Finally, Tanner nudged Greg towards José to the right and me to the left. He followed me. The scent was strong and easy to follow. The path through the snow was not well trod, though I detected the scents of several people and many different animals. After about fifteen minutes, the snow started to get thicker. We had passed the point most people had given up.

For a few minutes, I couldn't find their scent. I backtracked and sniffed around. Finally, I found where they had gone off the path. Following their trail, I located their camp site, and in one of the tents Chloe lay curled up looking cold and scared.

Her head snapped up when the tent opened. "Ja-Ja-Jade? Ta-Taa—" Her teeth were chattering too hard to get Tanner's full name out.

We ran over and rubbed up against her to generate some warmth. She felt like an ice cube.

After a couple minutes, her breathing evened out and her teeth stopped knocking against each other. "Do you know where my daddies are? Or Hannah?"

Tanner stared at me intently and shifted his gaze to my paw and then his paw. It was an indication of how badly my head hurt that it took me so long to figure out what he was asking. I placed my paw on his.

Yes?

I'm going to run back and lead your parents here. You stay.

Got it.

He turned and ran.

Chloe's arms wrapped around me like a big teddy-werewolf, and we waited. At a run, it didn't take long for Mom and Aunt Allison to return. Janet and Fred were with them. Once they got there, I headed out and started sniffing again. I found Hannah's scent uphill from the tents. As I followed it, I picked up traces of Chris and Andy as well. I increased my speed.

Suddenly, Tanner stood in front of me. I slid to a stop. His gaze was piercing and disappointed all at once.

Sighing, I placed my paw on his. *What this time? I have their scents.*

Why are you running?

To find them faster. This seemed obvious to me.

Jade, what if they fell off the edge of a cliff? What if they fell into a deep hole, one that you can't see? What if you're running top speed and fall and get hurt? Think. This is search and rescue, not run in like a hot head and become one of the hurt who needs to be rescued.

My head dropped in embarrassment.

He nosed me to let me know it would be okay.

The two of us headed in the direction we could smell the others, slower. After another two hundred feet or so, we saw the crevice. When I looked down, I saw three bodies below. They all looked hurt, lying prone and unmoving with their limbs spread. Tanner immediately turned and ran back towards the others.

I shifted.

"Hello? Chris? Andy? Hannah?" My voice echoed off the walls of the crevice, but I didn't hear a response. The drop was about thirty feet down and I couldn't imagine what had happened to get the three of them down there. I sat transfixed, watching them, willing them to move, to be okay.

I nearly jumped out of my skin when someone draped a jacket over my back. "You're going to freeze out here." I looked up to see Dad standing over me.

"I had to see if they would respond."

"And did they?"

"No."

Tanner and Greg approached in human form with Mom, Fred, and Janet. They all started to set up a rig to get down and save our pack members. Our family.

Mom looked at me. "Jade, dear, shift back, run down to your clothes, and get dressed. Then, if it isn't too much trouble, there is a cooler of food in our car, eat as much as you can stomach on your way back up."

I just gave her a level stare as the others chuckled.

On the run down the mountain, I met up with Clare and José on their way back, already dressed. José said he was going to wait for me.

After finding my humanity again, I felt dizzy. I searched the cooler and found a bagel with cream cheese to eat right away, then took a beef stick for the walk back up the mountain. Now it really did feel like a mountain, glaciers be damned.

When I met up with José, he demanded the cooler to carry. At my raised eyebrow, he said, "My guess is you're building your strength to do some Jade voodoo stuff. Then, you'll pass out. So, I'll carry this, so you have a pinch more energy before seeing stars."

Glaring at him, I continued to eat. As we walked, he kept handing me more food.

When we made it back to the others, they had a pulley system set up and were lowering Dad on a rope. Hannah was already lying on the ground, unconscious, being tended by Aunt Allison. Mom saw me and pointed. I knelt and rested my hands on her arm. Both animals charged forward, but I told Wolf to stay put and to take care of me.

Panther raced forward to investigate. Hannah was physically a mess and badly hurt. It looked like she had broken bones, and much more damage internally. If we didn't get her fixed, who knew how bad things would be… and then there'd be her emotional state when she woke up.

Then there was the fact she didn't have an animal to help her heal. She did have a seed, small and tender, deep down and hidden. We ignored that for now and began mending her internal organs and bones. At regular intervals, hands touched my shoulder and gave me more energy to work. Once Hannah was stable, I had Panther return to me.

Looking around, I found Andy and Chris lying on the ground. Aunt Allison sat close with Chloe on her lap. I surveyed the faces around me; they looked tired and worn down. "I can do more, if you can."

They all nodded back at me. I crawled to Chris, not sure if I could stand. I placed my hands on his arm and repeated my actions. His wolf was working hard.

Jade! Have you come to help?

I have. Let's get you fixed up.

My daughter?

Is fine.

I could smell the tension in Chris decrease as his wolf and I focused on healing his wounds.

I repeated my motions on Andy, though my vision was starting to fade. By the end, both Chris and Andy woke up, but Hannah was still unconscious. Though awake, I couldn't even sit on my own. I leaned against José and someone handed me food.

Dad monitored me to make sure I ate. "Chris, Andy, how did you three end up down there?"

Chris sighed. "Hannah wanted to see the mountain while Chloe took a nap. We told Chloe we would be back in an hour. Hannah saw a cloud that looked like a songbird and pointed up. We all gazed at it for a minute…"

Andy shook his head. "It was the dumbest thing I've ever done. We were running in a line, holding her hand so she didn't slip. We were being so careful with her. We didn't want her to get hurt. Can you imagine it?"

Snorting, I finished off my third stick of cheese. "That is the worst luck."

Andy gave me a sardonic smile. "Tell me about it."

When Andy, Chris, and I had eaten our fill, we packed up and moved down to the campsite. José wrapped his arm around my waist, supporting me. Tanner and Clare volunteered to pack up the campsite so the rest of us could head home. Andy and Chris refused, saying they could do it with Chloe's help. The rest of us shrugged and left them to it.

Janet and Fred decided to take Hannah to the hospital for a full checkup. My parents drove me and José home. We sat in the back and called Bevin on speaker. "Jade, did you find her?"

"We did."

"Who's 'we'?" Bevin asked.

"Don't let her fool you, amigo, it was Jade who found all the lost souls today."

There was a pause before Bevin continued. "Hi…José."

"Hi, my friend."

I just stared at José. It hadn't occurred to me that they still hadn't spoken to each other. *Gulp!*

"So, anyway, we found the four of them. Hannah is on the way to the hospital with your parents."

I summed everything up for him before signing off so he could find the rest of his family to get to the hospital.

José and I sat in silence for a few minutes before he turned to me. "I almost forgot. One of my new professors wanted me to say 'hi.'"

My lip curled up and my brows knit. I didn't know any professors except my mom and Sarah's mom. I just stared at him in my stupefied way as his grin continued to grow.

Finally, he broke. "Professor Falade, though he's told

the class to call him Kal."

My eyes widened and my jaw dropped. Kal Falade was the werepanther from Florida. He was the reason I now had two animals.

"Can you imagine my shock when I walked into class the first day to learn my professor was a cat?"

Everyone in the car grew quiet to hear the rest of his story. I gave José one last big hug. He gave me a big squeeze before returning to college and his new life.

Two days later, Hannah was out of the hospital and back to school.

Getting out of the hospital hadn't been easy. The x-rays showed evidence of a broken arm and leg, but both were healed, thanks to my epsilon abilities. There were no records of Hannah having broken her bones in her electronic medical record. Fred brought in a fax from a small doctor's office in Colorado, a town with no local medical connections to Madison, a town that hadn't updated to an electronic medical record. The fax was a paper copy showing a visit Hannah had to this clinic the previous summer for two broken bones.

Bevin told me about this when his family came over for dinner that Friday night to thank my dad for his IT magic. Apparently, the doctors and nurses had sounded close to calling in child services for child abuse.

CHAPTER 13

Track practice began in March. Every day after school, we had to do something with Mr. Nelson, which really messed up our afternoon practices with Aunt Allison. But with the town on the look out for wild animals again, Dad decided to hold off on those for the duration.

Wake up, home gym torture, breakfast, school, track practice hell, and special practice with Mr. Nelson two times a week. After that I had to focus on homework, which was starting to pile up.

The buzz about a black wolf being sighted got everyone in town excited. They needed something to liven up life after the holidays. Alyssa and Tiffany became instant celebrities. Not only had they seen the wolf, they'd survived it; mostly thanks to José and Owen stopping me from attacking them.

Friday, I sat at lunch and the others hadn't arrived. Tiffany scooted up to the table. "Hi, Jade, how goes school?"

My brow creased as I gaped at her, wondering if she was lost. "Um, fine. How are you?"

"Oh, I'm great. Just wondering. I watched you at practice the other day. Seems like you can actually run."

Nodding slowly, I took a bite of my burger. "Yep, apparently I came into my fifteen-year legs."

It was her turn for her brow to crease. Her head tilted and her mouth shifted to one side. "Was that a joke?"

Sighing, I sipped my soda. "Not if I have to explain it."

Her face lit up. "Oh. I get it. Funny. Anyway, if you wanted to sit with Alyssa and me, you and Sarah are welcome. Most of the track starters sit together, you know." She jumped up and headed off when she saw Bevin and Piper approaching.

My hand froze with my burger hovering just outside my mouth, jaw practically hitting the table. I must have looked like an owl gazing after her.

Bevin slid in next to me, looked me up and down, and snapped his fingers in my face. "Come back to us. How will we survive without you?"

I blinked and shifted my eyes to him. I took a bite

of my burger.

He smiled. "What's gotten into you?"

Piper and Sarah joined us. Jerking my head towards Tiffany, I said, "Apparently, now that I'm on the track team, Sarah and I can join the cool kids' table any time we want."

Piper stared at them for a second before picking up her pizza. "Just the two of you?" "Think so. It's for track starters." I turned to Sarah. "Am I a starter?"

Sarah shrugged. "Alyssa told me something similar earlier today. But she's been on me to sit with her for years. She said she never realized you were so down to Earth or some such nonsense."

"It must be the great picture she took of me." I fluffed my hair.

Bevin snorted at that. "Probably. So, ready for tonight?"

Piper's face lit up. "I am." She reached over and grabbed my hand.

Sarah smiled but it didn't reach her eyes. "I'm kind of jealous that I won't be joining you on this epic double date. Though, even if Owen were in town, I think he'd be a bit much."

We all nodded in agreement on that point.

After school, Sarah and I had track practice. I ran and jumped over hurdles. The system of running and jumping connected well to my logical mind. When I focused on counting verses on how my body moved, I got into a rhythm that let my body flow through the actions. It was probably why I didn't fall. Run, three steps, leap, three steps, leap, continue, until the end of the hurdles, then back to running and finish line.

"Wow, Jade, that was your fastest time yet. That was amazing." My head whipped around to Alyssa who was keeping time for me.

"What?"

"Yeah, that was like, epically fast."

"Maybe you started the stopwatch late, or maybe it's broken." Slapping my hands to my sides, I bent over a bit. "I actually had a stitch in my side and think that may have been my slowest run." Dread slammed through me. *The one thing Mr. Nelson warned us against.*

She tapped her foot and shook her head. "No, that was super-fast." She put her hand to her mouth like a megaphone. "Mr. Nelson, come see what Jade did."

Groaning in defeat, I dropped my shoulders. This was exactly what we had discussed avoiding. As he approached, I said again, "I really think the stopwatch is broken. My side is still aching. That had to be my slowest time."

Alyssa huffed in annoyance. "No Jade, you're wrong. Look, Mr. Nelson, check out her time. If she can repeat this time, no one can stop her. We can win in this event. It will be, like, the first time in our school's history."

Mr. Nelson grabbed the timepiece and nodded as if in thought. "Good work, Alyssa. Go work on your events.

Jade, walk off your stitch."

"Can I at least see this magical time I supposedly got?"

"No, I don't want the *stitch* to get worst. Take a lap."

Defeated, I started to walk. Though I didn't have a stitch in my side, my head was pounding. A persistent headache seemed to have taken up residence this semester. A headache in wereanimals was abnormal. One lasting this long was unheard of. I had to figure it out soon.

He went over to my stuff and found my book and the attached pen. He made some notes before putting the book back in my bag's side pocket. When I finished my lap, I gathered my bag. Practice was close enough to done to leave for the day.

"Ms. Stone, Ms. Baller, stay after please."

"I have an appointment, Mr. Nelson," I yelled, tossing my bag onto my back.

"It'll wait." He sat on a bench, compiling the notes he had taken during practice today. Everyone else was finishing up their last sets and starting to clean up. I found a bottle of water and sat impatiently.

When everyone had cleared out, Sarah and I headed over to our coach. "It's Friday, we aren't supposed to stay late with you today." I knew I sounded sulky, but I was tired of being at school.

"Ms. Stone, your time was just on the edge of unbelievable. You must be careful. I could sense your joy in the run that last time. That was why you went so fast. It's fine to have fun, but you must stay present and in the moment."

I rubbed my eyes. I didn't want him to be right, but I knew he was. "I'm sorry. I got lost in the counting. It won't happen again."

"If it does, I'll have to take you off that event. It'll be hard to explain, but better that than the alternative. Ms. Baller, as alpha, take charge."

Sarah's eyes bulged and I smelled her shock. "What?"

"You heard me. You can feel her emotions better than she can at times. If she goes to her happy place, stop it. You have better control. Probably because you've been doing sports your whole life. Step up, Ms. Baller."

"Yes, sir."

He nodded. "Good. That's it. Go."

We nodded and scampered off. Sarah grabbed her bag as we headed to the parking lot. We were about to hit the sidewalk when I heard a horn. Bevin drove up. "Thought you two might want a ride."

We piled in. Bevin went to drop Sarah off first. "No way," she said. "Jade can't be trusted to get herself put together for a date."

I huffed in annoyance.

Bevin snorted and headed towards my place. "I'll be back to pick you up in an hour."

I smiled. "I was thinking of driving separately. I'll drop off Sarah and get Piper, you get Phillip. Unless you were planning on hanging out with me afterwards."

He shrugged. "I kind of was, but you're probably right. We'll hang out tomorrow."

We reached my place quickly. "See you soon." Sarah and I ran into the house to get me ready for my date.

I searched through my closet and found a pair of black jeans and a nice blouse. I laid them on the bead. "Good?"

Sarah humored me by looking at them before saying, "No." She went into my closet. There was an area that only she and Pebble knew about that contained clothes I didn't understand. She came out with a navy-blue wrap dress with tiny white polka dots and an off-white shawl. She handed me the dress.

I yanked on it and rotated it but had no idea how to get it to fit on my body. Sarah harrumphed, grabbed the dress, adjusted it on me and ended by tying it at my side. I tried to see the magical movements she'd made, but I had no idea what she did to get the flat material to hug my body.

Afterwards, she pushed me into a seat and started in on my dark curls. By the time she was done, my hair was contained in a high, sleek ponytail and my face made-up. She had even found boots—like, nice ones—in my closet.

"Do you add things to my wardrobe when I'm not looking?"

She chuckled. "No, but that's not a bad idea." She finished the look by draping the shawl over my shoulders and handing me a purse.

She pushed me out the door. Pebble was at her bedroom door waiting. "Wow. Sarah, you did an amazing job!"

Of course I would get no credit.

"Thanks, Pebble. It took time and effort, but in the end, it was worth it."

Pebble giggled and followed us out into the living room.

Mom and Dad were there sitting on the couch in the living room watching TV. Dad's eyebrow went up in a very Mom-like manner. "Where did *that* come from?"

Shrugging, I turned to Sarah. "No idea. Sarah and Pebble seem to be able to magically find stuff in my closet."

Mom looked at me quizzically. "Candice's old stuff?"

Sarah grinned. "Yep. When we cleared out her room for Pebble, I stored her old stuff in the back of Jade's closet. Since Jade can fit into all Candice's old clothes, I figured it would eventually come in handy."

Mom nodded. "Saves on having to shop as well." She shivered.

Sarah rolled her eyes. "What is it with none of you being able to stand shopping?"

I laughed. "Come on, or I'll be late."

We headed out to Mom's car. I dropped Sarah off on the way to get Piper. I was bundled under too many layers for Piper to really see my outfit. When we reached the restaurant, we both got to appreciate each other's attire.

Piper had on a simple black tank dress with a burgundy lace long-sleeve shirt underneath. She looked great. I gave her a small smile. "You look lovely."

Blushing, she said, "So you do you…amazing."

We joined Bevin and Phillip at their table. They stood when we arrived, which made both of us blush.

Phillip checked us out. "You both look very pretty."

Both boys had on suit jackets and ties. "As do you," I replied.

We all sat. My head was still pounding. I gave my forehead a quick massage, trying not to have Piper or Bevin notice.

We each studied the menu and ordered. Afterwards, Phillip gently laid his hand on Bevin's. Bevin froze for a second before smiling. If I hadn't been watching for it, I wouldn't have noticed the pause.

Phillip faced Piper. "How are you enjoying our fair city? You're new, right?"

Piper looked shocked. She wasn't used to people noticing her. Phillip seemed the type to notice everyone. "I like it." Her focus shifted to me, and she smiled shyly. "It's the first time I've had a group of friends. My family usually moves every few months, but my dad says that this time we'll stay."

Phillip's eyes sparkled, picking up on the light green of his shirt. Lovely how his gray eyes could change with his surroundings. He smelled interested, like a vanilla shake. He leaned in towards her. "What changed?"

Piper froze, her uncertainty evident. She hadn't thought of an answer to this question that didn't involve werewolves. Phillip started to emit the minty scent of confusion.

I took Piper's hand and gave it a squeeze. "Didn't you mention that your dad really liked his current job?"

She finally took a breath and smiled. "What? Oh, yeah. Sorry about that. Yeah, he likes his job and has made some friends here he really likes, too. I guess he sees a future here."

Phillip relaxed and nodded. "Neat."

Who says "neat" anymore?

I turned to Phillip. "How did you do on that math exam?" I needed to change the subject and get the pressure off Piper. Otherwise, she would end up with her head pounding as badly as mine.

He groaned. "Really? The evening was going to be so nice. You had to bring *that* up."

Snorting, a smile broke out across my face. The other two looked back and forth between us, confused.

My eyes narrowed as I stared at him. "You know you aced the exam."

His smile slowly grew. "Maybe. But it was hard. That class is no joke."

"AP calc BC isn't a joke. Hard stuff," I agreed. "I can't wait for it to be over."

I smelled the spicy scent of Piper's anger flare up. "Calc? As in calculus? I knew you were in advanced math, but not calculus. What the hell, Jade?" My eyes grew big, and I slowly rotated to face her.

Bevin guffawed. "You've never told her what classes you take, have you?"

My head snapped to him. "Well…"

He couldn't stop laughing. "You haven't. You tutor her when she needs it, but she just knows that you're smart…. She has no idea."

I dropped my head into my hands. "Oh, gods." I had avoided this for months now. We'd discussed a bit about classes but never gotten too specific. She knew some of my AP classes, but not how many. She already thought I was a freak with what I could do as an epsilon wolf; I didn't need to add all my brainiac classes.

He flicked my head. *Ouch!* "It's your own fault, you know. You've both avoided the topic and brought it up now." He was laughing too hard to continue.

Phillip's minty scent intensified as his confusion grew. "Why haven't you told her?"

I moaned, still hiding in my hands. The pounding was taking over.

Piper's anger radiated off her and slammed into me like a fist. "She thinks I'm dumb. She doesn't want to brag about how smart she is."

I reached for her hand, needing her to understand. "No. That isn't it."

She pulled away, fuming. "Then why, Jade? Why not tell me what classes you're in? What classes *are* you in?"

Pressing my fingers into my temples, I tried to focus. "Because it wasn't important. You *are* smart. You've helped me figure things out plenty of times."

Her eyes narrowed. "Name one."

My eyes shifted to Phillip and back to her.

Her anger notched up. "See, you can't."

I could. But it had to do with my werewolf, and I couldn't talk about that in front of Phillip. "Piper, I can…"

"Just tell me Jade, what classes are you in?"

I sighed. "Bio with these two. Calc with Phillip. English and gym. History, Spanish, and physics. Actually, Phillip is in my physics class as well."

She gaped. "How many of those classes are AP?"

I took a long breath. "Six."

"You're in six AP classes? Wait, there isn't an AP option for gym. And if there was, there is no way you'd be in it. *All* of your classes are AP?"

I just nodded. Almost numb with pain at this point, I just wanted the night to be over. "It's a rough year this year…academically."

Phillip watched the whole fight happen, but the last bit stopped him. "Wait, I didn't know you were in AP English and history." He turned to Bevin. "Did you know?"

Bevin shrugged. "Sure, I did."

All this tension made the pounding in my head worse. "Hey, guys, as fun as this conversation has been, can we switch to something less intense? I think my brain is going to pound out of my head."

They all looked at me. Bevin smelled confused. "Your head hurts? Again, or still?"

I tried to breathe through the pain, I got out, "Still."

He took my hand, a motion that usually helped but seemed to make it worse. He asked, "Is that possible?"

I shrugged.

Shaking, I pulled my hand away, but the pounding continued. Nausea threatened to take over with the pain. Bevin stared at me as if he could see inside me. "Jade, are you okay?"

I nodded minutely. "I'll be fine"

Putting my elbows on the table, I began to massage my forehead. Piper's ice-cold fingers touched my forearm. I froze.

Phillip smelled more confused than Bevin. I heard him whisper, "Why can't Jade have a headache?"

Piper leaned close to me. "What's wrong? I've never seen you like this."

I slid my gaze to her as I started up the rubbing again. "I don't know." I tried to take a deep breath, hoping to dissipate a bit of the pain. "Piper, I'm really sorry. I never thought you were dumb. You aren't dumb."

I dropped my hands and stared at Phillip across the table. He had such concern in his eyes. He and Bevin were holding hands. I shut my eyes and tried one more meditative exercise to release some of the tension. It didn't work.

I rotated in my seat to face my girlfriend. I grabbed her hands. "I knew what you thought about AP classes; you made it clear to me when we met."

Piper snorted. "That was when I thought we were both teasing the mega-brains together. I never thought *you* were a mega-brain."

One side of my mouth twitched. "You did something this summer that no one else could do. Your ability to read people and situations, your intuition and insight…it's amazing. There is more to being smart than understanding what's in a book, love. So, never think for a second that I don't respect your mind. You're brilliant."

She snorted, but her shoulders relaxed.

I held her hands and knew right away it was too tight. The pain pulsated through my body, and I panted, but as I pulled away, my hands started to shake. Piper watched my hands, and I could feel that she knew I didn't want the boys to know. She snagged my hands again and squeezed, nodding. Leaning close, she gave me a quick kiss.

The waiter chose that moment to bring us drinks and appetizers.

Slowly, I sat back and regarded the boys and the food. A grin spread across my face as I stacked some fried cheese and nachos on my plate.

Bevin leaned towards Phillip. "Grab some food before Jade takes it all."

Phillip did but couldn't drop his previous question. "Why can't Jade have a headache?"

Everyone pivoted to stare at me.

Surveying those at the table, I grabbed my soda and

took a sip. My brain searched every possible reason I could think of that a person couldn't have a headache. Finally, I set the soda down and shrugged. "Well, it has to do with girly reasons. Are you sure you want to know?"

Phillip blanched and Piper dropped her face into her hands to stop herself from laughing out loud. Bevin rolled his eyes.

Smirking, I picked up a stick of fried cheese, dipped it in the sauce, and took a bite. Yum!

CHAPTER 14

Bevin came over Saturday as planned. I was sitting in the basement playing Kingdomino with Pebble. We'd just finished a round, so Bevin joined in.

"Sorry about last night. Is your head better?"

Pebble pushed her tiles to me so I could mix them up and I made a noncommittal sound. "It wasn't your fault. I'm the one who kept part of my life from Piper. She had every right to be upset. I'm just glad we talked. Did it freak Phillip out?"

Bevin dropped down next to me. "Not really. It was like dinner and a show. Why'd you really do it?"

I picked my piece from the domino options. "Don't know. I guess being in all these AP classes was just one more way to make me different, a freak. I'm tired of being weird."

"Stop thinking of yourself as weird; you're just you. You have great friends." He smiled at that. "If you have great friends, you must be great, right?"

Smiling at him, I couldn't fight such logic. A small bubble of warmth grew in my belly.

"What about you? You and Phillip seemed to do better than me and Piper last night."

Bevin's smile seemed genuine. "He makes me feel… well, normal."

I snorted. "Well, that's not true."

He punched my shoulder as he set up the dominoes for the next round.

"You know what I mean. We can talk about middle school memories or current classes and there isn't any weirdness. It's like us."

A warmth bubbled up and I slipped my arm around him in a half hug. Pebble, not knowing why the embrace was being given, but wanting in, launched herself at Bevin and gave him a tackle hug.

"Oof." He fell backwards with her on top of him.

She giggled. "You're better." She tapped his head.

We both looked at her as she scrambled down to select her next piece and place it down.

I stroked her leg. "What do you mean, hon?"

She gazed up at me. "Huh? I dunno. His head, it's almost all better."

"How do you know?"

"Cuz you know. It's your turn, can we play now?"

Bevin and I just looked at each other for a moment, and then I nodded. "Yeah, we can play." I decided on my next piece and placed it. It probably wasn't the best move, but my pounding brain had too many things to think about.

After a few more rounds, the game ended. I sent Pebble outside to play. Bevin and I climbed up onto a couch.

"Have you figured out the connections yet?"

"No. I try at night sometimes. My animals just tell me to do it."

"Helpful."

Letting my head drop back onto the couch, I gazed at the ceiling. "Yeah. Exactly."

"Do you and Sarah have big plans for spring break this year?"

"Like going to a different state and coming back with another new animal?"

He laughed. "Something like that."

"No. I think her parents might be planning another trip. Colleges keep asking her mom to sit on panels for her research. I don't think I'll go this time. Pebble is still getting used to living here and I don't want her to be here without either me or Owen."

"I could stay with her, if you think it would help."

I leaned into him, letting my head flop against his arm. "I do, but you can't go out on runs with her yet. You should stay and hang out with both of us!"

He smiled. "I can't go out on runs *yet*. But soon, right?"

"I think so."

"Phillip and I are going out again tonight…without you and Piper. I think it will be more romantic."

I snorted. "It couldn't be less. I don't know what's up with my head. It's made my torture time even more tortuous."

Bevin chuckled, then paused. "Oh, no. Is your dad going to set *me* up with one of those?"

Giving him an evil look, I nodded. "Absolutely. It's his perverse joy in life setting up training programs for new werebeasts. If you're really lucky, Mr. Nelson will give you a secondary one as well."

"I hope not. He isn't even my gym teacher. Maybe he'll never know." Bevin slid me a sidelong look. "So, when do you pick up a bear as your third animal?"

I froze. "What? No. Never. Can you imagine it? Just my luck, Mr. Nelson would be my alpha, or whatever they have." I groaned, imagining that hell. "That would be the worst."

Bevin laughed. "I figured you'd have a full menagerie by the time you were twenty."

A menagerie…. I narrowed my eyes and punched his shoulder. "No, thank you. Well, maybe if we could find a flying wereanimal, that would be cool."

Bevin snorted.

I could smell tomato soup heating up and grilled cheese frying. I slowly got to my feet and pulled Bevin with me. We made our way up to the kitchen and found Dad cooking.

He turned to us. "Sit, it's lunch time."

We sat.

As he put a drink in front of each of us, he asked, "Jade, any luck with the connections?"

"No, I've tried, but this headache has been making everything I do harder."

Dad reached over to feel my head. "Huh. No fever. How long has this been going on?"

I thought back. "More or less since I found the connections the first time."

"Have you thought about asking the beasts about it?"

My lip curled and I shook my head. "No, it seems so, I dunno, mundane. It's just a headache."

He shook his head. "There isn't anything mundane about a headache in a wereanimal, much less over a long span of time."

Bevin waggled his eyebrows at me. "Told you so."

A low growl bubbled up from my gut.

Dad served us each a sandwich and bowl of soup. "Eat, and then we need to figure this out."

After lunch, I moved to a couch in the living room. I laid down, closed my eyes, and found my beasts. They prowled in the mental landscape I'd created weeks ago. An image of a campsite with a firepit surrounded by logs for sitting on. There was a small cottage that I didn't think could be entered, and a forest with a lake behind it.

Do you know why my head has been hurting?

Panther sniffed me then circled me before bounding off. Wolf sat.

You are connected.

I broke off the connections.

No and yes. You must learn.

How?

I do not know.

Show me the connections.

You must show them; it is not me, but we.

And then, Wolf ran off, too.

I closed my eyes tighter as my head pounded in time to the pounding of her paws as she ran away. One more soothing breath and I faced Bevin and my dad.

"I really need to figure this out."

Dad handed me a mug of coffee and I drank deeply.

He patted my head. "No more answers?"

"No. They keep telling me they are me and I am them. I have to do it myself." I growled in frustration.

Two days later was my first track meet. Tiffany, the track captain, informed me that it was mandatory to wear the track uniform to school. Sarah confirmed this bit of unfortunate news. The very idea gave me mental hives. I wasn't sure if I could present myself to the school as a jock.

I put on the outfit, tight gray running shorts with a dark purple tank top. "Stolzburg Pumas" was printed across the chest in gray and my last name was splashed across the back, so everyone was sure to know it was me. Thankfully, I could hide in the track pants and a windbreaker. Both gray with dark purple down the outside of the arms and legs. "Stolzburg Pumas" was still emblazoned across the front of the jacket and my name was stitched across the back, along with "track starter." This way everyone not only knew that I was on a *sports team*, but *which team*.

I reached for my doorknob and hesitated. I backed up, took a picture, and sent it to Sarah.

She immediately texted a, Yes! And a photo of herself in her matching outfit.

Closing my eyes, I reached out, and opened the door. Hearing a squeal, I opened one eye. Pebble stood outside my door bouncing in delight. She leapt into my arms and gave me a huge hug.

I carried her to the kitchen and found Mom and breakfast. "You look great." She smiled, though I smelled her vanilla scent of mirth. "Great…school spirit, hon."

I groaned. "I hate this."

"No, you don't. It's just new. You'll adjust."

I huffed out a rush of air. "You're probably right."

After breakfast, I made my way to school, meeting Sarah at our usual spot. I tried to ignore everything on the way to the lockers with Sarah. Once there, I could hear the titters from students amazed that I was in a track outfit.

"Is that Jade Stone in a school uniform?"

"I thought she was a nerd, not a jock."

"Doesn't she always fall on her butt in gym class?"

Sarah started laughing at that last one. Bevin and Piper looked questioningly at her, so she filled them in. I sat on the floor, blushing, as the three of them giggled over the comments.

As the heat burned my cheeks, I tugged at the uniform and tried to figure out if this was better or worse than wearing a shirt proclaiming I liked 'grrls'.

Piper leaned over and draped her arm across my back. "The last time your outfit caused this much chaos in the halls, you ended up with a new girlfriend. None of that today, okay?" She gave me a mischievous grin, and a kiss on my cheek, then jumped up and left for class.

The bell rang and Bevin pulled me up so we could head to AP bio together.

The track meet was at a neighboring school, and we had to take a bus to get there. Coach Nelson had signed me up for four events: one-hundred-meter hurdles, sixteen-hundred-meter run, three-hundred-meter hurdles, and then the thirty-two-hundred-meter run. I sat on the bus next to Sarah and focused on how to navigate the meet, run each race to win…but not like a superhero.

Tiffany came up to our seats. "Okay, you two. I don't know where you came from, but this is your first year on the team. You're becoming stars in your events. I expect you to represent the school well. Don't lose." And then she sauntered off.

I eyed Sarah. "Was that a pep talk?"

Sarah chuckled. "I…think so."

"Wow…I feel…inspired."

Sarah nodded. "Totally."

When we got to the school, anxiety coursed through me. Because it was early March, there was still snow on the ground, and it was freezing outside, the meet was held indoors. The first event was a relay with Sarah competing as anchor. Though they were a bit behind, when she got a hold of the baton, she made up the time and we won.

Suddenly, I was up. One-hundred-meter hurdles. I got to the starting line and waited for the shot. I took off and found my pacing. Leap, three steps, leap, three steps…I made sure I could see the other competitors in my peripheral vision. Sarah and I discussed this strategy for not getting too far ahead of the others. I crossed the finish line just ahead of the next runner, gulping in air as if my lungs burned.

Next was the one-hundred-meter dash; back to Sarah. Again, she was brilliant. We went back and forth throughout the meet. There were some events that neither of us competed in. For those, we just sat back and watched.

The second to last event was the thirty-two-hundred-meter run. This was my last event, and I finally wasn't freaking out. I had already done two hurdle events and a shorter run. I was in the zone. I got to the starting line and waited. The shot rang out and all the competitors lunged forward, their stress and excitement perfuming the air. At first, I stayed back, letting one or two runners out-pace me.

As the run continued, I thought back to my first experience running when my brother explained gym class as a werewolf as being a "walk in the park." He wasn't wrong. That's what this felt like. I wasn't really pushing myself; it was more like a trot than a run. As my mind wandered, I kept pace with the other runners. Next thing I knew, I heard a whistle.

I suddenly slowed to a walk and looked around me, there were no other runners near me. I spun and saw the next runner half the field behind me. My eyes widen in fear. I bent over and grabbed my knees in panic.

Sarah ran up to me. "You okay?"

My voice wispy with fear, I asked, "What did I do?"

Her voice flat and matter of fact, she replied, "You went too fast."

"How fast?"

"Eight minutes forty-nine seconds."

"Okay, not a record. Almost, but not quite. Damn, damn, damn. This was such a bad idea. Is Mr. Nelson going to kill me?"

Sarah popped up and looked around. She bent back down. "Yep. Absolutely."

Sighing, I straightened. "You need to get to your last event. Let me," I raised my fingers to do air quotes, "walk it off."

Sarah snorted before jogging off to the starting line.

Alyssa ran up to me. "Oh, wow, Jade. That was amazing. I'm going to have to do an article on you for the paper. That was just…wow! You are just a wonder to watch run."

Taking a few deep breaths, I put my hands on my sides. "It was a fluke. I don't know if I can run that fast again. I've never done that before." *Liar, liar, pants on fire!*

Sarah's eyes narrowed as if she could read my mind.

Her eyes sparkled with excitement. "Just think, Mr. Nelson is amazing. He might get you to run even faster."

CHAPTER 15

By Friday, if felt like everyone at school had read the article about my run. Someone taped the insufferable thing to my locker, and every time I took it down, it showed up again. Afraid it would start to multiply, I decided to ignore it.

As I walked to class, fellow students would wave at me. Some even said "hi." To me. By name.

The second time this happened, I asked Sarah about it. She just shrugged. "You're famous now. You're making a name for yourself and the school. People want to know you."

Opening my eyes wide, I asked, "What about lettering in math?"

Sarah snorted.

I punched her in the arm. "I brought a trophy home for the school in both math and science. Are you telling me that that doesn't count?"

"Yep. That is exactly what I'm telling you. And though math was individual, science was a team effort."

I hoped it would die out by the following week, but it didn't. In AP bio, Phillip smiled mischievously, sitting on the other side of Bevin in AP bio, and asked, "Are you still allowed to be in all these AP classes while wearing your track uniform? Or are you breaking some track-star rule?"

I grumbled while Bevin slapped his hands over his mouth to avoid disrupting class. We were working on a lab together so talking was okay, laughing uproariously was not.

My head hit my folded arms before I sat back up and narrowed my eyes at both of them, I leaned in and hissed at Phillip, "Really? From you, too? You know there is no connection between being good at sports and AP classes." I glared at Bevin. "Sarah has always been in sports and she's in AP English. Can't I have one class?"

They both just smiled back and waggled their brows. Then Phillip held up a fist for Bevin to bump, who happily obliged.

After class, I navigated through the halls when Phillip grabbed my arm to slow me down. "Can I ask you a question before we get to math?"

"Of course. What's up?"

"I made Bevin a gift for our one-month anniversary,

and I was hoping you could check it out and tell me if you think he's going to like it."

I slowed to a stop and narrowed my eyes. "You two went on your first date in January. It's March. Uniform or no, I can count to one."

He cocked a smile. "Okay, I'll make it a three-month gift. It isn't done yet, and I want it to be special. Maybe I'll just give it to him because I want to give it to him…I don't know. I'll figure that part out later. But will you look it over?"

The happiness bubbled out of me, and I bounced. "Yes!"

He hooked his arm in mine and dragged me to class. "Privacy." When we got there, he dug through his bag until he found what looked like a navy-blue construction paper book, the type made by younger kids. It was about four inches by five inches in size. He handed it to me and blushed.

On the outside were the words *To My Bevin, From Phillip* in beautiful calligraphy.

"Did you do this?"

Phillip nodded. "I learned how a few years ago."

I turned to the first page. On the left-hand side was a picture. It was an image of a valentine that Bevin must have made for Phillip in elementary school. The two of them were standing arm in arm and they looked about seven years old. They were ridiculously cute standing there. It was well before Bevin and I had become close. Under the picture, in Bevin's handwriting, were the words: *BFF 4ever.*

I just stared at the image. Bevin was wearing jeans and

a blue shirt, and his hair was short. He'd always worn boy's clothes, but I thought this may have been before he started going by the name Bevin. Phillip's shirt matched Bevin's but was green.

"It's a journey of images I've kept of us. This was our oldest memory I could find. I've always loved this memory and I didn't want to exclude it or alter it. Do you think he'll hate it?"

I studied the picture again and thought about it, then shook my head. "I don't. It's his history, who he was, who the two of you were." I leaned over and gave him a quick side hug.

On the opposite page from the picture, Phillip had written about that Valentine's day and how that had been his favorite Valentine's card he'd received.

I flipped the page. The next image was the two of them in science goggles behind a miniature volcano. They were both covered in green goo, as was everything in the picture behind them. The two kids in the picture had huge smiles on their faces, eyes dancing. Again, Phillip wrote about that day on the right-hand side of the book.

The next page held an image of the two of them in seventh grade when the school went to Six Flags, Great America. They had gone on one of those rides where the ride takes your picture. Phillip had bought the photo and included it.

The fourth page had a picture of them in eight grade at the school picnic. The left side image was of the two of them sitting together laughing while eating lunch. On the right side, instead of words there was another photo from this picnic. They were pulling the rope from tug-o-war.

The next page was from their graduation; the left side had a picture of Bevin from that day, and the right side had Phillip. They both wore matching polo shirts and big smiles.

The final page had the two of them outside of the high school together. On the right-hand side Phillip talked about how this was the first day of high school and how excited he had been to start their new adventure together. It goes on to talk about the best thing that happened to him was me dragging him over to Bevin last December and reuniting them after all these years.

I put the book down and stared at Phillip. He wasn't breathing and his hands shook. His sour scent of anxiety took over. "This is…" I shook my head in wonder. "This is amazing."

"Do you think he'll like it?"

"I do. It's so thoughtful." I tilted my head. "What happened? You two were so close in middle school."

Phillip slumped. "When we started freshman year, he got really close to José. He joined GSA, something I wasn't ready to do. I think I knew I liked guys, but I wasn't ready to admit it. He was so confident in who and what he was. I guess I needed to figure out if it was just Bevin or boys in general who I liked. By the time I figured it out, you and Sarah were back in his life, and you all were closer than ever."

He finally relaxed, his scent shifting to a citrusy hope, as he gently picked up the book and stored it back in this bag.

Class was beginning, so we couldn't say much more about this treasure trove of memories he wanted to give to Bevin.

That night, I headed over to Sarah's house for dinner. Cindy and Tom had put together a gathering with me, Kal, and Dayo, Kal's daughter

I arrived early to help set up because I was only trusted to place dishes and cutlery on the table. I asked the room at large, "Did you know they were relocating up here?"

Cindy, who was finishing up dinner, chuckled from the kitchen. "Jade, dear, they arrived at the beginning of the school year."

"Why didn't anyone tell me?" I gave Sarah an accusatory stare. "Did *you* know?"

Sarah's hands flew up in the air as if I'd pointed a weapon at her. "I had no idea." Slowly lowering her hands and watching me as she did it, like she thought I'd attack, she asked her mom, "Why *didn't* you tell us they were in town? We could've shown Dayo around, introduced her to our friends."

"Well, dear, she's in college and has her own friends. I didn't think she'd want to be dragged over to Stolzburg to meet high schoolers."

Grunting, I finished placing the last of the items on the table. "There's always José. He could've introduced her to Madison. And she may've enjoyed a friendly face."

Tom shrugged. "José had just become a werewolf. We

thought he may be overwhelmed with everything else: new school, new people, dorms."

Scrunching my nose, I said, "It actually may have helped. Having another wereanimal who knows what you're going through can really give support when you have your freak-out moments." I shrugged. "But no harm, no foul. We'll tell them more about José tonight and let Dayo decide."

We focused on getting the house set up for the visit. Once Sarah and I were done, we slipped off to her room to finish some English homework. We had papers due that we could work on together for the remainder of the time.

When the doorbell rang, we headed back to greet our maker, so to speak. Tall and willowy, Kal hadn't changed at all. Well, everyone towered over me. But in the last year, Dayo had grown in both height and elegance; she also had an air of confidence. For a second, I stopped breathing. *Wow!* She and Sarah looked so similar; they could be sisters. The biggest difference was Dayo had green eyes like mine.

She dashed in and gave each of us hugs. Kal shook Cindy's and Tom's hands. Kal worked in Cindy's department, so they saw each other with some regularity. Then we all made our way to the dining room where Cindy set out pulled pork, roasted asparagus, and baked potatoes. I had been smelling the pork roast since I arrived, and my hunger oozed out of me.

We sat, served ourselves, and began to eat. Once the first pangs of hunger were alleviated, Kal turned to me.

"Jade, can you finally tell me what you are? Your scent has changed…again."

Before coming over, I had sat and discussed this with my mom. She hadn't met Kal yet, since she worked in a different department at the University, but she had decided she would invite him and his daughter over to meet the pack. She told me I was free to share information about myself in general, as well as the pack.

I took a drink of soda to clear my palate. Then I explained about my parents and the local werewolf pack. "When I visited Florida, I wasn't a werewolf. That happened later. I have a few theories as to why I smelled like a wolf when you met me, but I wasn't one yet."

Dayo's eyes narrowed. "But now you have two animals you can shift into?" Dayo's accent wasn't as strong as her dad's, but it was there. A hint of Africa seasoned her words.

I nodded.

She whirled to face her dad. "Have you *ever* heard of something like this?"

He stared into a far-off corner of the room. After a minute, he slowly shook his head. "No, I haven't. That's…I don't know what that is."

His confusion washed over me, and I had to slow my breathing. It was like he'd never learned to block any of his emotional output. Finally, Sarah touched my arm to help slow my system down. It helped.

Kal and Dayo watched us.

Dayo turned to her dad. "What just happened?"

Kal's eyes were wide. "Does that always work? Can the two of you always help with just a touch? How did you figure this out?"

Everyone watched us. Sarah's brow knit and her hand froze in place on my forearm. I searched each person's face, ending at Kal. "This is a werewolf thing. Werewolves need touch, need their pack. There are lone wolves out there, but most don't survive long because of the need for connections with other werewolves."

Placing my hand over Sarah's, I gave her a smile. I felt her relax as she smiled back at me. I focused back on Kal. "Sarah learned how to be a werepanther from a group of werewolves. I guess contact was part of her education. It's always helped her."

Tom cleared his throat. "It doesn't hurt that Sarah is Jade's alpha, or whatever word you use for panthers."

At that word, Kal froze, and Dayo looked confused. Her head cocked to the side and her brows lowered. She started off staring at Tom, then slowly rotated to Sarah, then reversed her movement, ending at her dad. Having my defenses up at this point, the emotions Kal and Dayo threw off weren't knocking me on my butt.

Cindy reached over and gently covered Kal's hand with her own. "Kal, are you okay?"

He jerked and his eyes snapped to hers. In a soft whisper he asked, "Did he just say, 'alpha'?"

Everyone around the table, except Dayo who already acted befuddled, began to emit a minty scent. Faces frowned in puzzlement. *What was so confusing?*

Cindy became the professor. My mom usually did this at home. "Kal!" she snapped. "What's going on? Why are you acting like we've said something foreign?"

Kal jerked back as if slapped. "Panthers are solitary creatures, Cindy. They don't have alphas."

Now it was my and Sarah's turn to pause in confusion. I held my breath, waiting for the next bomb to drop.

Kal nodded as he saw our uncertainty. "I've only heard of one other panther pair with an alpha—and that was more legend than fact. I'll have to find the story and bring it to you. Part of the legend involves Soul Sharing. Has that manifested yet?"

Sarah and I gazed at each other in confusion and then back at Kal. Sarah found her voice first. "Soul Sharing?"

"From what I understand, you two should be able to share…well…power. It's so rare, no one really knows what it means."

Thinking hard, I couldn't remember a single instance of this happening. "Is it a two-way street or just the alpha sharing my 'soul,' and do we need to be touching?"

Kal shook his head. "I have no idea."

Sighing in resignation, I faced Sarah. "You *know* we have to try it out now."

Sarah's eyes were a bit wild, but she nodded. "Do you

have a thought?"

The side of my mouth twitched. I knew exactly what I wanted her to try. I leaned over and whispered in her ear what to do. Then I sat back and watched her.

She closed her eyes…and nothing. "Stop staring at me, Jade. It really doesn't help this…at all."

Biting my lips to keep from laughing, I turned back to the rest of the table and realized everyone else was watching me. Oh…yeah…that really wasn't helpful. I smiled wide and waved.

Tom's eyes narrowed. "What did you tell her to do?"

Just then Sarah yanked a chunk of my energy away. The headache I had been trying to ignore ignited like someone had thrown lighter fluid on it. I nearly collapsed. At the same time, a wave of pure calm came out of Sarah. It was wonderful. It felt like floating on clouds on a perfect day while eating chocolates. I wanted to stay there forever… except for the headache.

Groaning, I piled more food on my plate, hoping eating more would help with my head.

Sarah watched me. "That was cool, but are you okay?"

"Yeah. Is that what the calming feels like?"

She smiled at me. "It feels like all kinds of wonderful. I love when you decide to put the calming smackdown on a room."

Kal's eyes were half-closed. He shook his head as if trying to clear his mind. "What did you just do?"

I huffed out a laugh. "It's my own special brand of werewolf. I can calm wereanimals and others down. That's what Sarah borrowed."

Kal's eyes became saucers. *Why did I have this effect on everyone?* "You're an epsilon werewolf?"

Slumping, my jaw dropped. "You've heard of them?"

"I really need to find this book. When I do, I'll gift it to you."

Rubbing my temples, trying to stop the pounding in my head, I said, "Everyone but me knows what I am."

Sarah laughed, throwing her arm around me.

CHAPTER 16

The following week on Wednesday, Kal and Dayo came for dinner at the pack house. Bevin came over to study bio with me and he decided to stay for the meal. In lieu of cooking, Dad brought home Chinese food. No one was in the mood to cook on Wednesdays.

Bevin and I were working through a study guide for an exam when the doorbell rang. I recognized Mom's tread to the door.

I closed the books in front of me and shoved everything back into my school bag. Bevin followed suit and quirked a smile. "Well, if we don't know it now, I guess we never will."

I nodded in agreement, and we headed up stairs. As we neared the front door, I heard introductions being made. Dropping my bag on the bench, I smiled up at Kal and Dayo. Dayo leaned in to give me a hug and I squeezed her back. "This is one of my closest friends, Bevin. Bevin this is Dayo and her dad, Kal. Kal is one of José's professors." Facing Kal I explained, "We're all close. We miss having José with us every day."

Kal nodded in understanding as he held his hand out to Bevin. "Nice to meet you, young man." After a subtle sniff he added. "You're not a werewolf like the rest of the group."

Bevin smiled and shook his head. "Not yet. Jade informs me that I don't have long to wait."

He turned to me. "I have the book for you, I found it very informative." He handed it to me.

Before any more could be asked, Dad interrupted. "Okay, let's move this to the dining room. I'm sure both what Bevin said, and the book opened up a lot of questions, but this isn't the most comfortable spot."

Snorting, I led the way through the living room and kitchen to the dining room. Someone had set it up, including transferring all the take-out to nice bowls. I took a seat and found myself quickly flanked by Bevin and Pebble. I wasn't sure where she'd been hiding but she hadn't been in the foyer to greet the guests.

Upon seeing her, Kal and Dayo froze. Disgust oozed out of them. My whole body tensed, and Pebble climbed into my lap to hide. Her body began to shake in fear and a tear rolled down her face.

Mom, taking in the scene, barked a single alpha command. "Stop!"

Everyone froze.

She slowly turned to our guests, the alpha glow in her eyes. "We did *not* turn a child into a werewolf. If you would believe us to be such monsters, you can let yourselves out, now. We have invited you into *our* house after you turned *our* child into a werepanther. Choose. Now."

At that moment she looked ten feet tall and scary.

Kal faced her; it didn't look as if he breathed. Dayo's eyes were huge, and her hands shook. Besides those two tells, she held herself regally tall. After a minute, Kal drew an audible breath. "I apologize for my assumption. I have not seen a child wereanimal in years. I will listen and share stories over food." He bowed his head in respect.

Mom closed her eyes then bowed her head back.

The dangerous moment passed. After another few seconds, everyone took their places. Pebble stayed on my lap until everyone was seated and the food was served. Before I moved her to her chair, she whispered up to me, "Can I sit between you and Bevin?"

Bevin's brows creased. Being the one norm in the group, he couldn't hear her.

I scooted over and plopped her in my seat, then switched our plates. I caught Bevin's attention. "She wanted to sit between us. I think she feels safest like this."

The vanilla scent of pleasure came from Bevin and Pebble giggled.

When most of the food was gone and we'd all caught up on Pebble's backstory, where Kal and Dayo came from, what some of what my special skills allowed me to do, and what the Soul Sharing was, we decided to move to the living room.

I sat on the couch with Bevin and Dayo. My parents were on the love seat and Kal occupied one of the recliners. Pebble dashed off to the basement to play.

Dad eyed the book in my hands. "So, this book you gave Jade has information on werepanthers, but also on werewolves?"

Kal smiled warmly. "Yes. Our area of Africa has plenty of both, so the book covers both creatures."

I leaned forward. "Do you know of *other* wereanimals?"

Kal smile widened. "Of course, young one. There are many wereanimals in Africa. Most of the larger animals have had clans at some point. Some have become extinct over the years. The panthers and the wolves, as always, are the biggest. The lions are a large clan, as are the zebras. They are one of the few prey clans that have survived."

Stunned, I sat listening to him. I forced my mouth to close. Gulping in a breath of air, I shook myself to restart my brain. "Do you know of any other wereanimals in America?"

Kal huffed. "No, child. I have tried to steer clear of the wereanimals here. Until I ran into you, I was doing a good job of it, too."

Bevin slid his hand in mine and mumbled, "Isn't that always the way?"

I shoulder bumped him.

Dad and Mom both chuckled at his words. Finally, Dad focused on me. "This weekend, you and Sarah will be beginning a new training regime."

Grunting, my head fell back onto the couch as my arms flopped to the sides.

Dayo, who had unfortunately been struck by one of my hands, asked, "Training regime?"

Bevin snorted. "Jade's dad is all about training new wereanimals. You should see their gym. He sets up strength, cardio—and I'm guessing now Soul Sharing?—programs. These programs are thorough."

I sat up while Bevin explained and glanced over at Dad. He just nodded as he started taking notes in a notebook he seemingly produced out of thin air.

Kal, who had been staring into space, focused on Dad. "Can I see your training program?"

Bevin and I stayed behind as the rest of the group moved off to discuss his torture programs. I already knew enough about that for a lifetime.

The following weekend, Owen was up from Whitewater. He, Sarah, and I sat on the floor in the gym ready to start the first of the Soul Sharing training sessions.

Dad faced us. "You did this once before, but Jade, you explained everything to Sarah. You were sitting there like a lifeline. The question is, can she do it without you? Also, is it only the calming or can more be done?"

My eyes widened at the implication of his words. Standing, I turned towards the stairs. "Should I just go lie down in the living room, or should I grab some protein bars first?"

Dad gave me a knowing smile. "I asked Tanner to come over and make you one of his shakes."

I moaned at the thought of the treat and dashed to the kitchen, where Tanner was pouring his liquid chocolate gold into a large cup. He held it out. I snatched it out of his hand and took a gulp before making my way into the living room. After taking another long swig of pure joy, I turned to face Tanner. "You are a god of the kitchen, you know that, right?"

He just quirked a smile and began making another one. My eyes got huge.

"If you finish the first one and haven't passed out, we'll talk about a second. For now, there's a house full of people who may want one of these."

Rotating on the couch, I concentrated on not passing out.

I knew passing out was a real possibility, so I took a gulp and set the cup down. Then waited. I repeated this until the cup was empty.

At first my muscles were stiff, while I waited for whatever they were doing in the gym to happen. I knew the tension would make my head hurt worse, it had become a background pain, but this would make it spike, so I forced myself to relax. But the waiting continued. Then, after about ten minutes, it felt like someone had taken an ice cream scoop and removed a chunk of my energy. Collapsing, I slid off the couch, landing in a pile on the floor. I didn't even have the energy to straighten up. I groaned in agony. My head pounded. I started to pant. All I could see were the legs of the table and the navy-blue recliner across from the couch. The world started to get dark, but I fought to maintain consciousness.

Eventually, I saw Tanner's blue eyes glowing from his dark umber skin as he reached down and picked me up like a rag doll. He gently lowered me to the couch, straightening my limbs and draping a blanket over me. "You okay?"

Trying to nod, I couldn't get my body to work, so I grunted.

"Would sitting you up make you pass out?"

"Don't think so," I managed to get out. The words sounded breathy.

He adjusted my position so that I somewhat resembled a sitting person. Then, he disappeared into the kitchen. He reappeared and held a straw to my mouth, and when I drank more delicious shake slid into my mouth. I almost swooned in happiness. I sucked down as much as I could stomach. After a few sips, I reached up to take the glass, but an eyebrow raise told me what he thought of the idea.

A herd of elephants came tearing towards us from the

basement. Sarah's voice led the charge. "Did you feel the pull? I did it. I healed Owen! Your dad had to injure him first, but it was only a cut."

When they arrived and saw my state, they all paused. "Sis, you okay?" Owen plopped down next to me and took the glass from Tanner, taking over the nursing of the invalid.

"I didn't pass out. I think I'm fine. It just takes a big pull. It's one of those things. You can use my skills, it just takes more from me than when I use them myself…apparently. So, be careful. Also, healing takes a lot of energy. We should test the calming again. That didn't seem as bad…just not today."

Over the next few weekends, Soul Sharing became a regular training item. Sarah could calm by borrowing my epsilon powers. It seemed that the closer we were to each other, the easier she could draw on my abilities, and the less it took of my energy. We practiced healing one more time but decided that should only be done in an emergency.

When we tried the connection from Sarah to me, it seemed the Soul Sharing went both ways; I could pull Sarah's dominance and drop Owen to his knees, or even Tanner when I tried with him. The Sharing didn't seem to take quite as much from Sarah as it did from me.

CHAPTER 17

The next few track meets went by without fanfare. I figured out my headspace and didn't daydream while running. Before I knew it, it was spring break.

José's family decided to travel to Mexico for his spring break, which coincided with ours. There would be a full moon during his trip and his parents wanted to check in before heading out. José took the opportunity to visit with me. It was cool outside, but we sat in the treehouse while Pebble played in the yard.

José leaned back. "So, chica, two news articles this year. You're a superstar."

I gave him a level stare. "I'm working on it. The wolf story has fizzled out since no one has seen the black wolf again." Taking a deep breath of the cool air, I asked, "Did Bevin start taking your calls?"

José shifted his gaze to watch Pebble run after bubbles made by an electric bubble-maker. "How did you know about that?"

"I know everything."

His eyes slid to me, and he grunted.

I smiled and wiggled my eyebrows. "What? You didn't know I'm omniscient? I distinctly remember telling you."

His scent shifted to earthy sadness. My smile faltered. "If you knew everything, you wouldn't be asking me about my friend."

Bumping him with my shoulder, I winced as a squeal of pure happiness erupted from Pebble below and sent a spike of pain through my skull. I still battled a headache.

"I don't know why you don't ask *him*, but yes, we're back to talking."

I smiled, my whole body vibrating in happiness. "Good."

"I miss him."

"He's why you joined our group last year, isn't he?"

José shifted to face me. "When Bevin started high school, I introduced him to GSA. He didn't really have anyone for that first year. By the end of his second year, my junior year, we had talked so much, hung out so much, I realized that he had become my best friend."

He paused to look up at the clouds. "Hanging out with Owen was purely habit. Hanging out with Bevin fulfilled something deep within me." He looked down at his hands. "Then, a few months ago, something in me changed. I don't know what it is, but I don't want to lose my friend."

"What do you mean?"

"I don't know, ya know. I go out on dates with guys. They're great. But halfway through the date I think about wanting to get home to call Bevin. I probably think about him too much."

"You know, Bevin had a theory about that. Did he tell you?"

"The alpha theory?"

I nodded.

"Yeah. He told me. That could be it…maybe. But, Jade, this started before the wolf. It got worse with the wolf but wanting to end dates to talk to him started…a while ago."

He smelled conflicted, like there was more, but I didn't want to push.

"How about you? How's track?"

I snarled. "Really? You, too?"

He snorted, and the first real wave of amusement rolled off him that I had felt in some time.

"That good?"

"I can't believe Sarah dragged me to that damn meeting. I train with the team. We decided I would do long distance running and Sarah would do the short distances. I'm also doing anything with hurdles. I'm oddly good with them. I'm practicing the long jump."

José snorted. "How do you stop yourself from bounding too far?"

"That's the best part. It's like precision jumping. I'm almost to the point that I can decide how far I want to jump and jump to that spot. I'm thinking of practicing blindfolded. I mean, there isn't a practical application, but it's sure a fun trick."

José shook his head as if in disapproval, but his eyes danced. "I can't believe you sound excited about something athletic. As I live and breathe, chica, as I live and breathe."

"Hush." I slapped him lightly on the chest with the back of my hand. "I know it's weird. I keep thinking of it more as a puzzle then a sport. The worst part is practice. I have to do one type with the team and then some nights Sarah and I stay late for a special session. Then there's still our morning sessions. Dad has shifted to mostly strength training. He coordinates everything with Mr. Nelson." I might have had a bit of whine in my voice at the end.

José laughed at me.

We sat in silence for a few minutes, watching Pebble play on the new swing set that Dad and some other pack members had built for her. The bubble-machine, still pumping out bubbles, made the backyard look ethereal.

José leaned over and rested his head on my shoulder. He sighed, the minty scent of confusion still flowing off him, but he also had the woodsy smell of determination. "Jade, can I tell you something? I need to tell someone, but you can't tell anyone. Not Sarah, not Piper, no one."

I slid my arm around him and rested my head against his. "Of course. You're like my brother. Your secrets are my secrets."

He tensed before letting out a big breath. "Those dates I go on…"

"Yeah?"

"Sometimes, when I kiss the guy, I wonder what it would be like if the guy was Bevin…"

I gave him another squeeze, still watching Pebble. I could feel his whole being relax. It felt like he had taken off a jacket of stress and put it aside. I knew the tension of carrying this deep secret would return, but for just an instant, he was free.

The next day, Monday, was a full moon night. Because of spring break, the pack would come over earlier than usual. Between Phillip and track, Bevin and I hadn't spent much quality time together in ages. He came over right after breakfast so we could hang out together.

I got up, ran, and did my weights before most of the house woke up, as usual. While I finished up my homework in the basement, I heard footsteps on the stairs. I looked up to see Bevin. Happy that he had arrived, I rose to embrace him. He paused for a second and then returned the hug.

"It's not like I didn't see you a few days ago, what's up?"

"I dunno, I feel like we never *really* see each other, just the two of us."

"That's true. Our catch-up time, bio, has been usurped by Phillip…sorry about that."

I dragged him to a couch and pulled him down. "No worries. Tell me about it. Are you happy as an item or what? I can never tell. Your scent wavers when you're around him. Though he's all in."

Bevin blushed. "I don't know what to tell you. We've been going on dates, but it doesn't feel any different than when we hang out. I know he really likes me, it's just…" His head hit the back of the couch. "Jade, I want to like him. He should be perfect. He's cute and smart, and he knows about me…. He gave me the most romantic gift."

I smiled at that.

His eyes widened. "You know about the book?"

My face heated. "Yeah. He asked me what I thought about it. He wanted it to be the perfect gift."

"It was…. It may have been too perfect. He's wanted to ask me out for years. We were friends for so long and when I started to transition, he was all in."

"Is that bad?"

"I don't know."

I rubbed his arm. "It's fine, you don't have to like someone because they like you. But you should tell him. Stringing him along isn't cool."

Bevin's arm was warmer than usual. I could feel the heat through his shirt. I moved my hand to his forehead and froze. *Now!* went through my head.

I snatched my hand back. My eyes went wide with shock, and my hand trembled.

Bevin grabbed my hand. "What? What is it?"

I shook my head. "Ummm. I don't know." But I did. As we sat there, hands together, I knew. I looked up at the ceiling as if I could see the sky and the moon. Then I dropped my gaze to his eyes. My heart raced and wildness filled me.

Mom's voice preceded her as she came racing from upstairs. "Jade, what's wrong?"

Mom, my alpha, could feel my emotions. I couldn't get my heart rate down and she knew it. I sat there, staring at my friend. My friend whose life was about to change.

Mom stood there, waiting for an answer.

Bevin finally pulled his gaze from mine and looked up at her. "I'm not sure. She just started freaking out."

"Jade, what's wrong, dear?"

Wrenching my focus from Bevin's forehead up to Mom, I said, "It's time."

Bevin froze next to me. I think he finally understood. Mom put the back of her hand on his forehead and nodded. She patted my head. "You are such a wonder, dear. This will make things easier in the future. So, tonight? I wonder if I could force things now and make it even simpler. Jade? Do you know?"

"What?" I looked at her, confused.

She waved her hands at Bevin. Bevin, for his part, smelled sweet with his terror. He sat frozen in fear, staring at Mom open-mouthed.

Comprehension hit. "Bevin, are you okay with this?"

Wild-eyed, he just nodded.

My headache threatened to split my head open. I slowly took his hand and closed my eyes.

Neither animal moved forward.

What's wrong, why don't you help?

They looked at me, heads cocked. *You know the answer. You are connected.*

I closed my eyes tight and searched for the connection. It was there, deep down.

End the connection, it isn't needed.

There was a snap and Bevin drooped. Instantly, my headache stopped. I felt like I could float with the sudden cessation of pain.

I reached out towards Bevin and found his wolf.

Do you need to wait, my friend, or can our alpha help you out now?

I am ready; I want to run.

I backed out gently and smiled at both Bevin and Mom. "The wolf is ready."

Bevin gripped my hand. "What happened?" His whole body shook.

"We were connected. I don't know how or when, but

that connection was causing my headaches. I think my wolf was trying to help you. I just don't know why."

He closed his eyes, forehead scrunched up in concentration, breathing slowly. "It was Phillip."

"What?"

"I had so many doubts, there was so much turmoil, but every time my emotions threatened to overwhelm me, there was a coolness that flooded me. I bet those times correspond to your worst headaches."

"Gods, I need to figure out how to control this. You did not need me to help you with that."

"Agreed!"

Mom smiled down at us. "Well, one thing figured out. About a dozen more to go. Bevin, you ready?"

He paused. I could smell his fear as he nodded.

I still held his hand when I stood so I pulled him up with me. He trembled as we made our way to the backyard. In the kitchen, I hesitated. "Do you want privacy? Do you want me to join you?"

His grip on my hand tightened. "Don't you dare leave my side."

"Wouldn't think of it."

Mom met us in the kitchen with her phone in hand. "I'm going to call your parents before doing this."

Bevin nodded and we sat down to wait. After making the call, Mom scrambled some eggs and served them with toast and a sliced orange. By the time Bevin's parents arrived, Owen, Dad, and Pebble were up as well.

We all headed for the backyard, except Pebble, who went to play in the basement. Most of us stayed near the house on the porch. Only Bevin and Mom went out into the grass.

Bevin blushed, faced away from us, and stripped. He got down on his hands and knees. Mom knelt next to him and, placing a hand on his back, and whispered some words to him. It took a few minutes to start, but then his transformation began.

Bevin's shift took a while. First shifts often did, and this one was early. It looked painful as body parts shifted, thick, coarse fur grew, his face transformed, and then a sleek black wolf stood before us, almost a twin to mine. He attacked. Mom was the only one near, and he leapt for her throat. She had been ready for it and caught his snout.

Dad watched for this. His smile was huge as he jogged out to help. By the time he reached them, Bevin had backed up, tail tucked, aware of who he was and what he had done. I took a deep breath and stared at him. "Mom, Dad, Bevin's wolf is male."

Everyone in the backyard stopped what they were doing and sniffed the air. Bevin, for his part, yipped and started trotting around the backyard. His excitement infused us all.

Finally, Dad got a hold of Bevin and trapped his snout. "Alright, wolf boy. Give me your best." And he did. They sat there looking at each other until Bevin's tongue lolled out and he yipped. Dad slapped him on the rump. "Go, run, be back soon."

And Bevin was off.

Owen just watched. "That was amazing. Like his wolf knew. I always knew our animals were smarter than us."

Fred, Bevin's dad, had a dumbfounded look of pure wonder on his face. "This is so amazing. Hazel, did you see that? His wolf is male. My son's wolf is male!"

CHAPTER 18

Bevin stayed in wolf form for the rest of the day. Pebble transformed and the two of them played all afternoon, mostly chase, Bevin learning how to move on four paws.

As pack members arrived, they met the new wolf. After lunch, I went out to join them. The three of us tumbled and played until the rest of the pack had turned wolfy. Only Owen joined in our play. At dusk, Estrella came out and took Pebble to the tree house. The rest of us followed Mom on a run.

A dusting of snow coated the ground, and the fields were open and wide. Bevin ran next to me, two black shadows amongst the gray and red wolves. Eventually, we found animal trails and split up. Bevin and I veered away from the others, found a new trail, and followed a few rabbits. He started to run after them, but his clumsy approach alerted our prey and they escaped. I laughed with a wolfy tongue loll.

Bevin charged and tackled me. We rolled. I twisted and yipped, nipping at his ear and leg. He bounced away, rotated, and splayed out his legs for better balance. He lowered his head, ready to attack. I stood and got into position, staring him in the eyes. His dominance flowed over me, making me shiver. I held my own only because I was epsilon.

He growled low in his throat and attacked. We clashed and then flew apart. I landed on my back, rolled, then flipped on my paws and ran. He pursued. We found the rest of the pack. I nosed my mom to signal I was heading home. It was late and I was getting tired. I could hear Bevin running behind me.

When Bevin and I got home, I leapt up into the tree house and curled around Pebble. Bevin mimicked my motions and curled around her other side. Between having my people around me and my head finally not pounding, a sense of contentment flowed through me.

I woke up early, threw on a robe, and trudged into the house. I got coffee started and began making breakfast. Yesterday, some industrious person prepared a breakfast casserole: layers of potato, bacon, cheese, and sausage. All that was left to do was the baking. I put the casserole in the oven and sat at the kitchen table, drinking my liquid gold.

While I caffeinated myself, I found my phone to catch up on text messages. Piper sent some pictures from last night of the kiddos playing with Pebble. Owen had gotten a few shots of Bevin, Pebble, and me before joining us. Bevin and I were intimidating, two black wolves. Because José was in Mexico, I probably wouldn't hear from him until later today. Curiosity was killing this cat about how they had handled the full moon away. I sent a quick "hi" to José, asked for an update, and then closed my phone.

I wanted to tell him about Bevin, but that wasn't my story to tell.

I finished my coffee, then made my way to shower and get dressed. When I returned to the kitchen to check on the casserole, a crowd had gathered. Someone had taken the food out of the oven, so I grabbed a plate and sat at the counter to eat. Bevin slowly made his way over with a full plate and sat next to me.

We ate for a few minutes in silence, clearing our plates, though Bevin was buzzing with worry. It made me shiver.

"Jade." He finally turned to me. "I need to talk to you."

I checked the room; no one was paying attention. "Okay."

He shook his head. "Not here. And…I need my dad." He looked around frantically. "And my mom." A nutty, almond scent of nervousness surrounded him.

His parents stood in a group talking to Dad by the back door. I slipped off my seat, gave his shoulder a quick squeeze, and made my way across the kitchen to Bevin's parents. "Fred, Janet, Bevin needs you…right now."

They paused their conversation to face me. Fred put his hand on my shoulder. "Do you know what about?"

I shook my head. "No, he said he had to talk to all of us."

I headed back to Bevin. As I approached, he shot up and led us towards the medical room.

When we got to the room, Janet gave Bevin a hug. "Your wolf is so beautiful, son. I'm so excited for your first run."

Bevin leaned into the hug for a second, visibly relaxing. When he backed up, he searched all our faces. As he surveyed the room, jerking when he saw my dad. "Oh, River. I…I didn't know you were going to come." He blushed.

He backed up a few steps and his blush deepened.

My dad just stood there silently.

Bevin nodded. "Okay, so, I noticed something when I woke up. I don't understand. It's not complete, which is why I'm really confused."

We all just stared at him. I quirked a smile. "Bevin, what you're smelling right now, that's called confusion. This is your first lesson in smelling emotions."

His parents laughed. Bevin just looked at me, eyes wide. Shocked.

After a few beats, he sniffed the air. It was such a delicate move I couldn't hold back an eruption of laughter. He glared at me as he continued to sniff.

His dad, still chuckling, said, "At this point, you're

probably smelling amusement, not confusion. Now, why did you want all of us in here?"

Bevin stopped sniffing and stared at his dad. "Right. Okay." He grabbed the bottom of his shirt and stripped it off.

Before anyone could say anything, he stood in front of us naked from the waist up. More than that, his chest was flat and squared off. If I didn't know better, I would think I stared at my brother.

My jaw dropped and my brows flew up. "What the… where are your…how? Bevin…. Is it the same?"

I waved my hand to encompass his whole body.

He shook his head. "Only this. I'm not sure what happened or why, but when I woke up my body was like this." He backed up and sat on a chair.

I tore my gaze from his very muscular chest and gazed at Dad questioningly. He looked as confused as the rest of us. I turned back, ran over to Bevin, and gave him a huge hug. "This is amazing."

Finally, his face broke out in a smile, and he hugged me back.

Our hug seemed to break the tension in the room, and everyone started talking at once. Dad went out to find Mom and Aunt Allison, though they didn't have any more idea about what had happened. Finally, Aunt Allison suggested I try to have my wolf talk to his.

Bevin put his shirt back on and we all traipsed into the living room, where there would be room for both of us to sit comfortably. I sat next to Bevin on the couch, close enough our arms touched. Even that felt a bit different. I slowly reached out and slipped my hand into his. We interlaced our fingers, and I closed my eyes.

Panther and Wolf were waiting to help. I entered Bevin with Wolf.

I found Bevin's wolf, so similar in looks to mine except for the brilliant sapphire eyes. *Friend, Bevin has changed. Can you explain what happened?*

The wolf gazed up at me, laughing, head cocked. I felt the confusion. *He was hurt. I healed him.*

Now it was my turn to be confused. *What do you mean…hurt?*

He wore bandages. Bandages mean a wound. I wanted him to be healed, so I healed him. Was it wrong?

I shook my head quickly. *No, just unexpected.*

He yipped and ran in a circle.

I felt Bevin tense next to me, then shiver. I wasn't sure what he felt when his wolf got excited. No one but Dad seemed to have the same relationship with their animals as I did. To them, their animals were ideas, not separate entities to communicate with. It must be weird.

Thank you, and welcome to the family.

Bevin's wolf came over and rubbed his head against my wolf. I slowly backed out and opened my eyes.

Everyone watched the two of us. I snorted. "This has got to be the most boring thing to watch."

Mom raised an eyebrow. "Jade." Her tone was serious. "What did you find out?"

Licking my lips, I gave Bevin's hand one more squeeze. "Apparently his wolf saw the binder as bandages." I faced Bevin. "He thought you were wounded. He wanted to fix it so you would be better, you know…healed."

Bevin's face dropped in shock as I finished my explanation. His color drained away as the implication of my words hit him. He started breathing in choppy breaths. I squeezed his hand trying to help him to calm down.

His mom came and sat on his other side, pulling him into a hug.

I got up so that his dad could take the side I was on. The rest of us moved off, giving the family some privacy to digest what had just happened.

We went back to the kitchen to finish our breakfast. No need to let good food go to waste.

CHAPTER 19

The next morning, Dad and I decided to take a run down the bike path…in human form. We had never run together before in human form, so this was a new activity for me. I wanted to talk, and he agreed to give this a try.

We were about twenty minutes from home when Dad asked, "How's school?"

"Good. I may have dug myself in deep with six AP classes, but the year's almost over."

"We warned you against it."

I snorted. "But I'll have fewer college bills this way."

"I'm less worried about that than you overextending

yourself. Did you leave any classes for next year?"

"Maybe. There are a few. I might need to head over to the college campus for some classes." I sort of shrugged as I ran. After a few more steps I darted a quick look at him. "Dad, speaking of college…"

He groaned.

I took a bigger breath than needed. "I think I should check out some campuses. I've applied to a few but need to apply to more."

"You know how I feel about you traveling alone."

"I know, but I have a plan."

I heard him mumble, "This ought to be rich."

I tried not to get discouraged. "Okay, hear me out. What if I went with José and Tanner? I would want others along as well, but if they went, I'd have strong wolves with me."

Tanner was pack security and second only to Mom and Dad. He was over six feet of visual danger. He and I didn't always get along, but I knew he would represent safety in Dad's eyes. His side-job of bounty hunting was just a bonus.

We ran in silence for a few minutes. When I shot Dad another look, his brow was furrowed. "Have you spoken to either of them?"

"Yes," I replied. "Tanner can take off time in June; so can José since his finals are in May. If we leave after my finals, we'd have almost three weeks before the full moon."

"Who else would you want to bring?"

"Ideally? Piper, Sarah, and Bevin, of course, but I

haven't actually talked to them about it."

Dad shook his head. "If you're driving, everyone in the car should be able to drive. That eliminates Piper and Sarah. Bevin is an option; so is Owen if he doesn't have to take summer classes."

I almost stopped running as his words sank in. "Wait… are you saying yes?"

We got to the turnaround point and found new surveillance cameras up. I shook my head in disappointment. Apparently, someone was determined to find the dangerous black wolf of doom. We turned to head back.

After noting the placement and type of equipment in the trees, Dad continued our conversation. "Just figure I'm not saying no. You have thought this through. I need to see an itinerary, as well as a list of places you'll overnight. You'll probably be passing through Colorado, so we'll have to contact that pack. It would be polite to check in with them."

This time I did stop, but just long enough to shake my head in disbelief before running to catch up. "Wait, there's a pack in Colorado?"

"Yep."

"I didn't know you knew where all the packs were."

"Of course we do. It would be dangerous to not know. We are in contact with all the alphas somewhat regularly. Let me know if you don't go through Colorado, then we'll avoid the whole issue."

My mind reeled at the idea of meeting a new pack.

"How many packs are out there? Where do they live?"

Amusement rolled off my Dad. "There are five packs in America. You know of ours and the one in Florida. Then there's the Colorado pack, a pack in Massachusetts, and one in Tennessee."

I pondered that. "All the packs are east of the Rockies."

Dad nodded. "Yeah. It just happened that way. No real reason."

After a few minutes Dad asked, "What do you make of Bevin?"

My mind went blank. "No idea."

"It's good, you know."

"What do you mean?"

"We avoid hospitals because our blood is different. Fred and I had been trying to figure out how to get his surgery done."

I thought about it. "Were you thinking about refusing Bevin his surgery?"

Dad sighed. "No, we just weren't sure how to get it done safely. Bevin deserves this. Now it's halfway there. That's something."

As we veered off the biking path and onto pack land, I warmed at Dad's words.

"I was just thinking..." Dad started as he quickly faced me before we returned on the dirt path to the house. "Could you try talking to his wolf? Convincing him to finish 'healing' Bevin?"

My mind stopped working and my foot missed its step. The next thing I knew I was on my face on the sloppy wet ground.

I rolled onto my back and saw Dad's hand a few inches from my nose. I raised my hand and he grasped it, pulling me to my feet. "Sorry about that. It was just a thought."

I wiped the mud off my face, then slipped my arm around his waist and rested my head against his arm as we walked back home. "It's a good thought. I just don't know if it's realistic."

He stroked my arm. "Pumpkin, nothing about you is realistic."

When we got home, I went straight to a warm shower. My fall ensured dirt had covered every inch of my hair and body. Afterwards, I met my parents, Pebble, and Owen in the dining room for lunch—burgers and fries.

I moaned in pleasure as I sat down and stuffed my face. After I had cleared half my plate I looked up. Mom handed me a mug of tea, and it reminded me of José. Gods, not having a pounding head was amazing. "I almost forgot. I've been meaning to ask. Is there some special meaning behind a wolf seeking a specific mate?"

Owen and Pebble continued eating, interested if their smell was any indication, but not enough to ignore their food. Dad's eyebrow raised. Had he heard of this before? Mom paused, burger halfway to her mouth.

Her piercing gaze felt like it wanted to see through me

into my brain. "Jade, honey, when did this come up?"

"A while ago. It was what José's wolf was talking about before he initiated the connection. I totally forgot about it, what with school, finals, track, and my headaches."

Mom nodded. "Wolves can partner up, like your dad and I did. It's common. Some wolves find their mate. It's a more spiritual thing. Something in their soul, I guess, connects. I've only known of one other mated pair. Once they met, the two knew and that was that."

I thought about it for a few minutes while finishing off my fries. "Aunt Allison and Uncle Jackson?"

Dad snorted. Owen finally stopped eating and looked up, interested. Mom just smiled, nodding. "The moment I brought Allison home, the two of them were inseparable. It took some time to figure out what was going on since none of us had heard of mated pairs. Well, your grandparents had."

Dad finished off his lunch. "José's wolf says he's mated?"

I shrugged. "He said he was looking for his mate… like he knew who it was or had run into his mate. It was confusing."

Owen's eyes got wide. "What if his wolf was hinting that his mate is you?"

CHAPTER 20

Thursday morning, I sat in the living room reading a book for English class. We were halfway through Spring break, and as much as I enjoyed the time off, part of me was ready for it to be over.

The front door opened, and I looked up to see Bevin and his family come in. His sisters ran to the basement to play with Pebble. Putting a bookmark in my book, I set it on the side table. "Morning."

Bevin and his parents just stood at the entry of the living room and watched me, awkwardly. Bevin hugged himself and his parents shifted back and forth.

I sat up straighter. "My parents are in the barn if you want them."

They continued to fidget, looking uncomfortable. Scrunching up my face, I gazed at them, confused. "What?"

Janet kissed Bevin's cheek. "Go on, son."

Bevin slowly crossed the room before standing over me. He clenched his fists and then relaxed his hands. He searched the couch pillows near me but wouldn't look at me. I could smell how nervous he was.

I huffed in annoyance. "What is it?" I grabbed his hand and pulled him down. "Sit, you're going to give me a crick in my neck."

He flopped down and mumbled, "Sorry."

"Grrr. Just talk to me. You're all making me nervous, and I don't know why. What's going on?"

Finally, Fred crossed the room and knelt in front of me. He grabbed my hands and stared me straight in the eyes. "Jade, we want to ask you something. Something big. We just don't know how to approach this…"

I tore my gaze from him and shifted it to Janet and finally to Bevin, who curled himself into a ball, small and scared. He had scrunched himself into the corner of the couch as if ready to bolt. *Huh?*

Closing my eyes, I released my calm. I felt everyone in the room take a breath as the tension went down. When I surveyed them, they were all less fidgety.

"Better," I mumbled to myself. I faced Bevin. "Is this

about what Dad mentioned to me?"

His eyes became blue saucers. "What did your dad say?"

I lifted my gaze to Fred and raised an eyebrow.

Fred shrugged. "I don't know. We haven't spoken to River or Hazel. We've just been talking at home." He quickly looked down at Bevin and Janet and then back to me. "We were wondering if you could talk to Bevin's wolf…"

Biting my lip, I shrugged. "I can try."

Their excitement almost overwhelmed me. I pulled my hands out of Fred's and put them up. "Whoa. I don't know if I can do anything. I didn't do anything the first time."

When I faced Bevin, there was such hope in his expression, it hurt. Slowly, he slid over so that we were close enough to touch. I tucked my hand in his and found his wolf.

Friend.

The black wolf stared up at me bouncing. *You're back!*

Yes. I have a request.

You need something from me? He cocked his head to the side, confused.

You healed Bevin, but you only healed part of him.

His wolf whined. Mine approached, nosing his. They each bowed their heads.

I have failed.

No! No. You haven't failed. You have done something amazing. I just wondered—hoped—you could do more.

More? The blue of his eyes sparkled like stars in the night sky.

There is more... I faltered, unsure how to explain this. *There is more healing to be done.*

Can you show me?

Staring between the two black wolves, I blanched. *Er...*

I backed out and dropped my head back onto the couch. Looking up at the ceiling, I scrunched my nose in frustration.

Fred, still kneeling in front of me, squeezed my knees. "What's wrong? Can it be done or is this too much to ask?"

Groaning, I lifted my head to look at him. "I have to be able to explain...to show..." I waved my hands vaguely. "...Bevin's wolf what he needs to fix. I don't know how to do that."

Bevin made a noise, something between a groan and a strangled laugh. I glared at him as Fred nodded. "Let's talk about this over lunch."

I needed to think, and sometimes letting my mind wander helped. I picked up my book and continued to read. Bevin ran into my room and grabbed another book. We sat together reading while his parents went to the kitchen to prepare lunch.

About an hour later, Owen came bounding up the stairs that connected the underground passage to the gym. "Do I smell lasagna?"

At that, I sniffed and realized what I had been smelling. I put down my book and headed to the dining room, Bevin close on my heels. Owen grabbed plates and cutlery as he joined me.

Mom and Dad arrived just as I served myself and Pebble and passed the dish along. Dad looked at Fred. "To what do we owe this pleasurable lunch?"

Fred quickly filled Dad in on what we had tried.

Owen snorted. "You have to explain the fix? Of course you do. Maybe *show* the fix, but how when you don't have the parts?"

I took another bite and thought.

Mom glared at Owen. "Not funny. This could be amazing if we could figure it out."

Owen, shaking with mirth, nodded in agreement. "I know, but it's just hilarious. We need a male epsilon. Any leads on that?"

I stared at Owen, thinking. I kept eating while I watched him.

Dad snapped at Owen, "I know you find humor in these things, but think about someone other than yourself. This is a serious matter for Bevin."

Owen sighed, dropping his gaze to his plate as he dug in. After a few bites, he surfaced and glared at me. "What? Why are you staring at me?"

I cocked my head to the side and narrowed my eyes. "A male epsilon wolf…"

"Yeah, that isn't me, so what gives?"

"No, you're not, but you *do* have two animals. I wonder if I could use your wolf. Maybe I could bring him over to help."

Everyone at the table except Pebble froze, then

stared at me.

I shrugged. "It's a thought." I ducked my head and went back to eating.

After lunch, we all gathered in the living room. I sat between Owen and Bevin and everyone else sat in various places around us. I laid one hand on Owen's and another on Bevin's. Closing my eyes, I found my animals in my mental landscape I'd created.

Connections. I had to find a way to bridge the wolves.

Wolf, can we join Owen's wolf over to Bevin's? He has his panther to keep him safe.

Wolf looked at me then ran off, too fast for me to follow.

Panther padded up to me and sniffed. Then she, too, trotted off.

Confused about what I should do, and about to give up, I felt Owen stiffen. I focused on my wolf until I was with her. *She is me and I am her.* She had moved into Owen.

Friend, can you help?

Owen's gray wolf gazed at us. *Lead me.*

I closed my eyes and focused on Bevin's black wolf. I felt the pull. When I opened my eyes, he was in front of me. I did a quick search, and Owen's wolf stood beside us.

Owen's hand trembled in mine. I wasn't sure if it was in fear or amusement, but I knew he was aware of what was happening. I focused on his wolf.

Are you okay?

Yes. I'm learning. I'm growing. I'm becoming.

We approached Bevin's wolf.

Owen's wolf will show you how to heal Bevin. I will stay as a bridge. Let me know what you need from me. From us.

The two wolves gazed up at me, then they dashed off. I didn't follow.

As I sat there, I felt Owen shiver and then Bevin stiffen. I tried to emanate calm. Next to me, they both sagged and breathed more freely.

After some time, the wolves returned. Owen's wolf hopped a few times before yipping and disappearing. Bevin's wolf slowly lowered itself to the ground.

Do you understand?

I do and do not.

I don't follow.

*Bevin is not hurt, but he is not well. I will try to heal him during his next shift. I will try…*With that, he buried his nose in his paws.

I backed up and released their hands. Rubbing my fingers together, I tried to get feeling back into my numb digits.

I sat up. Mom leaned forward. "Did it work?"

Owen smirked. "Of course it did, I'm here." Then he slumped, nearly passing out.

I elbowed him in his side. "Maybe. Bevin's wolf is confused but will try."

Owen faced me. "That was trippy. Do you always see the animals like that? Like, traveling with your animals and speaking with them? I could see and feel them. I actually spoke with them there at the end."

A smile blossomed on my face. "Yes. That's what it's always like for me."

"Wow. That's just…wow."

Dad stood. "So, what now?"

Bevin sat stock-still next to me, barely breathing. I reached for his hand; it was ice cold. I squeezed it. "Now? Now Bevin changes, runs around, and changes back." I shrugged. "The rest is up to his wolf…" I turned to face Owen. "And someone brings Owen some food before he passes out."

I could feel the tension in the room amp up as everyone but Mom waited for Owen to get food. Mom returned from the kitchen with a plate of food.

Bevin didn't move. "I don't know what to do…it's so… oh, my gods, I feel sick."

I stood and pulled him up into a hug. "Do you want someone to run around with? I mean, Owen's here…" I pulled back and searched his face.

He snorted and softly punched my arm. Gripping my hand, he dragged me to the backyard. We each found our own corner and stripped down to shift. I focused on my wolf paw and let the wolf flow over me. The pain was sharp and quick and soon it was over. I turned and found my twin low and ready to attack.

Mom ran out and stood between us. As Bevin leapt at me, Mom intercepted, taking him down, grabbing his muzzle in both hands. They rolled in the muddy yard. By the time the rolling stopped, Bevin's mind caught up and he froze, standing over Mom. Mom, for her part, laughed.

She slowly stood and wiped off some of the dirt. "Well, hell, I'll have to shower while you two run and play."

Bevin and I darted out into the woods. We sniffed out a rabbit trail. This time, I took the lead and modeled what to do to catch the rabbit. After I brought one down, Bevin copied my motions and caught one himself. After our meal, we ran to a small river and found a bit of flowing water to lap up.

We ran home and let our human selves back out. Mine was a quicker shift since this was still Bevin's first full moon. I was slipping back into my clothes when I heard him gasp and start to cry. A gingery scent came from him. Shock, confusion.

I was crushed. I finished getting dressed when I realized the emotion I was smelling wasn't defeat, but relief, maybe excitement? "Bevin?"

"I don't know what's wrong with me." He sniffled. "I've wanted this my whole life…"

He sat in the grass holding his knees, rocking, and crying.

I ran up to him and hugged him from behind. "Did it work?"

He nodded, twisting around to return the hug. "Oh, my gods, thank you Jade. I can't believe this…but it worked."

I gave Bevin privacy as he slipped his clothes on. We went into the house, and everyone mobbed us.

Once back in the kitchen, Owen slapped Bevin hard on the back. "You know, now you have a whole new skill set to learn…and you better figure it out before school starts."

Bevin's eye's popped as he looked down the length of his body and back up at Owen. The people in the room tried to hold back their laughter but the air filled with citrusy amusement. Bevin's scent shifted to a nutty nervousness as he moaned. "Oh, my gods, I have to learn how to pee!"

CHAPTER 21

While the excitement grew over Bevin's success, I slipped off to my room to let him have his moment. I sat at my desk making a calendar of the homework I needed to finish in the next few days. Just as I pulled out my history assignment to make an outline for a paper that was due in three weeks, someone knocked at my door.

I swiveled in my seat and sniffed the air. "What's up, Bev?"

He slowly opened the door. "Why did you leave? Are you okay?"

He glowed and it made me happy. I gave him another hug and he felt different. *Gods, this is so weird!* I backed up and sat on my bed, pulling him with me. "I'm great, I just wanted you to have your time. Did I hear Aunt Allison come over?"

"Yeah. She gave me a checkup."

"How did that go?"

"Good. I'm all male. She's running some tests. She pulled some labs for you as well in case you needed to run any tests, but she thinks everything is good. She said she wants to talk to you about what supplements I still need."

I quirked my mouth to the side and rubbed my eyes. "We may need to bring in an expert. I know Dad has someone on payroll. This goes beyond what I know…"

He leaned in, wrapping his arm around me. "I get it. I'm just reeling right now. This spring break has gone way different than expected."

"I'm just so happy for you. I don't know how we're going to tell the school…or rather you, or if you should. You're going to have to pretend to be your old self. You're excited about finally being you, but you can't show them who you are—not without medical records."

He stared at me. "I hadn't thought about that. This just got more complicated…but I can continue doing what I have been doing."

I laughed, giddy with excitement for him.

He squeezed my hand. "I think it'll be okay. I change in the men's locker room, but in the bathroom. I'll continue to do that. No one should be the wiser."

I leaned over and kissed his cheek.

He started to vibrate. "I'm so freaking excited. It's done. I can be me. I'm no longer icky."

A laugh erupted out of me. "I love how happy this makes you. When are you going to tell the others?"

"I don't know. Maybe we can have the girls over on Sunday, before school. I'll probably tell José tonight or tomorrow, whenever we talk next."

I looked up at him sharply. "You two are talking regularly again?"

Bevin blushed. "Yeah. I couldn't stay mad at him long. You know how I've always felt about him. I mean, at least since high school when I was promoted from annoying kid to friend…maybe even best friend. He also wasn't wrong about Phillip…neither were you. I finally broke down and told him that we should only be friends last night. I realized that even without you and Piper there fighting, there really wasn't any romance between us—at least not on my end. That book he gave me was too much."

"Well, that sucks."

"It does, but at least I know myself and my heart enough to know I'm better than just nice. Not to mention, can you imagine me trying to explain this?" He waved his hands at his body.

I snorted.

The following morning, a phone call interrupted me while I worked on my history homework. It was ten in the morning, and I didn't recognize the number, but answered anyway. "Hello?"

"Kid team leader?"

Shutting my eyes, I thought for a minute, trying to dredge up a name. "Zack?"

"You remember me!"

"How did you get my number?"

"I called Allison. I was rock-climbing up at Devil's Lake and saw this great perch and launched for it…"

"And missed?"

His voice dropped, sounding hurt. "What do you take me for? Of course I made it. I'm great at rock-climbing. I had my lunch and took a nap. I rolled off the perch during my nap and I'm not sure what I've broken. I thought the kid team would be in school, but I hear it's spring break!"

Grumbling, I organized my papers so I could pick up again later. "Where are you? I'll collect Bevin and we'll drive up."

"I'll text my location to you."

After signing off, I called Bevin as I headed to the kitchen to find food.

Before I could suggest picking him up, he said he'd be at my place in five and hung up. I grabbed my medical bag, slipped on a coat, and went out to the stoop to wait for him.

After a forty-five-minute drive, we reached Devil's

Lake. We got out and Bevin froze. He stared at me. "So many scents."

I found Zack's scent in and amongst the trails and dragged Bevin over. "Do you smell the wolf scent?"

Bevin sniffed gently, almost like he was afraid of what he might smell. He shook his head. "I smell—" he sniffed again, "—people, and a dog—" sniff, sniff, "—and…food?"

I gave a quick nod. "Good. Take a deeper sniff. Think about how your parents smell. That scent of wolf."

Bevin shut his eyes, took a deeper breath and froze. "I smell it. Under everything. It almost smells like pack, but it's not pack."

Smiling, I patted his back. "Good, now lead on."

"What?"

"Lead on. Find our wolf."

Face pale, Bevin's hands shook. He curled them into fists before starting up the path. A dozen feet up, the path split and, closing his eyes again, he sniffed. It only took a few seconds for him to find the right path. At the next split, he didn't even need to pause. He had the scent and followed it true.

A thirty-minute hike later, we found Zack. He lay on his back at the bottom of a cliff. It appeared as if he rested on the ground sunning himself, except he sat prone in the shade on a rocky ground.

"The A-Team!" he yelled as we approached. "And Bevin, my man, you've turned wolf since last we met. Kudos!" He snuffled the air and his eyes widened. "Wait, more than that has changed. What's the story there?"

Bevin paused and faced me, eyes wide. "I hadn't thought this through. Will I have to explain this over and over?"

I shook my head. "How many wolves are left for you to run into?"

His shoulders dropped and he gave me a small smile.

Zack just watched us as we worked through Bevin's fears.

I knelt beside Zack but kept my eyes on Bevin. "How about I do my thing and you distract him with a story?"

As I was about to touch Zack's arm, Bevin stopped me. "Food first. I'm tired of watching you pass out." He handed me the bag and glared at me until I had eaten what he considered enough.

Zack watched, smelling confused, but didn't interrupt our dealings.

Full to bursting, I thrust the bag aside. "Gods above, you're bossy." Wrinkling my nose at him, I smiled, then put my hand on Zack to see what had happened.

Bevin knelt as well, knocking shoulders with me, and began regaling Zack with the story of his week.

Panther came forward with me and I did a quick triage of Zack's injuries. He had three broken ribs, a broken arm, and a broken leg…the same one I had fixed before. His wolf was working on fixing his internal organs, which was why he could breathe and talk. Panther and I started on the bones.

After I finished with the ribs and the leg, I tried to

determine the order of issues that would allow him to walk himself out. I felt a hand on my shoulder and knew Bevin fed me more energy. Bevin gasped and he started shaking where his body touched mine, but I focused on Zack's arm. Once I knew everything was sufficiently healed, I backed out.

I flopped back on my butt with a grunt. I found the bag with the supplies and grabbed a soda and drained it first. Then I started on some food. After I had eaten a protein bar, I realized the boys weren't talking and looked up. "What?"

Bevin just gazed at me, while Zack had a half-smile, shaking his head. Bevin finished off a ham and cheese sandwich. Where did that come from? I went searching for one for myself.

Bevin snorted. "I can't believe how much energy you give to other people, Jade. Which animal do you use for healing?"

"Mostly my panther."

"Well, your wolf put me on my backside in seconds. I just put a hand on your shoulder and down I went."

Zack let out a dry laugh. "Truth. I thought he was having a seizure. Once he explained what happened, I understood all the food he forced into you before you started working on me. That said, nice work, Doc. I think I'm good to go."

"I didn't completely fix the arm. I just got you far enough that your natural healing should finish it in the next week or so. I kind of like the idea of people walking out on their own cognizance."

"Fine. No rock-climbing for a week. Got it."

Bevin rolled his eyes, and I sighed, but we got to our feet, packed up, and headed back to the car.

On Saturday, José's family returned from Mexico and stopped in to let us know they'd made it in safely.

Finally, a warm day. I didn't want to waste it, so I read my English book in the treehouse. I looked up as José climbed up and joined me.

"Welcome back to the cold tundra of the great Midwest."

He snorted. "Well, it is cold compared to where we were, but not too bad." He bent to give me a huge hug, then plopped down next to me.

Closing my book and setting it aside, I asked, "How was it?"

"Wonderful. It was so nice swimming in the ocean and experiencing a different piece of my ancestry."

"And you found a safe place to run?"

"Yeah. Apparently, my grandparents are part of the pack down there and they have stomping grounds. They let us join them on their run."

"Even with how dominant you are?" Most packs didn't like including unknown dominant werewolves, even if they are family.

"That was tricky at first, but since my family has been

part of the pack for so long, they allowed it. I guess my dad is the first person in my family to leave the pack. My uncle and aunt still run with the Mexican pack, so that helped."

"That's amazing. I had no idea you had so much family down there, and that they were wolves."

"Honestly, neither did I. Dad doesn't really talk about his family back home. I guess he got into a fight with someone in the pack and walked away. He wasn't even sure of our welcome. His sister begged for our visit and finally got him to agree."

Arms flopping to the side, I shook my head, dumbfounded.

José closed his eyes, pausing before taking a deep breath. "Is it true? Did you help Bevin's wolf change him?"

I shrugged. "I guess. Owen helped, too. The wolf saw it as healing him. Dad was thrilled because going to the hospital for an operation is tricky with our blood and healing abilities."

José nodded. "I bet. It's just…so…Jade, you're magical, you know that, right?"

"I didn't do it this time."

José shook his head. "You didn't do all of it, but if it weren't for you, it wouldn't be complete."

"Me *and* Owen."

José's eyes narrowed. "Chica, you need to learn to take a compliment."

I smiled. "Maybe." I gazed at a cloud for a second. "Oh, my dad said yes to the road trip out west this June. His one condition was that everyone going has to be able to drive."

"He said yes?"

"Well, no…he just didn't say no."

José huffed out a laugh. "If everyone has to be able to drive, that eliminates Piper and Sarah, doesn't it?"

I sagged. "Yeah, I'm pretty sure it does. I think Piper plans on getting her license in June and Sarah…who knows. She's happy getting rides."

"No worries, we can have fun, old-school style. We can bring Owen and Bevin."

I nodded. Just then, I heard his parents open the back door. His mom said, "We're heading out. If you want a ride to the dorms, it's now or never."

José gave me one last hug before leaping down and following his parents.

I pulled out my book and continued to read.

The next day, the last before spring break was over, Sarah, Piper, and Bevin came over. We decided to have a game day.

I dealt out the cards from Bonanza. Sarah squinted at Bevin. "Something looks different about you, what is it?" She sniffed. "You even smell different, wolf…male?" Her eyes grew wide. "How is that possible?"

Piper stared at him. She poked his arm, then his upper chest where the top of his binder would be. She snatched her hand back. "Bevin? What happened?"

His eyes danced. "The wolf part is obvious."

Piper punched his arm. "Why didn't you tell?" She whipped her glare to me. "Or you?"

I held up my hands. "Not my tale to tell. Get it? Tail." I snorted.

Bevin smiled. "I asked her to let me do this my way." He took a shaky breath and just like the first day, he quickly slipped out of his shirt.

Both Sarah and Piper gasped. Sarah's gasp quickly transformed into laughter and applause. Piper just gaped, mouth open, eyes wide.

Bevin blushed. After a few seconds he fixed his shirt and slipped it back on.

Piper found her voice. "But how?"

Bevin shrugged. "My wolf wanted to heal me. He thought my binder meant I was hurt."

"Your wolf is male? That's so great!" Piper's eyes dropped down to his lap. "And did he fix that, too?"

Bevin's blush deepened, but he nodded.

Sarah froze. "Oh, my gods, no way!"

We filled them in on the story as we played our game. Their reactions were priceless and completely supportive.

CHAPTER 22

Monday morning came earlier than I wanted it to, but at least the sky was a light blue and the temperatures reasonable. My head didn't hurt; it felt like it had been months…years since I could say that. I felt light as air as I squeezed into my exercise clothes and ran over to the barn.

After thirty minutes of strengthening my arms, I jogged back to the main house for a quick shower and a clean outfit. Then it was time for coffee and food.

I found Mom in the kitchen. She read the news on her phone at the table. A plate of eggs and toast and a mug of coffee awaited me in the spot across from her. I slid into my seat and started eating.

Mom took a sip of her coffee. "Do you think Bevin got enough practice at the mall last week?"

"Nope. We went twice. We went to the movies once. Owen's suggestions were great. But nothing prepares you for how awful high school is."

Mom nodded. "Where are you all meeting?"

I checked my watch to see how much time I had. Ten minutes. "At our normal corner. Sarah and I will help him out."

"Good. Why not drive? He has an appointment with Dr. McBey after school."

I paused, looking up at the ceiling, thinking. "I thought she moved out of town."

"No, hon. She just didn't want to join the pack. She prefers being a lone wolf and running alone, but she likes the area. She moved out of the greater Madison area, but she still works here."

"Huh." I returned the conversation to the matter at hand. "We decided to approach the crowds slowly. Walking together is our thing."

Mom nodded. "A slow approach makes sense."

I quickly finished my breakfast and suited up. Grabbing my bag, I headed out to meet my friends.

I was the first to the corner but could see the other two approaching. When Bevin arrived, I waggled my eyebrows at him. "Ready?"

"Not even close." His eyes looked a bit wild as he hugged himself. "I mean, I thought I was, but this isn't just one change, is it?"

Sarah joined us and we faced the school together. "You'll be great. Just remember the boxes, or whatever it is you two do."

That got Bevin to huff out a laugh. "Boxes. Maybe I should write that on my hand."

When we reached the parking lot, we stopped at the edge. Sarah and I waited for Bevin to adjust. He nodded minutely and we continued through the cars.

When we got into the hallway, there were a lot of students. They were all excited to tell their friends about what they had done over their week off. As I listened, Bevin shook and stiffened. I squeezed his hand, trying to lend him calm.

Sarah said under her breath, "I bet no one had as great a week as you."

Bevin relaxed as he smiled. He took the lead up to the lockers where Piper waited for us.

Bevin's breathing roughened. I could feel his stress, practically taste it. His movements were almost robotic as he loaded his bag for his morning classes.

I rubbed his back and sent quick looks to Piper and Sarah. "Let's just go to class. We're early, but I think you need quiet."

He nodded quickly, eyes moist. He seemed like he barely held himself together.

We were the first two to arrive to AP bio, even before the teacher. Bevin crossed his arms on the table and dropped his head down. "How did you do this? How *do* you do this?"

Slinging my arm over his shoulders, I gave his back a rub. "It may take a few days, but you'll figure it out."

He groaned, and then tensed.

I whipped around, trying to figure out what had set him off, then I wanted to hit my own head. A year later and I still didn't always use my nose. Phillip had arrived and I could smell both his interest and concern. He arrowed straight towards us.

Bevin moaned. "No, no, no, no, no. I can't. It's too much."

I didn't know how to help. It had been clear to me that Phillip was way more into Bevin than vice versa, but until now, Bevin probably hadn't known. It would be hard to miss now.

I stood and blocked Phillip. "Hey, Phillip."

"Hi, Jade, have a good break?" He bent to see around me. "Is Bev okay?"

"Yep, it was good, lazy, ya know. Bevin isn't good. He's feeling sick. I know this sounds awful, but could you not sit with us today. If he…" I waved my hand in front of my mouth in a throwing up motion. "You know…he would be really embarrassed if you were close."

Phillip's scent became sad and concerned—an earthy sandalwood emanated from him—but he agreed and moved back to where he used to sit. Guilt filled me for sending him off, but Bevin's needs came first.

Bevin smiled weakly at me. "Thank you. I'll try not to throw up on your shoes."

Snorting, I bumped shoulders with him.

Once class started, Bevin seemed to perk up. Afterwards, his eyes seemed a bit wild, but I squeezed his hand as we separated until lunch.

At lunch, I found Sarah sitting outside. It was cool, but not too bad. Bevin found us and his relief at sitting outside was intense. He sighed and his whole body relaxed. Piper was the last to join us, but she had her jacket on to protect from the cold.

"I don't know if I can do this." Bevin's hands shook. "I just…it's too much."

Sarah reached out and patted his arm. "Okay, this is Owen's trick. Imagine a fortress, and you are the queen… or king. Build up a wall that nothing can penetrate."

Bevin closed his eyes and took a few deep breaths. "Okay, I'll try that this afternoon. Maybe if my castle is filled with boxes."

"And an incinerator," I mumbled.

Sarah snorted as Bevin stared at me open-mouthed.

"What? Not everything is worth reevaluating. Some things are best just being destroyed…like all the stupid scents."

Piper rummaged through her bag. I watched her for a minute before asking, "What are you doing?"

"I need to take notes. One day this will be me and if you all are at college, I may be on my own. Boxes, fortress, incinerator…this is good stuff."

Bevin pointed at the notebook. "Don't forget the chocolate."

I peeked into Piper's bag, "Oh, yeah, chocolate is *very* important."

Her eyes narrowed and her hand dipped down into some secret compartment before she produced a handful of bars. "One each. I figured Jade always needs one and Bevin would need one today. I couldn't just offer half the table chocolaty goodness."

Bliss.

I heard the door behind me open and smelled Phillip. He headed to our table and slipped in between Sarah and Bevin.

Facing Bevin, he asked, "Feeling better?"

Bevin looked a bit strained but nodded. "Yeah. My head is still tender, but I'm good."

I took a bite of the chocolate and enjoyed it melting in my mouth before tilting my head and asking, "Don't you have a doctor's appointment after school? Is it for your headaches?"

Bevin's confusion was apparent to everyone at the table. "How did you know about that?"

"Dude, how many times do I have to tell you?" I pointed at myself with both my hands. "Omniscient."

Crumpled napkins and chocolate wrappers came flying

at me from every angle. I ducked and protected my head with my arms.

Bevin sighed. "Yeah, I do have an appointment for my issues. My parents are picking me up right after school." He turned to me with a mischievous smile. "Don't you have a home track meet on Thursday?"

I groaned, dropping my chin to my chest.

Sarah started bouncing. "Yes! It will be awesome. I'm so excited to be competing here, *finally*."

I glared up at her.

She raised her hands to the sides, palms up. "What?"

"Do you think people will show up?"

Her eyes almost glowed. "Oh, yeah. After that article Alyssa wrote about you last month, I think *everyone* will come. They all saw you land on your butt during dodgeball. No one believes you're on the track team, despite you always wearing the track uniform."

"Maybe I'll call in sick."

Sarah's shoulders danced with her glee. "Who would be less convinced, your dad or Coach Nelson?"

Damn.

Phillip's head bounced back and forth as we spoke, and his scent went from citrusy amused to minty confused. "Why wouldn't they believe you if you faked an illness? Especially the coach?"

Rolling my eyes, I gave him a sheepish smile. "I wasn't the most willing participant in joining track."

Phillip gazed at me. "Then why did you join?"

I took a second to control my expression to make sure I didn't show my annoyance at him or Sarah. "It was brought to my attention that I needed something on my college application aside from pure academics."

Sarah snorted and I glared at her.

"Anyway. My dad and I run together—" *once,* "—and I thought this would be something I could do without ending up falling…again."

Phillip snickered. "Have you fallen that many times?"

This got everyone at the table but me and Phillip laughing beyond speech. I sat and watched them, disgruntled. Phillip looked confused.

Piper got out, "That many times." And then she snorted.

The snort got Sarah laughing harder.

I rolled my eyes and waited, but apparently this wasn't ending any time soon.

I sighed and faced Phillip. "Piper was in my gym class last year when she started here. It was her first impression of me. I don't fall *that* often."

Piper, still laughing, squeaked out, "Just a couple of times a week."

I rolled my eyes. "No. Maybe a couple times a month." I realized that didn't sound that much better as Phillip bit down on his lips to stop himself from joining in on their mirth.

Glaring at them, I ate my lunch and couldn't wait for the bell to finally ring.

I didn't see Bevin for the rest of the day and had track practice right after school. I texted him when I got out and Sarah and I were changing.

How did the appointment go?

His reply was quick. Headache all better.

I'm going to kick you when I see you.

And end up on your butt?

I growled aloud. How did it go????

Where are you?

Changing.

I'm in the lot, hurry.

I showed my phone to Sarah, and we headed out to Bevin and a ride home.

I got in the front. "Talk."

"Dr. McBey was great."

Sarah leaned forward. "Who is Dr. McBey?"

I sometimes forgot how new she was to the pack. "She's a lone wolf I thought had left the area years ago. Apparently, she just left the greater Madison area."

Bevin took up the story. "Yeah, she likes it here and has a great job at UW-Health. I guess she's agreed to see pack members in an emergency. I became an emergency. She did a complete work-up on me. She said my testosterone levels are in the average range for a cis male. I don't have to take hormones. I have no idea what the wolf did to me. It really was magic."

I gaped. "Are you kidding me?"

He shook his head. "No, I'm…me. It's done. I'm all Bevin now."

Shocked, I fell back into the seat.

Sarah started whooping in the back. Once she got it out of her system, she asked. "Can they tell you used to be different? Female?"

Bevin shook his head as he said, "No. There aren't even any scars." He quickly glanced at me before pulling up in front of Sarah's house and parking. He turned off the car so we could talk. "Dr. McBey said that your dad will have to do some major hacking to change all my medical records. They'll have to be changed to reflect my assigned sex as male…I don't know what I think about that."

"You've lost part of your past."

His eyes dropped as he faced me. "That's how it feels. I mean," he waved his hands as if presenting himself. "This is great, it's what I always wanted, but now my history has to be rewritten."

I wrapped my arm around him in a half hug. "Not in the pack. We'll always know. I'll keep a record of your real medical history."

He squeezed my hand. We all sat in silence, our smiles bittersweet.

CHAPTER 23

A gruff, disappointed voice cut across the field over the shouts and laughter of hundreds of students. "Ms. Stone, you're better than this!"

I wasn't sure he was right. The stands were full. It felt like the entire school body sat watching us…me…as we competed in each race, and all those eyes watching us had been intimidating. It hadn't just been the students, the bleachers also held staff, and parents, all cheering for the pride of Stolzburg. My win represented the school well, and they stomped their feet, clapped, and cheered. I had proven the news article correct. I won my last race.

Their shock, then cheers, overwhelmed me. During the race, I had forgotten they were there. Focused on running and jumping the hurdles, I had been in my zone, enjoying the process. After crossing the finish line, their positivity washed over me. A wave of emotion from the crowd crashed into me and I lost my footing, tumbling to the ground just across the finish line. Luckily, I hadn't taken anyone with me.

As I slowly pushed myself to my feet, I imagined the next issue of the school paper with a picture of me on the ground splashed across the front page. I made my way to Sarah.

Bumping shoulders with me, she snickered. "Nice work there, champ."

I let out a gusty breath. "When is track season over?"

"Not until the end of the year. Suck it up, babe."

"Any chance this is the last meet the school, as a whole, comes out to support us?"

A smile split her face. "Not a chance."

The Monday before the full moon, after I got my food from the lunch staff, I turned to see Bevin pacing the outdoor patio. It was a cool, windy day so everyone else had chosen to sit indoors. I felt a mantle of power emanating off him through the windows. It froze me for a second.

Snapping out of my shock, I made my way out to him,

dropped my food on the table, and situated myself so that his back would be to the lunchroom. "Bevin?"

Snarling, he faced me with the fluid grace of a dancer… or a wolf. His eyes glowed with alpha intensity and his blast of strength rolled over me, making me want to roll over and show him my belly. Being epsilon, I could withstand it, but this was Bevin, and he was hurting. After a beat, I took a breath and lowered my eyes to stare at a point between us.

Shock pierced me like an arrow as I heard Bevin approach. I watched his feet as he got closer. He used a finger under my chin to force my eyes back up to his. His hand moved to my shoulder. His breathing was ragged. Slowly, I raised a hand to brush his bangs from his eyes and then I rested it on his shoulder. That contact was enough to even out his breathing. Pack. Friend. Connection.

He lowered his forehead until it touched mine. We stayed like that until I heard the door to the patio area open. A slight breeze brought Piper's distinctive aroma and Sarah's familiar feline scent to me. Once their trays hit the table, Bevin and I separated and joined them.

I sat down between Bevin and Piper. Leaning over, I gave Piper a quick kiss before digging in to eat. We all ate in silence for a few minutes.

Finally, I reached over and took Bevin's hand. "Hey, what happened?"

He took a calming breath and said, "I really hate the lunchroom, ya know?"

Sarah huffed. "It will get better."

Bevin shook his head. "I probably won't be here long enough. I graduate in a month. Anyway, you know that one group? The group of close-minded jerks? Most of them came from different feeder schools, and the ones from our old school seem to have forgotten my past. They never talk about me. Well, your new habit of kissing when sitting down hasn't gone unnoticed." He pointed at me and Piper.

I shot Piper a look. She hid a sly smile. My shy girlfriend was proud of our display of affection every day.

Bevin saw the smile as well, and it made him relax; he smelled pleased. "That group was talking smack and it put my wolf in protective mode."

A low growl built in my gut as he went into protective mode over me. I didn't need protection. I tried to pull my hand from his, but he tightened his hold. "Bevin, you aren't my alpha. This doesn't make sense."

"I know. But my wolf was screaming for blood."

"More than that, you aren't *anyone's* alpha." I pulled again, but Bevin held on, not letting me go. "Was it even determined whether you're alpha level?"

Bevin closed his eyes and let his head fall back. After a few seconds he faced me again. "I don't know. I only had that first run and that wasn't enough, I was still zeta. All I know is that when they talked about you and Piper, I got hot…angry hot." He took another calming breath, looking me in the eyes, a look of desperation, needing me to understand. "It wasn't until I saw you submit to me—an action I knew was wrong—that my wolf calmed down."

I narrowed my eyes. "Is your connection to your wolf always this agitated?"

"Yes and no. It helps when you or other pack members are around, he's calmer, especially when it's you. But I do wonder if there is something wrong with me."

Sarah laughed. "She has that effect on everyone."

Piper leaned in with a smile, sliding her arm around me.

"Have you talked to your dad? He's one of the best people I know for advice."

Bevin sighed. "He's dealing with my sisters right now."

"What about José?"

"Yeah, we're back to talking just about every night. I'll ask him about this. We should be talking tomorrow night. He has a big exam tomorrow, so he has to study tonight."

I didn't think Bevin would get the chance to discuss his agitation with José. The next day at lunch, I sat at the table alone, waiting for the others to arrive. Bevin sat down heavily beside me. "I have to go. Now."

Confused, I turned to him. "What?"

He handed me his phone. "My grandma died. My dad wants me home as soon as possible. We're driving up north for the funeral. It's in a couple of days."

I pulled him into a big hug. His head rested on my

shoulder. He trembled and his breathing was rough. "I'm so sorry, Bev, that's awful."

He clung to me for a second before pulling away. "She was old; it isn't a surprise. But it changes everything, doesn't it?"

Thinking about the timing, I froze. He'd be home with his family of norms over the full moon. "What about Thursday night?"

"We'll figure it out." He handed me a piece of paper. "This is a list of my classes and teachers. Can you talk to everyone? Gather homework?"

Nodding, I took the paper. "Of course."

He gave me a hug and then headed out.

Sarah and Piper showed up a few minutes later. Sarah glanced around. "Where's Bev?"

"Gone. His grandma died. He'll be out of town. My guess is through Sunday, at least."

Both their jaws dropped in shock, then the earthy scent of sadness filled the air.

After school, I went around explaining to teachers about Bevin and gathering his homework. I arrived late for practice, but Sarah had explained my lateness and I didn't seem to be in trouble.

Bevin returned in time for AP exams. He hadn't been terribly close with his grandma but had spent part of each summer visiting up north. Though he was back, his heart was not with us; he was grieving. He spent time at the pack house so he could be with family and friends, but he didn't talk, and he didn't joke. It was like the mantle of adulthood had settled on him. He acted like an adult with bigger responsibilities who had mentally mapped them out.

After the AP exams, he and his dad returned up north to close up and sell his grandma's house. His grandpa would be moving in with some cousins. Because Bevin had good grades and was a senior, he was excused from taking finals. They planned on being up there for weeks. They needed to sort through all the stuff in the house and either pack up, throw out, donate, or sell every item. The process was going to be difficult.

While Bevin, Fred, and Janet were working on his grandparents' house, Hanna moved in with Chris and Andy, and Heather moved in with Clare and Alejandro, Estrella and Jose's family. Bevin didn't plan to return to walk the stage for graduation but appeared at our doorstep that morning anyway.

There was a knock at the door before it opened. I had been in the living room, and I jumped up when I saw him, engulfing him in a hug. "Bevin! You're back!" My powers of observation acute at the end of the school year.

He squeezed me tight. "We decided I should walk the stage, though I'm not as convinced as my parents are that this is that important of a memory for me.... Will you come?"

I stepped back but kept ahold of his hands. "Of course

I'll come…I wouldn't miss it for the world. I've missed you, and I think it's great that you're walking the stage."

With a few quick nods, he finally managed a small smile. "I'm heading back afterwards."

His words hit hard. "You won't even stay the night? José won't be able to make it today, and I'm sure he'd love to see you."

Bevin shook his head. "No, I promised my parents… and…no, I'm not ready. I'm too emotional right now."

Only a few of us managed to make it to watch him. I saw a tear roll down his cheek as he shook the principal's hand, and my heart went out to him. We got ice cream afterwards before he slipped away back north. He missed the college tour because he felt his family needed him more. I understood the decision, though it made me sad.

CHAPTER 24

With finals behind me, Tanner, Owen, José, and I packed up to leave. We planned on driving to Stanford and then back via Colorado. The others wanted to visit Las Vegas on the way back and since they agreed to drive me to California I couldn't really object. My main objection being I was too young to gamble.

The plan: drive from Stolzburg to California, take a tour and stay in the area a day or two, then return via a different scenic route. We would stop in Las Vegas on the way back for fun and frivolity, staying there a couple of nights before moving on to Boulder and meeting the Colorado pack.

The plan was to see the Garden of the Gods while driving through the state and maybe visit a local college as well. Decisions could be made on the road.

After meeting the local wolves and seeing the sites, we'd probably be ready to head home. The plan was to be back in Wisconsin before the full moon at the end of June.

When Dad had looked over the plan, I had been a nervous wreck. "This has decent details." He sat at his desk and narrowed his eyes.

I shook nervously on the other side hoping I'd get the final thumbs up.

He tilted his head. "Sit, Jade. You've given a few alternatives along the way. Tanner will appreciate the flexibility and the lack of teenage idealism in your itinerary."

I flopped in a chair and snickered. "Well, I'll have to change it now. Needling Tanner is my goal in life."

Dad laughed and handed my papers pack, eyes dancing.

We left on Monday morning after finals. Tanner drove. I sat up front in the passenger seat, the boys were in the back.

"Did I see a suitcase in your car?" I asked Tanner as we pulled out of the driveway.

Tanner didn't answer right away. As we turned out onto the beltline heading towards I90, he broke his silence. "Easton and Greta are staying at the pack house while we're gone. Easton can play with Pebble and Greta can get help with childcare."

"Oh, man, I'd like to hang out with Greta for a few

days," I mused.

Tanner shot me a quick look before focusing back on the road. José spoke up. "Me, too. She's great."

Tanner just sighed. "This is going to be a long trip."

Owen piped up. "You can't help that your wife is just the bomb."

I heard a punch. "Yo, who says that word anymore?"

Tanner chose to ignore the two in the back. "I saw the plan and the big picture. What's the goal for tonight?"

"Well, I had two plans worked out. It's up to you which one we do."

He grumbled low in his throat. "I don't like the sound of this."

"No, it's fine. The drive to Stanford is about thirty-three hours. If we drive ten to twelve hours a day, we'd have to find hotels or shift and sleep in the wilderness. The other option is to take advantage of youth and just drive through the night."

I gave him a huge, wide-eyed smile.

"No."

José laughed. "Told ya, chica. There's no way he'd go for sleeping while we drove through the night."

"Okay. Sidney, Nebraska is just over twelve hours away. Cheyenne is just over thirteen. We can figure out if either of those are possible destinations for today. Maybe they're both too far, but if we could make either of them, that would be a great chunk of our drive out of the way."

Tanner gave me a longer look before focusing back on the road. "Okay, I can work with that. Do you have multiple plans for the rest of the trip?"

"Mostly. I have a skeleton plan because we're driving, and I want us to have flexibility. The only school that is a must-see is Stanford. Beyond that, we can have fun."

After that, I took out the latest Rick Riordan book and started reading. The boys put in earbuds and start playing on their phones. Tanner tuned in to a radio station.

Tanner drove until lunch and then José took over. After a few hours, he got bored, and Owen took the wheel. He continued after dinner. He got into his groove and took us all the way to Cheyenne.

We found a cheap hotel and got two rooms. I woke early the next morning and dragged everyone to the car, grabbing a travel mug of cheap hotel coffee; a bit gross, but it did the job. I drove while they slept. After a couple hours, they all gained enough consciousness to demand breakfast. I stopped at a breakfast buffet—all-you-can-eat pancakes, sausage, bacon, and coffee.

I almost swooned in anticipation.

After breakfast, Tanner took over. The second day was a repeat of the first, except that I sat in the back with Owen. At just past two in the afternoon, I checked the itinerary on my phone and figured out our next stop.

"Hey, Tanner. If you're willing to push through until about eleven tonight, we can make it to Reno. Then we'd be just over four hours to Stanford. We can sleep in. I'll make an appointment for the tour on Wednesday afternoon. What d'ya think?"

He thought about it for a few miles before he grunted.

Owen would understand the secret language of grunts that all men seemed to share. I turned to him. "What does that mean?"

"I think it means yes."

I smiled, scheduled the tour, and then went back to reading my book.

By Wednesday afternoon, we made it to the tour. I had planned on going alone, but José wanted to join me to check out the campus. Then Owen said he didn't want to be left out. At the last minute, Tanner growled that he was coming as our chaperone.

The four of us followed a student who led us walking backwards.

Owen turned to me. "You could never be a tour guide. You'd make it a step and then fall on your butt."

I glared, but José and Tanner chuckled. I moved ahead of them, trying to ignore them. Less than a minute later, almost all my energy drained away, and I started to black out. José and Tanner were on either side of me before I hit the ground.

José's worried voice hissed in my ear, "What happened?"

Shaking my head, I shrugged. "No idea, but I think I'm okay."

Tanner growled. "No, you're not. We're leaving."

I growled right back at him. "No. We did *not* drive halfway across the country only to not do this tour."

José slipped his arm around my waist. Gazing up at Tanner, he nodded. "I've got her. It's fine."

My phone buzzed. I pulled it out of my pocket and saw I had a text from Sarah.

Sorry about that. Call later to explain.

I showed the text to the others, and we continued the tour.

Halfway through, Tanner got a call. He ducked out for a few minutes to take it. I thought about listening in but realized the likelihood it had anything to do with me was miniscule, and I didn't have the energy. He had two jobs, one in security and one as a bounty hunter. Both had him on speed dial.

The University was beautiful. I felt my heart connect to it right away, like when you meet someone you know will be a friend for life. The people with the tour were nice and answered questions about applying and school requirements.

After the tour, we found a local restaurant and sat for lunch.

While I ate my mac and cheese, I asked Tanner. "What was the call?"

He wiped his face of non-existent pasta sauce. "Your dad called to tell me there was a sighting of a rogue wolf in the area."

Owen sat up straighter. "Like, here, in California?"

Tanner shook his head. "No, closer to Colorado. The Colorado pack is dealing with it. But, that being said, we need to be on high alert."

I groaned and dropped my head into my arms on the table. "Have I lost all of my freedoms?"

Owen snorted.

Massaging my back, José said, "You have us to hang out with; it won't be that bad."

We decided to spend a few extra days at the beach in Santa Cruz since we were so close to the ocean and then head to Las Vegas. It was nice, but with us being on high alert, it was also frustrating. The four of us were always together, and that killed any feeling of it being a vacation. Nothing like a snarling Tanner to ruin the relaxation.

We were on the beach when I got a call from Sarah. I flashed the screen to the boys and got up to walk while they continued to soak up the sun, what little there was.

I answered when I was a few feet away. "Hiya, tell me what happened."

"Are you alone?"

I saw the seagulls around me and decided they didn't count. "Yep. The others are on their towels out of hearing range. I'm walking along the water."

Sarah let out a huff of air. "Good."

She went silent and I watched the gray water, looking

out as far as the horizon. The flat hazy clouds dotted the sky. The day was cool and drab, so the water and the sky matched closely enough it was hard to tell where one started and the other ended. The only discernible difference was the white waves as the water broke in the distance.

Finally, Sarah took a breath and began. "I was walking with Bevin on the bike path. He's returned from up north and needed someone to talk to. His normal confidants are all out west, which is hard for him."

A stab of guilt pierced me, and my steps faltered.

"None of that," my alpha commanded. "Even at this distance I can feel those strong emotions if you don't put up blocks. We figured it out."

"Sorry. I'll text him when we're done."

"Not a bad idea, though we worked through most of it. Some of it was his grandma, which was just him needing an ear. I know you've been over that with him the last month, so has José. But he also needed to figure out his heart and head."

I perked up at that. "Anything solved?"

"A bit. He really wanted to like Phillip. Did you know that he's been half in love with José since forever?"

I laughed silently. "Sarah, I grew up with them both, of course I knew. He's always been subtle and got better at hiding it, but yeah, I knew."

"But, Jade, it never went away, not even when they became friends. Bevin just got better at hiding it. He knew that was all they would ever be. This was his problem. He wanted more with Phillip but couldn't convince his heart to drop this boyhood crush he'd always had on José."

I found a large rock to sit on and gazed out over the calming ocean. I breathed deeply of the salt and sea. Sadness for my friend filled me. "They need to talk. Bevin needs to let José know how he feels."

"That's what I told him. He's thinking about it."

"Good." It felt like a weight had been lifted off my shoulders.

"Anyway, in the middle of talking about his grandparents, and his facing his feelings about José, Bevin started to panic. So, I tried out our Soul Sharing. Hope it didn't affect you too much." She ended with a small, embarrassed laugh.

I rolled my eyes, not that she could see, and sighed. "If it was for Bevin, it was for a worthy cause. I'm just glad José and Tanner were there to catch me before I landed on my nose."

"What?"

I told her about the tour, and she laughed, the intended outcome. Then we signed off.

I sent a quick text to Bevin with a picture of the ocean, letting him know I was thinking about him. Then I sat and debated things in my head for a bit.

Before heading back to the boys, I searched the area on my phone for other colleges and found a small local college between Santa Cruz and San Francisco. It was due east of Half Moon Bay in a small town called Santa Arcoíris. The college had been established over a hundred years ago and its focus was on science and medicine.

I jogged back to the others and plopped down on my towel. "José, have you ever heard of Arcoíris University? It's in a small town north of here, Santa Arcoíris. Maybe we could drive up and take a look. They focus on STEM majors."

José, who wore nothing but a tiny speedo, rolled his head in my direction. "Chica, we are on a beach. Can't we enjoy the California sun? Why do you always have to be doing something?"

I huffed. "What sun? The sky is gray! We're already out here. Why not take advantage and see one more college?"

Tanner, who leaned back on his elbows, dropped his head back and sighed. "She's not wrong. If she can set up a tour, may as well see what this college is about."

I awarded him with a huge smile and made the call. I set up a tour with one of the administrators for nine in the morning the next day.

When we arrived at Arcoíris, we met with a no-nonsense woman wearing a tight bun and a lavender business suit. Tanner wore black slacks and a black button-down shirt, but the rest of us were in jeans and t-shirts. She evaluated us and didn't look impressed.

She barely stood taller than me in her tall, spiked heels, yet she looked down at us. "Yes, who would be interested in Arcoíris U?"

I cleared my throat. "That would be me. I have my transcripts if that would help."

She looked me over and sighed. "Very well, hand them over." She held out a perfectly manicured hand with light pink lacquered nails. She wore exactly one ring and a fine bracelet.

I gently placed my paperwork in her hand, trying not to mess anything up.

We all stood outside the main campus building. I had a feeling that if she didn't like what she saw, we wouldn't pass entry. In a previous life she must have been a sphynx.

She opened the manilla folder I handed her and looked over my paperwork. Slowly, she paged through the file, sheet by sheet. The words summed up my life. I tried not to fidget, knowing that the real-life version of me didn't impress, hoping the black-and-white version did. After a few minutes of close inspection, she let the pages fall flat and slowly closed the folder. "So, Ms. Stone, have you considered early graduation?"

CHAPTER 25

The drive to Las Vegas took almost nine hours. Car-dwelling began to get tiresome. Tanner parked and we dragged our tired bodies into the flashy lobby of the hotel he'd chosen.

The center of the hotel had a huge indoor water feature with jets of water and beams of colored lights. To navigate to the check-in desk, we had to walk through a gambling room with signs all over letting me know I was too young to be welcome. Once we arrived at the lobby, the atmosphere of the hotel overwhelmed me: large, gold, and surrounded by stores selling overpriced clothing and fancy jewelry. The whole place pierced my eyes, made my ears want to melt, and combined into an amalgamation of sensation I wanted to escape.

Owen, José, and I hung out by the water feature as Tanner went to check us in.

"Heeey, handsome, looking for a single?" The voice floated over from the check-in counter, and we all froze.

I smelled Tanner's cinnamon scented annoyance before I could react. He had a ring tattooed on his finger underneath his wedding band so that no matter what no one could mistake his attachment. I heard a low growl come from his direction as he said, "No."

I swung towards Owen. "Did you know she worked here?"

Eyes wide, he lifted his hands in my direction. "I had no idea. After we broke up, I cut off all contact with her and her group of friends."

Placated, we all faced Brooke, Owen's ex-girlfriend and my nemesis. Tanner pointed towards us as I heard him say, "I need a room with at least three beds, four would be better."

Brooke's eyes widened and then narrowed into a glare. I could smell her cayenne-scented disgust at seeing me. Then she glanced at Owen and her scent shifted to something chocolatey. She gave a small wave as her smell shifted again to a deep vanilla interest and something else that made no sense. She went back to her computer and started typing before I could figure it out. "I think I can find something for you, gorgeous."

José snorted. "This trip just got a lot more interesting."

Several minutes later, we walked past the flashing lights and garish stores to the elevators. It zoomed us up and deposited us on the ninth floor. Our suite had a queen bed, two doubles, and a couch. After dumping our luggage, I sagged from travel fatigue—too much time in a car.

"I think I'm going to go take a walk. I need to move."

Tanner checked his watch, then looked at me. "You can't go out alone. You know the rules."

I sighed. "These rules are dumb. I'm sixteen. I'm old enough that I should be able to do some sightseeing without causing a stir. No one, save Brooke, even knows we are here."

José watched us with a half-grin. "I'll go with her. I could use the walk as well. Stretch my legs."

Owen beamed. "Cool." He smiled mischievously at Tanner. "Then we can go gamble."

Tanner shook his head. "It's just past five; be back by seven so we can try out their famous buffet. All-you-can-eat is the best part of Las Vegas."

I perked up at that. "Sounds great."

José and I headed out. Our hotel was at the end of the strip, so we had a straight shot to walk. The crowds ensured we didn't walk fast, but the point was moving.

José's tension surrounded us like almonds and minty incense. I took his hand. "What's up?" At my touch he relaxed, but not by much.

"How does he look?"

It took me a second to realize he meant Bevin. "You haven't seen him?"

"No. I was at school, then in Mexico. Then with his grandma…"

"He looks like him…not really different, maybe a bit…I dunno, less willowy? He's more comfortable with himself, though."

José smiled and seemed to relax a notch.

"If you were worried, why didn't you ask before?"

"This is the first time we've really been alone."

"That's true, our trip out to California has been so busy. The tours were nice."

"Did you like Stanford? Is it on your short-list?"

"It's on the list. It was amazing; it seemed to fit my soul, but I can't imagine not having any pack around me. Running alone would be rough. I really liked Arcoíris. Think I could convince Bevin to join me out west?"

José growled low in his throat, then shook his head. "Yeah, probably. I could see both of you enjoying either of those two colleges. Personally, I'm glad I chose Madison because of the pack. I always have others to run with and lean on." José squeezed my hand. "Speaking of, how goes the figuring-out-pack-connections adventure?"

I groaned. "Horrible. My animals just tell me 'I am them' and 'they are me' and I should just do it."

José chuckled. "Helpful."

"I know, right?"

We walked down the block, weaving in and out of the crowd, hand in hand, when a wave of disgust flowed over me.

We both shivered and our steps slowed to a stop. I pushed him to the side to avoid the other people around us as I sniffed.

José pointed subtly with his chin to the left. I rubbed my chin on my shoulder to survey the sidewalk behind me and saw her: Brooke.

Brooke sashayed up to us, navy-blue mini-skirt tight and high on her legs, heels clacking on the sidewalk. I wasn't sure how she, or anyone really, managed to maneuver in them, especially on the crowded street. She wore a stylized cream top to finish off her outfit. *Why did she always have to look so good?* When she reached us, she raised an eyebrow. "I totally thought you two weren't each other's type. What gives?"

I tipped my head to the left and right, stretching out my neck.

José started to tense. I used a bit of my epsilon calm to relax him. Dad had added limiting the area of where I calmed to my practice schedule. I'd worked on it over winter break and spring semester and had gotten to the point I felt I could calm José without worrying about causing everyone on the sidewalk to feel like they'd suddenly taken drugs. Thankfully, it didn't seem like many of the tourists noticed a difference. He sighed as his tension dropped and he mouthed a 'thank you.'

Turing to face the center of our stress, I asked, "Brooke,

why are you following us?"

"I'm not. I just saw you two and then you stopped." She swung around in a circle, searching. "Where's Owen?"

"He's back at the hotel. Shouldn't you be there, too, working?"

"Not that it's any of your business, but my shift ended at five."

"Well, I would say it was a pleasure, but I don't like lying. Bye, Brooke."

Before I could turn around, her hand snaked out and she grabbed my arm. "Wait, no reason to rush off. How long are you all in town?"

I could have pulled out of her grasp, but I didn't want to cause a scene. "Just a day or two. You should know; you made the reservation."

She twirled her hair with her other hand. "Oh, yeah, right. Is Owen still with that friend of yours?"

I raised a brow. "You mean Sarah?"

"Whatever." Being from Wisconsin, her valley girl twang was an act.

"As far as I know, but I am neither of their keepers."

"Just let him know I'm available while you're here." She looked José up and down. "You, too, if you've switched teams, sweety."

"Chica, even if I had, you aren't my type. Too…plastic."

Brooke's face contorted into a mask of fury. The arm holding me whipped back. Completely taken unaware by the move, I staggered to where she pushed me, running into a pair of men approaching from up the street, upwind. Focused on the battle of wills between José and Brooke, it wasn't until they snatched me that I realized they were werewolves.

A hand clamped over my mouth, and they contained me before I could scream. The last thing I saw were José's eyes widened in fear and anger as he watched me being dragged away. Two more men held José and he struggled to escape them. A fifth had secured Brooke.

They dragged me down an alley and tossed me into the rear of a van. I hit the back wall, hard. I scrambled up just as another body bowled into me. The doors slammed shut. Everything went dark. I heard a lock click.

Panting, I tried to slow my breathing with a deep breath. I tasted the air to see if I could figure out who was in the truck with me. Brooke. The truck lurched into motion and my head knocked forward and then back. I tried to brace myself, but Brooke and I slid and then collided with the back door.

She moaned.

Where is José? Did they take him, too?

I checked my pockets. They had taken my phone during the grappling. I had nothing; no phone, no watch—just me and Brooke. She wasn't moving. I gently touched her wrist. Panther leapt to the forefront. We entered. Brooke was unconscious, but we couldn't sense anything wrong with her. There was nothing we could do. I backed out. The ride was bumpy and all I could do was wait.

CHAPTER 26

We bounced about in the back of the van for twenty minutes. Brooke remained unconscious the whole time. I pulled her away from the door and prepared to launch myself at whomever opened up the doors.

A key snicked into the lock and a growly male voice spoke. "We've got guns pointed at the back. We know you're…something. We're not sure what. We know your friend is human. If you fight, she dies."

Friend? They think Brooke is my friend?

Then the lock clicked, and the doors swung open. Four men stood outside the van; three of them held guns. The tallest had a set of keys clipped to his belt. There was a short man with glasses, one with greasy hair whose body odor wafted up to me, and one with beady eyes. All of their scents informed me they were all werewolves, not just the two who'd originally snagged me. I lowered my arms; I couldn't fight all four of them and win.

"Smart," the one who had the keys said. "Now, pick up your friend and follow me."

I looked down at Brooke and shivered.

The wolves all smiled and the tall one asked, "Not your friend, huh? I guess we misread the situation. Well, the choice is yours: bring her, or she dies."

Apparently, they knew how to use their sense of smell to read emotions that much. They weren't complete idiots… that wasn't good.

As much as I disliked her, letting Brooke die really wasn't an option. I squatted next to her and lifted her using a fireman's style hold. She was about six inches taller than me, but I was strong.

The tall wolf grinned. "Good. Now that your hands are occupied, you won't be able to fight back."

I just stared at him as blankly as I could while I analyzed the situation. I probably could fight, but they still had guns. Though I could probably survive a few gunshot wounds, it wasn't as many as they could inflict at close range. Moreover, Brooke couldn't.

"Follow," he growled.

I obeyed. What choice did I have?

When I got to the edge of the truck, I saw the bed of the van was about three feet off the ground. I sighed and jumped down. It was awkward with Brooke over my shoulders, but I managed. The men laughed at me, enjoying the show.

They led me through a compound that smelled old, dusty, and mildewy. The walls were a greenish-gray metal and dirty. Reddish-brown mud covered most surfaces. As we went deeper and deeper into the compound, I realized we were treading over the same path. I recognized signs on the wall so old the words had been worn away with time. It occurred to me the compound wasn't that big; they were walking me in circles to get me lost.

Eventually, they pointed to a room with bars on the walls. The room was small, maybe ten feet by ten feet. From the outside it looked like a regular room, but they'd installed bars inside to make it a jail. Before they left, I asked, "What do you want from me? Us?"

The tallest of the group said, "All in good time, girly, all in good time." When they left, they secured both the cell's door and the room's door

A fluorescent light flickered from the ceiling, so we weren't in darkness. There was one bed, a table, and a chair. Everything was bolted down. The bed had a mattress, but no pillow or bedding. Everything smelled new and clean, thankfully.

I lowered Brooke to the bed and sat on the chair, looking at her. I sighed and waited.

About fifteen minutes later, Brooke moaned and stirred. I watched as she slowly woke up. She rubbed her eyes and finally spotted me. "What the hell are you doing here?" She looked around the room. "Where *is* here?"

"Remember ambushing me and José?" I asked. "Well, when you tossed me aside, apparently you tossed me into some guys who wanted to capture…well, I'm not sure. It may have been you, or me, or girls…"

She looked around. "How long have we been here?"

"By my estimate, about an hour."

"Did they take José as well?"

"Not sure. I saw them grab him, but he might have gotten away. He's scrappy."

She massaged her head as she sat up. "Damn. Well, there goes my date for tonight."

I raised an eyebrow. "You had a date?"

She closed her eyes. "Well, no. I was hoping to tempt Owen."

I chuckled. "I don't see why. You don't like me, or anyone in my family *but* Owen. Obviously if he and I are here together, we get along. You have made it abundantly clear you don't want someone who is a family guy. Why him?"

She sighed. "I like him. I can't help it. I always have. He's cute and nice. Then last spring, something changed, and he got even better. I know I messed it up. I was going to see if I could rekindle something while you all were in town."

"Well…your approach is a bit heavy-handed."

She flopped down on her back. "I am who I am, Jade. Take it or leave it."

"If only I could," I mumbled.

She rolled onto her side. "What did you say?"

"Nothing."

Brooke sat up with a blank stare. "You don't think I'm good enough for your brother."

I couldn't hold back a snort at such a ridiculous question. "No, you don't think *I'm* good enough. You made that painfully clear. I don't know what I ever did to you, Brooke, but you gave me hell for existing. All I did was be Owen's sister. You thought that was enough. I didn't know what your deal was then, and the situation between Owen and I hasn't changed."

She squinted, but before she responded, the doors opened, both the room door and the barred cell door. The tall wolf entered with a set of handcuffs. He eyed Brooke like she was a tasty morsel. "Come along, my pretty, we have a present for you."

I narrowed my gaze. "What do you want with her?"

"You two aren't really friends, what do you care?"

Crossing my arms over my chest, I glared at him. "I care because I don't trust you. I like you even less than her. She's not like you and, one on one, I think I could take you. Leave out the guns, and your goons, and you are nothing."

He laughed. "Now why would I do that? And she's so pretty. We just want someone to join us who's lovely to look at." *Darn it, they're going to hurt her. Maybe even turn her. This is bad, bad, bad!*

I leapt to my feet, standing between him and Brooke. "No."

He snarled. "Yes." He pulled out a gun and aimed it at my head. My heart pounded in my chest, but I couldn't let them take her. I started to think of another argument, something that may save her.

The bed creaked. "Jade, I'll go with him. Don't get shot over me."

My mind went blank for a second and I almost couldn't speak. *She doesn't know what she's doing. Think, Jade!* "Brooke, stay back, you don't understand."

Before I could stop her, she shuffled around the small room to the man. He grabbed her wrist and dragged her out. The door slammed shut and locked. They were gone. Brooke was gone.

I stood there, frozen, unable to breathe, watching the door, willing it to open. Demanding this to be a bad dream. How could I be standing in a jail cell, in the middle of nowhere, with lone wolves who had just taken Brooke? *What nightmare am I in? How can I fix this?*

Eventually, I had to breathe. I backed up until my legs hit the bed and I sat down, hard. My arms flopped down as my back hit the wall behind me.

Sometime later, the door opened, and food was slid through a small opening at the bottom built between two bars to fit a tray of food. On it was a slice of pizza and a bottle of soda rolling on its side. I wanted to go on hunger strike, but that would hurt no one but myself, so I got up and snatched the tray. The food was fine.

With a belly full of food, I closed my eyes and reached for my animals. I needed to find the connections to find Tanner, José, and Owen. Even with all this extra time, I couldn't find them.

A few hours later, I slept. The next morning, the tray was gone. I woke and did a few stretches and squats. I heard the slot open and a tray with eggs, toast, and coffee was slid in. Coffee. I moaned. I asked the air as I moved the tray to the table, "Can I get extra coffee?"

Time slipped by. The light stayed on. Food came in intervals. No one would talk to me. I slept. I exercised. I became numb with boredom. Brooke didn't return.

Eventually, the food slot opened, and handcuffs slid in on a tray.

"Put those on and I'll open the door."

I sighed. From what I remembered, not only were the werewolves all bigger than me, they all had guns, too. The sooner I figured out what was going on, the better. Besides, I could slip out of these in either of my animal forms. I put on the hand cuffs.

The door opened a crack, and I stared down the barrel of a gun. "Back up."

I obeyed. "Do you have a name?" My voice cracked. I was dehydrated.

The gruff voice replied. "I'm Jonny. You?"

"I'm Jade. Why'd you take me if you don't know who I am?"

"I'm not supposed to say. Dalton'd kill me if I did."

"Okay, no worries." He'd already given me more information than I'd expected. I held my cuffed hands out in front of myself in a pacifying way.

He yanked the chain between the cuffs and dragged me. Our path was direct this time. We only took a few turns before reaching a central room bigger than my cell.

The center housed a huge table with chairs around it. Dalton, who I assumed was both the driver and the leader, sat at the head. Three of his goons sat around the table, two to the left and one to the right.

The room smelled awful. There was a sour smell coming from my right. When I quickly surveyed the room, I saw a woman lying on a cot, chained against the wall. She was under a dirty blanket. She had blond hair, messed up and tangled, and her blue eyes were flat and vacant.

The men around the table smelled like they hadn't seen soap in days; not that I had either, but I was living in a jail cell.

I quickly checked over my left shoulder and saw another woman lying on a cot. She wasn't chained but was in just as much disarray. Her dark hair spilled out over her face, messy and tangled, and her body looked gaunt in its torn, barely-there clothes. Suddenly, I recognized her: Brooke.

Brooke looked horrible, all mangled and bloody. Her

fashionable shirt was torn to shreds and barely clinging on her body. Her skirt was rucked up around her waist and her shoes were gone. Her hair, which I'd never seen anything but perfect, was a mess. I ran to her, but one of the rogue wolves grabbed my arm, yanking me back before I reached her.

I whipped around to face the leader. "I can help her. I'm a healer."

"You can't heal her wounds. You're a baby." He sneered.

"Yes, I can," I snarled back.

His eyes narrowed as if he were calculating. "Not without equipment. I'll make a deal with you. Do to her," he pointed at the dead-looking woman in the other cot, "what you did to your friend on the street, and I'll let you take your *friend* to the medical suite." He sneered when he said 'friend.'

I didn't need a medical suite, I just needed to find out what was wrong with Brooke. I needed to slow down and think and stop reacting. I paused and took a few breaths. I slowly turned to Dalton. "What are you talking about?"

"Don't play coy with me, little girl. You know *exactly* what I'm talking about."

I didn't. I closed my eyes and my brow crinkled as I tried to search my memory back when I stood on the street with José. My nose wrinkled up and I shook my head as I tried to remember. *Think, Jade, think.* Nothing.

Snuffling noises came from the group around the table. My eyes snapped open. One of the goons kept looking back and forth between me and the leader. "Hey, boss, she don't smell like she's lying. She smells confused."

"Hush, Brett. You don't know what you're talking about."

He lowered his head as his shoulders came up, cowering in his seat.

I blew out a breath. "Can you help me out here? I'm really not trying to be evasive. What exactly are you talking about?"

The leader sat back, steepling his hands in front of his mouth. "What exactly are you, Ms.... I never did catch your name."

"Jade. My name is Jade."

"Ah, nice to meet you, Jade. I'm Dalton. This here is Brett and next to him is Tony. Over here is Rex. Your escort is Jonny. They are my pack. Now that we're friends, maybe you can help me out."

I nodded. "Who's the one on the cot?" I tilted my head to my right.

"That's my old lady. She's been a bit wild ever since we turned her. She didn't take the change very well. None of us are sure why. Can you imagine our shock when we were minding our own business walking down the street—and bam!—we all wanted to curl up and take a nap? I thought to myself, we can sure use some of that to calm Pam down."

Oh, that. I kept my face blank. "And you think that this is something I did?" I raised an eyebrow, channeling as much Mom as I could.

"Honey, we know it is. We smelled your scent shift and then your friend smiled at you and mouthed 'Thanks.'"

"I'm not sure what you want. If I help your friend... what's her name?"

"Pam."

"Right. If I help Pam to what, want to take a nap? Which I don't know that I can, it won't be a long-term fix."

"But it will allow me to talk to her for a few minutes. Give her some relief from her pain."

My head dropped back, and I searched the ceiling for inspiration. Nope. Nothing. I slipped my hands into my pockets and shut my eyes as I weighed my options. At this point, I didn't think I had any. They knew I could give them what they wanted and instead of threatening me further, they offered me Brooke to heal.

I straightened and closed my eyes again. I took in a deep breath and found a center of calm. I released it at full force to fill the room. When I opened my eyes, they all stared at me wide-eyed, slouched in their seats with slow smiles. Their breathing had deepened, and their pulse rates decreased.

Rex surveyed the room. "Whoa. It's better than drugs."

"Can you show me to the medical suite now?"

Dalton rose and crossed the room to Pam. Her breathing had evened out, and her gaze seemed sharper. As he observed her, he nodded.

The other men collected me and Brooke and then took us to a new room, this one clean and bright. They placed her on a sterile-looking bed in the center of the room. There were two other beds against two of the walls.

Medical supplies lined a third wall in a similar setup to our pack house medical room, just much bigger. Jonny stayed while the others shuffled away.

I held out my hands to him and his eyes got wide. Face hardening, I said, "You have the gun, and I can't do much with cuffs on. When I was given permission to help her, I'm sure taking these off while you watched over me with a gun was part of it."

His face scrunched up and he looked confused. After a minute of seeming to parse through my words, he slowly lowered the gun and took out a key to take off my cuffs. I massaged my wrists before turning away from him.

I inhaled sharply. Brooke was a mess. It looked like they had used her as a punching bag. Teeth marks dimpled her arms. Human teeth marks. Confused, I unbuttoned her shirt to see if I could make sense of her other injuries. Maybe they'd punched her while wearing metal gloves or whipped her with a chain. Whatever they'd used to hurt her, there were a few lacerations needing stitches. The gashes on her torso had not been done by tooth or claw. Most of her abrasions just needed to be washed out and bandaged.

I got to work cleaning her up and patching the bigger abrasions. Once done, I covered her with a blanket and pulled a chair up to the bed to sit next to her. I turned to Jonny. "Can I stay with her tonight? I don't want her to wake up alone."

His eyes narrowed and he patted his gun. "I have my piece," he reminded me. "So don't do anything stupid."

CHAPTER 27

I took Brooke's hand, and my panther flew to action. Brooke was a mess inside. Her internals were almost all damaged. My wolf wanted to help but I needed one animal to stay home and keep me safe.

We started with the vital organs—heart, lungs, kidneys—and worked our way out to less life-threatening injuries. There were a few bruised and broken bones. I wasn't sure why they had done so much damage, but they had. I knew that I was using too much energy as the hours dragged by, especially considering how little they'd been feeding me.

I sensed a hand on my shoulder and felt Wolf drink

energy from that source. I told Wolf to drink deep. I didn't know who it was, but it wasn't a friend.

Once I knew Brooke was stable and would survive, I started to back out. Before I left, I heard a whimper from inside her.

I froze. I knew my energy was low; I hadn't eaten enough. But I searched.

It took some time, but eventually I found her—a small gray wolf.

No!

It snapped its head up and looked at me, tail tucked. *Did I do something wrong?*

I groaned. *No, friend. Nothing at all. Come out and let me see you.*

She shivered in place; large gray eyes like saucers gazed at me.

Don't be afraid.

I saw you healing. I tried to heal, but there was so much. I can help now.

I nodded. *Yes, you can. We came to help. I didn't even know you were here.*

Throughout my discussion with the leader, I had forgotten that they were going to make Brooke a werewolf. Their attack was wrong for the process. It looked like they had just beaten her up. I wondered if they even knew how to make a werewolf without this kind of damage.

I'm going to leave now. You will be okay.

The wolf vibrated with excitement. *Will I see you again?*

I believe so.

When I opened my eyes, the room was dark and silent. I turned to see Jonny lying on the floor next to me. I stroked Brooke's hand and she stirred before falling into a deeper sleep.

I needed sleep and decided to use one of the other beds in the medical suite. I grabbed a piece of paper and wrote a note for Jonny: *Please bring a large breakfast. We are both hungry.* I curled up on a bed and fell asleep.

The next morning, I found Brett standing at the door with his gun. As I sat up, he got his gun ready. I heard the click as he pointed it at me. I held my hands out. "Unarmed. Bathroom?"

He pointed to a door in the back. "What did you do to Jonny?"

I went over to the medical supplies. "What are you talking about?

Brett's voice snapped out. "What are you doing?"

"Looking for a rubber band. I want to put my hair up. I don't think a rubber band will do any harm to you or yours." After a few seconds of rummaging around, I found two. I held them up for Brett's inspection before slipping them in my pocket.

I trudged into the bathroom. It was semi-private with no actual doors. After washing my hands and face, I wrestled my hair into a ponytail. It no longer fell into my face and blocked my view. I returned and found a plate with four sandwiches, all PB&Js. They had also brought sweatpants, a t-shirt, and flip-flops for Brooke, so she didn't have to run around mostly naked.

I shook Brooke and woke her. She quickly dressed and then mocked the food but dug in all the same. We each ate two sandwiches. My stomach grumbled for more, but I felt better.

Brett eyed us suspiciously as we ate. "Jonny said you were holding her hand last night. Then when he grabbed your shoulder, he passed out. So, what did you do to him?"

I continued to eat my sandwich as my brow furrowed. "I sat with Brooke. She slept. I'm not sure what you're talking about. After Jonny shook my shoulder and woke me up, I moved to the bed and fell asleep over there." I pointed, giving him a look of indignation. "That's where you found me. I don't know what you or he is talking about."

"I found him on the floor by her bed this morning." He pointed at Brooke.

Brooke sat tall, eyes narrow, following the conversation with interest.

My brows flew up to my hair line. I leaned in conspiratorially. "Whoa. What was your man doing by her? Do you trust him?"

Brett let out a low growl but dropped the topic.

After eating our food, I checked Brooke over. Most of her wounds were gone. She gave me a questioning look.

"What happened yesterday?"

"Don't really know."

"No, not with them." She waved her hand towards Brett. "But you."

"What do you mean?"

"I mean, I remember talking with you when I was asleep. You kept calling me 'friend.' It was weird."

My elbows hit the table and I rubbed my eyes, willing the headache to stay away. "Tell me about the attack."

"They said they wanted a lady wolf. I mean, I've been called a fox, but never a wolf."

"Did they just hit you?"

She scowled. "Yeah, and one of them bit me, the idiot brute."

I nodded. They *were* idiots. "Can you look me in the eyes for a sec?" I tried to channel Mom or Dad, José or Bevin, someone with dominance.

She rolled her eyes, but then did it. She gave me her best arrogant Brooke stare, but immediately dropped her gaze to the floor. She gave a huff of shock and tried again. Again, her gaze dropped to the floor. After the third attempt I couldn't keep a smile from my face. "Stop."

"What's happening to me?"

"It's a rather long story. I don't want to get into it now."

"Jade, I want to know immediately. Why can't I hold your gaze anymore?"

I turned to Brett. "What's your boss's end plan here?"

Brett shrugged. "He don't want no submissive brat, that's for sure."

I knew I could take the men down one at a time, but the idea of that much fighting made me feel sick. "Can we get more food?"

"Sure." He cracked open the door and yelled. "More grub for the chicks."

Leaning back in the chair, I shut my eyes. I found my beasts in my mental landscape sitting outside the tiny cabin by the fake fire pit.

Okay. We have to find the connections. No more playing around. Just show me the string to Tanner. I closed my internal eyes and focused everything I had on the connection to Tanner. I thought about him and about seeing a string attaching him to my wolf. I put everything, everything, I had into that and pushed it out.

Please, Tanner, hear me.

Jade? Is that you?

I almost leapt out of my seat. A hand landed on my shoulder and shook me. "Hey, girl. Wake up. I brought more food and some coffee. You seemed to really like coffee."

My head spun as he pulled me to a sitting position. I smelled eggs, toast, and coffee. My stomach growled as my head began to pound.

I smiled and grabbed the mug of coffee. Taking a sip, the warmth centered me before I started in on the food they brought. Brooke dug in as well. We both concentrated on eating and drinking. Brett went back to his spot as sentry.

When the food was all gone, I shifted my focus to Brooke. "How do you feel?"

"Like I was hit by a truck."

A brow rose. "Really?"

"Yes," she snapped back. After a pause she shifted in her seat, then, looking confused, said, "Well, maybe not."

"Good. Leave it at that for now."

"But why?"

"He's listening."

She faced Brett. "No way. He's by the door, there is no way he can hear us."

Brett snorted. "That's what you think." Brooke slapped her hands over her mouth.

I rubbed my temples and dreaded the thought of how long the day was going to be.

After breakfast, Brett returned us to the tiny cell. I sat at the table while Brooke rested on the bed.

"Okay, nerd girl, talk to me. I remember them beating on me. Why are all my cuts almost completely healed?"

I sighed. "Why am I stuck with *you* of all people?"

"What does *that* mean?"

"It means you are not nice. This would be so much easier if I were stuck with someone who wasn't so…you."

"Whatever. Just tell me what I need to know, already."

I closed my eyes. "Look, I need to lie down and take a short nap. I was up most of the night patching you up. After that, we'll have a nice, long heart-to-heart. If you wouldn't mind just sitting and…I dunno, not being you for a bit."

She made a sound of annoyance but switched places with me, taking the seat I vacated. I shut my eyes and found my beasts.

I focused on the connections. Nothing. I growled.

"Did you just growl, Jade?"

"Brooke, please let me…sleep. You're not helping by talking to me."

"Whatever."

Tensing, then forcing myself to relax, I tried to find the connections and my hope to locate Tanner, Owen, and José. I focused on my need for the strings, and I pushed that need out. Something deep inside me shifted. It felt like something blossomed out. When I opened my eyes, the strings were there.

I almost whooped in glee. All the connections were there, including—I noted with a sinking heart—one to Brooke. I groaned.

I touched Tanner's string. *Hello?*

Jade! Is that you?

Yes.

Where are you?

Don't know; some industrial base. Five lone wolves have created a pack. I guess it's six. There's one who is uncontrollable; they want me to calm that one. Is José with you?

Yes. When they tried to grab him, he got away, but he

couldn't follow you or find you. You and that Brooke girl were gone. They threw you in a truck and took off too fast.

Can you follow the string?

What string?

Damn! Ummm, okay. I focused on my wolf. *Can we show Tanner the string?*

Yes. I am you, you are me. We can help his wolf. Make it so.

Aye, aye, captain. I focused on something deep within me again and made my connection tangible. I heard a gasp. Then a tickle.

I felt that.

Tanner laughed. *I see the string now. I think I can follow it. You're southeast of here.* There was a pause. After a few minutes he said, *About ten miles away. We're on our way.*

Can you and the boys do it alone?

We aren't alone; we have you to help on the inside. But once I told them you were abducted, your dad, Fred, and Bevin got on a plane.

One more thing. They beat up Brooke…and bit her. They were in human form, but it was enough to turn her.

Well, hell. Good to know.

I'm going to say hi to the boys before I disconnect.

Sounds good. It'll take about five minutes to gather everyone.

I lightly touched both Owen's and José's strings. They were in a room together. That was good because my ability wouldn't let them hear each other, otherwise.

Hi, I said gently.

I sensed them both jump.

Oh, my gods, sis, you're alive.

I couldn't stop the smile from spreading across my face. *I am. And I'm stuck in a cell with Brooke.*

José's sadness traveled down the line. *I'm sorry I couldn't protect you, chica.*

Not your fault. Nothing anyone could have done.

Chica, what can we do?

Two things. One, Tanner knows how to find me. Two, help Brooke when you get here. They bit her. I haven't explained anything to her yet. I just don't know how.

Owen's shock clogged my throat. *They did what now?*

Yeah, they turned her. But they did it as humans. They beat her up and bit her. Oh, and she's trying to win you back, I think. Just an FYI. Oh, crap. Got to go. I smell them coming. Love you both lots.

I broke off before they could say anything more. I rolled to face the wall as the door opened.

My nose told me it was Tony. "Boss said to bring her."

Brooke stood up. "She's asleep. She just fell asleep. She was up all night tending me. Can't he wait?"

I heard flesh strike flesh, Brooke gasp, and a thud. I turned and sat in one swift motion. Tony was standing over her, snarling.

He shook his head. "She's so damn submissive. I barely have to look at her and she's on her hands and knees. Boss ain't gonna like it one damn bit. He likes them with a bit of fire in 'em."

I stood and glared at him. He glared back. He tried to bring me down with a dominance stare. He must have done that after hitting Brooke. I just raised an eyebrow at him, unimpressed.

As if!

CHAPTER 28

Back in the main room, I stood in front of Dalton. Pam, still chained to the bed to my right and the other goons scattered about the room all emanated hostility towards me. The men were armed. Two had guns out, ready to point at me.

Dalton smirked down his nose at me. "Will your friend survive?"

"No thanks to you. Why did you beat her up? Were you trying to kill her?"

"I've heard that the closer you bring 'em to death, the stronger the wolf is."

I stared at him, utterly baffled. "Where did you hear such nonsense?"

"From the wolf who changed me."

My face contorted at the stupidity of his words despite my attempt to keep a poker face. "And you were changed by being beaten? Punched and bitten like Brooke?"

"How else would you make a werewolf?"

I shook my head and snorted in disgust. "You can't create strong wolves because you're all too weak."

Dalton leapt up from his seat and snarled at me. "How dare you?"

I laughed. "How dare I? This isn't me being insulting, it's me being real. You're here playing at being a pack, but none of you are strong enough to hold a pack together. The first true werewolf that comes along will tear you all to pieces."

His voice dropped low, and the wolf took over. "You have no idea, little girl. We've taken down wolves, lots of them, and we'll take down any others that dare to come here."

"How, by shooting them?"

He slammed his fists into the table. "With whatever it takes to win."

His anger and frustration flooded the room with a strange mix of pepper and mint. He just needed to be pushed a bit more.

I sneered. "You couldn't win in a fair fight if it bit you in the butt. I bet you tied Brooke up just to ensure she didn't fight back...and she's a girl."

"Enough," he roared. His eyes started to glow, and his hands twitched.

I backed up a few steps.

His nose flared. "You aren't scared of me, little girl, are you?"

I gave him as much blankness as I could muster. "No."

He roared again louder. This time more of his beast infused his voice. The four men around the room cowered at the sound.

I dug deep within myself. I found the string that belonged to Mom and pulled. I pushed out an alpha command. "*Change.*"

I didn't know if it would work. I had seen Mom force the change on members of the pack, but these weren't members of my pack, her pack. A heart beat passed where nothing happened, and then they all dropped to the floor. Keys rattled as they fell, and I darted in to grab them. I turned on my heel and dashed for the hybrid room and cell I shared with Brooke.

By sheer luck, it only took two tries to find the correct key to unlock the door. I slammed the door open and found her sitting on the bed. She leapt up, searching behind me for our captors. I clasped her hand and said, "Run!"

She followed me as we made our way through the compound. The hallways were straight, and a light glimmered ahead. We located a door leading to the outside, but it was locked. I fumbled with the keys. There were too many of them and I kept glancing over my shoulder, expecting an attack from behind.

"Jade, work on the keys. I'll tell you if any of the men come."

"Not men. Wolves."

"What? They have animals here, too?"

"What? Um? Yes. That."

A chorus of yips and howls came from behind us. The click of wolf nails on the metal floor echoed as they ran down the hallway.

Brooke froze in fear. I finally found the correct key. The lock clicked open, but the door was jammed. I slammed my shoulder into it, once, twice, three times before it gave way slightly. The gap slivered open, barely enough to squeeze through, but neither of us were large. I dragged Brooke through the tiny opening into the bright sunlight.

As I burst into the open, hands grabbed me, and I screamed. "Stop it!"

"Jade, it's me." I looked up into Dad's eyes.

"Dad!" I collapsed into his arms. He held me a moment before putting me aside to face the wolves snarling at the cracked-open door. Tanner, José, Owen, and Fred were in wolf form. Dad and Bevin were not. Bevin helped Brooke to the car. I followed them.

When I got there, I found water bottles and energy drinks.

Bevin engulfed me in a hug. "Have you told her yet?"

I gave him a sheepish look. "No."

He sighed. "Should we tell her or wait?"

"I'm all for waiting. Or maybe never telling her."

Brooke tapped that obnoxious foot of hers. She crossed her arms and gave me her superior stare. "You know I can hear the two of you just fine, right?"

I sighed. "Probably better than you."

"What does that even mean? And those dogs with your dad—Will they be safe with the wolves in the compound?"

I saw Bevin's mouth twitch as he tried not to smile.

All sorts of horrible sounds came from around the corner at the door we had exited. The snarls and yips of pain had me darting a look over my shoulder before I gaped at Bevin. We both jerked at the sound of a grunt and thump. "Should we go help?"

He shook his head. "I was told to not let you or Brooke anywhere near the fighting."

"Tell me the story."

"Well, your dad got here first, and we decided on a plan. Owen, José, and Tanner were already…you know. Your dad changed. I was put on rescue duty. They needed a friendly face. In lieu of that, well, me."

Brooke surveyed the surroundings. "Where are Owen and José? You said they were here."

Bevin just gave me a look. Before I could start, Dad came running around the corner. "It's all clear. There were five wolves. Anyone else in the building?"

Brooke pushed past me, taking command of the

situation. "The five bad guys and the woman, Pam, who they had chained in the main room."

Dad just gave me a deadpan stare. "We'll deal with the…riff raff. You'd better explain things to her." With that, he walked away.

I wrinkled my nose. *I'd rather deal with the bodies than talk with Brooke.* I yelled after Dad, "Can one of the boys come and change over here? It would certainly help."

"Yes, but not until *after* you explain things to her."

I hit my head against Bevin's bicep a few times. "Ouch, your arm is harder than it was before."

He smiled down at me.

"Jerk," I mumbled. His smile got bigger, and his eyes twinkled.

I glanced at Brooke. "Okay, suspend your disbelief for the next ten minutes, will ya?"

She eyed me suspiciously but nodded.

"You were attacked by werewolves."

With a huff, she spun on her heel and started to walk away.

"You can leave but it won't change anything. In a few days, when there's a full moon, you're going to grow claws and become furry."

She froze and slowly turned. "What?"

"The full moon. You'll change. And then you'll attack someone, and then things will get really ugly. Or…you could just listen to me."

She crossed her arms and began to tap her foot, again. Oh, gods, not again.

However, she allowed me ten minutes of explanation before demanding answers. "Is that why everything suddenly smells so…distinct?"

I nodded. "Yep. Ready to see the proof?"

She rolled her eyes. "Whatever."

"Owen, José, time for your moment of glory."

They trotted over.

Her eyes widened, her body stiffened, and she stepped back.

I smiled. "Think of them as dogs. They can be dangerous, but in this case, they won't hurt you." José gave me a look, and I added, "Probably. Why don't you meet them first?"

Shaking, she knelt, and José approached. She couldn't even begin to look him in the eyes. Instead, she turned to me. "Is this Owen? He's so manly and powerful."

José sneezed in laughter and backed up. Owen trotted up and Brooke actually managed to meet his eyes before dropping her gaze. "Oh. This must be Owen. The eyes are the same blue as his."

Both wolves backed up and started the change. I reached into the car and threw their clothes next to where they shifted. Owen's change was relatively quick, as always, though it looked painful. Once human, he slipped on his pants and shoes.

"Hiya, Brooke. Welcome to the world of the strange."

Despite knowing what was happening in theory, the reality seemed to have temporarily short-circuited her brain. She just stood there staring at him, open-mouthed.

José's change took a minute or so longer. He slipped on his pants and then turned to face us. And then his attention switched completely to Bevin.

Bevin froze, staring at José. It was their first time together in the same form since the party in January, since Bevin had become a wolf…since a lot of things.

Bevin's face lost all color and he started trembling.

I looked at him. "What's wrong?"

His eyes remained fixed on José's as he said, "José is my mate."

CHAPTER 29

A wave of shock and terror rolled off Bevin. I smelled sadness coming from José.

I placed my hand on Owen's arm. "Why don't you take Brooke for a walk that way?" I pointed in a random direction. "Answer her questions about werewolves."

Like a man waking from a dream, he shook himself, grabbed Brooke's hand, and forced a smile. "This way, my dear."

I heard a giggle come from her—a giggle! Gah! "So, how long have you been…?" She waved a hand up and down his body.

They walked away quickly enough that I didn't catch

more of their conversation.

Taking a steadying breath, I faced the boys. "Do you two know what mates are?"

They both stood like statues, staring at the ground between them. Almost as one, their focus shifted to me.

José broke the silence. "You never got back to me."

I hit my head with the heel of my hand. "Between Bevin's transformation, and his *transformation*…then track and then school amping up for the APs, I forgot." I slid his hand into mine. "I'm really sorry. It happens sometimes. It's not common, though not unheard of."

Bevin lightly touched my shoulder. "Jade, babble mode."

"Oh, sorry. Some wolves find their…" I paused. They both hung on to me as if I were their lifeline. Bevin's hand rested on my shoulder, and I still held José's hand. I shifted my gaze back and forth between them.

José finally spoke. "It's their other half, isn't it? This is why I've been so anxious this last year, isn't it?" He turned and reached out his hand to Bevin. "I needed Bevin to find his wolf…and then to find me." A sense of peace followed his revelation.

Bevin stared at José's hand; his confusion so thick it was hard to breathe. "Jade, José, I don't understand any of this."

I laid my hand on his. "I know. I should probably leave you two to talk."

He gave an almost imperceptible nod before his hand fell from my shoulder. I let go of José's hand and trotted off to find Owen and Brooke. I couldn't believe I actually decided to find Brooke over my friends, but José and Bevin needed some privacy.

As I approached, I heard Brooke ask, "What is she, anyway?"

I snarled low, "Don't you dare."

They both jumped before gazing at me. Owen shot me a questioning look, his eyes darting to the boys and back to me. I shrugged.

Brooke started tapping her foot. I wonder how long Mom would put up with that if she ended up in our pack. A shiver ran down my back at the thought. "What do you mean by that?"

"Owen can talk about himself and anything in general. He can't answer questions about others."

Brooke seemed to consider this. "Okay, that makes sense. But the men in there were confused by you. They kept saying you smelled weird."

I waited. She hadn't asked me a question.

It was Owen who broke first. "What do you smell?"

Brooke's face contorted in a sneer. "What kind of question is that?"

Owen's brow furrowed and he stared at me. "I thought you said she was one of us."

I shrugged. "She will be. She hasn't shifted, so she hasn't developed all of the superpowers yet. You *know* this. It's close to the full moon, they're developing, but not fully developed."

He shook his head. "I haven't really slept since you

were taken."

"About that—how long has it been? Do you have my phone? My watch? Any way for me to connect to the world at large?"

Owen snorted. "It's Friday."

"How have I lost a day in there? I thought it was only Thursday. They fed us two breakfasts."

Owen shrugged. "Maybe you were drugged, or maybe time in captivity is like being in the twilight zone."

I rubbed my head. "Yeah, maybe."

"Anyway, your stuff is with Dad."

Brooke was vibrating at this point. "Friday? Friday! I'm going to be fired."

Owen and I just stared at her.

"What? I just got this job. It leads to working the floor and maybe to the stage. I can't lose it."

My hands went from rubbing my forehead to rubbing the back of my neck. I looked to the sky for help. She was going to try my patience.

Amusement emanated from Owen. I lowered my head and gave him a patented 'Mom look.'

His eyes danced merrily. "You two were locked up for three days together? That's comedy gold."

Facing Brooke, I took a deep breath. "Listen. Listen carefully. In just over a week—a week from Sunday to be exact—you will turn into a gray wolf. You need to come with us so we can help you do this safely."

Brooke squared her shoulders. "No. I need this job. I need the money. I left Wisconsin for a reason." Her head tilted. "How do you know the color of my wolf? Owen and José were different."

I forced myself to smile. "I'll explain everything wolfy to you later. As for Wisconsin, you went back in December."

"That was to visit friends." She huffed, then her eyes narrowed. "How do you even know that?"

I sighed at my own slip. "I'm omniscient—and the sooner you get used to it the easier," I waved my finger back and forth between us, "*this* will be."

Owen's voice snapped out in a perfect impersonation of Mom. "Jade."

My hands clenched into fists as I leaned towards her. "Brooke. Are you prepared to shift into a wolf on your own? Are you prepared for the consequences of attacking someone? Are you prepared for what may happen if you bite a human? Are you ready to go hunting for small furry animals in the wild?"

As I spoke, she paled. She actually seemed to shrink into herself, getting smaller with each word. I felt a bit bad…and a lot not.

"None of that's true," she whispered.

I had heard the approach of others as I had spoken. It was time to leave. Dad put his hands on my shoulders. "Actually, it's all true." I leaned back against him.

She looked up and glared at him. He shrugged. She

pointed at me. "Why can I look you in the face, but not her?"

Dad's hands tightened on my shoulder. "Pumpkin, what have you been doing?"

Well, hell.

Owen gave me a questioning look. "What is she talking about?"

Brooke looked at everyone in the crowd, one by one. She ended with me. I just stared back, blankly. Her face tightened and her foot tapped faster as her ire grew. "What the hell, Jade?"

I let my head fall back onto Dad's chest. "The men in there," I tapped my head on my dad, in the direction of the compound, "always had their wolves in their eyes. They were playing games. I had to put them in their place."

Tanner came into view. "But you aren't dominant."

I shifted my eyes to him. "No, but *you* are. And so is my mom. I mostly pulled from mom, but I did what I had to do to get us out."

Tanner's eyes widened. "Is *that* why I started to get headaches and felt the need to eat more than normal these last couple of days?"

I smiled at him sheepishly. "Sorry. We had connected and you were the only one I could pull from easily. I don't have that kind of oomph myself. At first it was a fluke, but I think it was easier as I went along."

Brooke's gaze was bouncing back and forth between us as we spoke, like a ball in a tennis match. "None of this makes sense."

A snort escaped me. Dad's hands tightened on my shoulders in apparent disapproval. *Ouch.*

Dad's cool voice came from over my head. "Brooke, according to my daughter, you'll become a werewolf with the full moon next weekend."

Her eyes narrowed and she crossed her arms. "According to her? What, she's the word I have to trust? Why can't Owen verify this, or handsome over there?" She tilted her head towards Tanner.

I felt Dad tense behind me, but otherwise he had no physical reaction that I could sense. "Jade has a special ability that neither Owen nor Tanner have. She met your wolf. Now, while this has been edifying, we all need food and rest. We'll go back to the hotel for the night. But tomorrow we need to go back home."

Brooke's eyes narrowed. "This is my home. You can't make me leave. I'm not going back to Wisconsin."

Before Dad could answer, Owen touched Brooke's elbow. "You're right, we can't. But, Brooke…this will be safer for you. My family is trying to help you. Being a lone wolf is dangerous. That's what those men were. There may have been a group of them, but they weren't acting like a pack. They were attacking people and they weren't being careful. There are standards that pack wolves follow; it makes being with us safer. On top of that, you're a submissive wolf, from what I understand. You aren't dominant enough to protect yourself."

"I don't even know what that means."

I pushed away from Dad. "Exactly." I glanced at the cars and saw Bevin and José facing each other, holding hands, foreheads touching, and quickly turned back. "You need to learn about what those creeps did to you. We're trying to help. Gah!" I threw my hands in the air. "I give up." I knew the boys needed privacy, but I couldn't be part of this conversation. I'd already tried. I wouldn't help anymore. "Dad, can I have my stuff?"

He absently waved at one of the cars. I headed over and got in on the passenger side. My phone and watch, with a broken band, sat on the center console along with a second phone, which I assumed belonged to Brooke. After turning my phone on, I heard the back doors open. Twisting, I saw Bevin and José crawling in.

"You two okay?"

Bevin shrugged. "Sorta. This is really weird."

José barked out a laugh. "That's putting it mildly. But my wolf is the calmest I've ever felt. I've been agitated since my change. It's been rough." He looked at Bevin and his expression softened. "It's the first time I haven't been on edge."

"You two should talk to my aunt and uncle. They're also a mated couple."

They both smiled. Bevin seemed to relax into his seat. "I could get down with hanging out with Allison and Jackson. But can we talk about something less tense? Like what happened in there?" He jerked his thumb towards the compound.

My laugh was only slightly hysterical.

CHAPTER 30

I had just finished my story when Fred slid into the driver's seat of the car and started up the engine. The air conditioning felt amazing on my sweaty skin. Fred asked, "Everyone doing alright in here?"

I looked out the window; the others were piling into Dad's car.

Fred addressed my confusion. "I wanted to talk with all of you…and not around that Brooke girl." He made a face. "She's a pill, isn't she?"

I flopped back in the front seat and secured my belt. "You don't know the half of it. Are we leaving her in Vegas?"

I asked hopefully.

Fred smiled as he pulled out onto the road. "I believe your dad and Owen have convinced her that returning to Wisconsin would be in her best interest." I groaned and could smell the cinnamony disappointment from the back seat.

I watched as Fred navigated the car out of the compound. "I was just filling in José and Bevin on my time in there." I pointed. "Can you fill me in on the bits I missed during and after the fight?"

Fred's eyes slid to me for a second before returning to the road. "Well, when we got you and Brooke out, there were five wolves in hot pursuit. That fight ended fast; they were mean, but not good fighters. Then your dad, Tanner, and I searched for the sixth wolf—Pam? She was chained to the wall and only halfway through her shift, but she smelled sick." He sighed. "Her death was more of a mercy killing."

Remembering what I knew about Pam, I had to agree. "She didn't seem well the times I saw her. Sick and vacant. I don't know what happened to her before, during, or after the change, but it wasn't pretty."

Fred merged into traffic before continuing his part of the story. "Since we have a car in town, I'm planning on remaining in town and doing a cleanup with anyone who wants to stay with me before heading back to Wisconsin. I'm guessing Tanner will help, being the expert on this sort of stuff."

I thought about how much work there was going to be in breaking down the lone wolves' hideout and eliminating any evidence. "Will you just burn it all down? I'm sure there's biological matter all over that place."

A growl bubbled up from Fred's gut. "Maybe. Whoever stays behind with me will help with a survey of the place starting tomorrow. We'll see what can be done in a day or two. But enough of that. I would like to discuss the two of you." He said the last with a quick glance in the rear-view mirror.

Rotating halfway in my seat, I could see everyone in the car.

Bevin's hand rested on the seat and inched closer to José's. I wasn't sure either of them were aware of the action. He stared at his dad. "What's up?"

"Well, you're both strong dominants. I know that it's been stressing you out, José, and I can see that same thing eventually happening to you, Bev."

They both dropped about an inch as their stress released. That wasn't the topic they'd expected.

José cocked his head to the side. "Well, you know I didn't want to be a werewolf, Fred. I wouldn't have chosen to be bitten if it hadn't been natural. Then to be this dominant…" He shook his head. "I dunno…"

Fred spared a glance back as we headed into the city. "Well, what *do* you want? Do you want to lead a pack and be alpha? Do you want to be part of a pack? Do you want to be a lone wolf?"

José froze. His and Bevin's pinky fingers were overlapping. Suddenly, he snatched Bevin's hand and squeezed it as he closed his eyes, his scent a whirlwind of hope and confusion.

Finally, he surveyed everyone in the car. "I...I..."

He gaped at me, and his eyes were misty. He shook his head as if to clear it. "I didn't think it was a question. I have options?"

Fred smiled. "Everything in life contains choices. The world is full of them. This isn't a path set in front of you that you have to take. It's an opportunity, son, a choice, and what you do with it is up to you."

Fred's focus snapped to a patch of nasty traffic he had to navigate, and the car got quiet.

After a few minutes, José said. "This was all thrust on me. First becoming a wolf. Then a dominant wolf. Then the idea of a wolf with a mate. I feel like I've been running a marathon with rules I don't understand."

He spun to Bevin and his gaze dropped to their hands. His brows furrowed as if he wasn't sure how their hands had gotten linked, but a small smile appeared on his face. He then faced Fred, concentrating on the conversation. "But I like how Hazel and River run the pack. They do it with love and intelligence. It's more about family. If I could have a pack that was about family," he focused on Bevin, "then I could see being alpha to a pack."

A small smirk quirked Fred's lips. I had a feeling he knew more of what went on than any of us knew. "Well, then," Fred said. "If you want to continue on the alpha path, talk to Jade's parents and figure it out. I'm sure it's something that could be in your future."

José's eyes narrowed as he stared at Bevin. "Is this what

it was like growing up in your house?"

Bevin barked out a laugh. "Pretty much."

A few minutes later we arrived at the hotel. I got out of the car and almost collapsed in the parking lot. My head swam and I grasped the roof of the car to steady myself. José scrambled out of the car to help support me.

"What's up, chica?"

"Don't know, feel weak."

Fred made it around the car and slipped an arm under my shoulder. "Is it any wonder? You've been running on high for days and it sounds like you haven't been eating. I'm surprised you're still standing at all."

José maneuvered himself under my other arm despite my protest and the two of them all but carried me to the elevator and up to my room. They headed toward a bed.

"I need a shower," I protested. I was dirty and felt gross.

"No, chica, you need food and sleep. You can get cleaned up when you can stand on your own."

I growled in lieu of words as they lowered me on the bed. I had a great argument, but the bed had a pillow, and that was an unfair advantage.

When I cracked my eyes open, it was dark outside. I was confused because my mind told me five minutes had passed. Stiff and sore, someone had tucked into the bed, and snores came from elsewhere in the room. Intent on getting up, I blinked heavily. The next thing I knew, the sun shone through the windows.

This time, I forced myself up into a sitting position. My jeans and shoes had been removed. When I stood, the room spun and my stomach felt like a black hole demanding sustenance, but I made it to the bathroom.

I grunted at a knock on the door; I wasn't up for more talking. The door cracked open a hair and Dad's voice floated in. "Hey, pumpkin, here are some clothes. We're going to mosey on down for breakfast after you get cleaned up. Do you need help in there?"

He slid the outfit into the bathroom.

"I think I can manage, thanks," I mumbled.

After I cleaned up and dressed, Dad, Tanner, and I made our way down for food. Despite my protests, they both stood close enough to touch my arms in case I felt the need to topple over.

Dad pushed me down into a chair at a table. I looked up at him, confused. The hotel, as well as Vegas, was famous for buffets. "Pumpkin, you can barely stand, much less walk safely with food." With that, he walked away.

The crowd at the buffet swallowed him up just as Tanner emerged with a carafe and a mug. I looked up at him with hopeful eyes. He chuckled. "Yes, it's coffee…but it's decaf." He poured a mug-full for me.

At my horrified expression, his face finally broke. "Kidding, but that just made my morning…" Shaking his head in amusement, he left to get his own food. He passed my Dad who was returning with two plates.

My brain started working halfway through my plate of waffles and after my second, tiny mug of coffee. "Where is everyone else?"

Dad looked around as if he expected they'd all jump out and say 'boo.' "Probably still asleep."

I went to check my watch before I remembered it was no longer on my wrist. Although it had been recovered, the band was broken and needed to be replaced. I pulled my phone out of my pocket and saw it wasn't even seven yet. Then, I noticed my plate was empty. *How does that keep happening?*

I slowly stood. Everything seemed to be okay with that action. Tanner's hands instantly went up to catch me if I fell.

Dad checked me out. "You got this?"

With a bright smile, I went to get more food.

When I got back, Bevin entered the dining hall. He waved as he swerved toward the buffet.

I sat down and Tanner eyed my two heaping plates of food. "Are you really going to make it through all that?"

"Look, it's logical. One is sweet, one is savory."

"That doesn't answer my question."

"If I don't, I'm sure Owen will make it down before too long."

Tanner snorted, shaking his head. But he conceded the argument.

Bevin plopped down next to me with a carefully crafted plateful of food. He looked over at my two plates enviously. "Damn, that's genius."

Ha! I made a face at Tanner. He ignored me.

I started to dig in. Between bites I asked, "What's the plan?"

Dad pulled out his planner app on his phone. "Check out's at eleven. Four of us will drive, four can fly. We can either do it by lottery or by voting; I don't really care."

Savoring a sip of coffee, I set the mug down, considering. "Were the lone wolves the ones we were worried about? Are we still thinking about stopping in Colorado?"

"I'm pretty sure they were and no. We need to get Brooke situated and educated."

I had blissfully spent the morning not thinking about her. "Where will she be staying?"

José chose this moment to slip in between Tanner and Bevin. Like me, he decided on two plates. Tanner just threw up his hands, chuckling at our exuberance. "Teens!"

Dad laughed with Tanner and said, "She'll probably be staying with us. She's adamant on not staying at her own home. She does have friends she can stay with, but not right away."

Choking on the bite of donut I had just taken, I gulped down some coffee to clear my system out. "What? Where? I had the misfortune of thinking you said she would be staying with us."

"I did. Our house is the pack house. She needs to start learning and our place is the best place for it."

"Um, no." I shook my head, looking around frantically.

"Okay, then, I'll move in with José." Fred walked up with a relatively conservative serving of food, smiling at my panic. "Wait, Estrella lives there, she is way too…well, just too much. Um, Bevin, I'll move in with you. Except you have two younger sisters, and your house is full. Crap…Sarah. I'll call Sarah. I'm sure I can stay with her for the summer."

Dad touched my arm and my heart rate slowed down. I took a deep breath. "What?" I asked him, mind still spinning with places I could flee and wondering if I could take Pebble with me.

"You need to be at home to help train her. You are one of the best at that. Besides, the rest of us have to work."

"What about Owen? He's home for the summer and she actually listens to him. She likes him."

Dad stroked my arm. "I know this won't be easy, but it's necessary. And he has a job, too."

I had conveniently forgotten about that. "What if *I* got a job? Or she could go to one of the other four packs. She doesn't like Wisconsin. She has too much history in our city. Come on," I whined.

Finally, Bevin put his arm around me. "It'll be okay. You won't be alone." He kissed my cheek and took my hand.

My heart rate slowed. I stared at him, still feeling lost.

José took my other hand and squeezed. "Chica, it won't be just the two of you. You'll have all of us helping you train her. It will be great."

Their combined concern centered me, and I finally

brought my body under control.

Bevin laid his head on my shoulder and said softly, "Better."

Nodding, I whispered, "Thank you."

They released my hands so we could all get back to the important matter of food. When I checked out my plates, I noticed they were empty, again. I shot an accusatory look at Tanner. He just rolled his eyes. I went to stand up.

He glared at me. "You are *not* eating more food."

Dad laid a hand on Tanner's arm. "It's included in the price. Why pay for more later?" Then he looked at me. "You *will* have a job this summer, pumpkin. Trainer."

I drooped at his words before sauntering off to get more food.

At ten-thirty, we stood outside the hotel, ready to leave. Brooke joined us, having asked for leave for a death in her family. They gave her two weeks off.

Fred and Tanner decided to drive back. Originally the talk had been four staying to clean up, but they decided they could do it faster without having to teach clueless kids what to do. They could get the cleanup done fast and hit the road home. The rest of us would be flying. Dad wanted to get Brooke situated and her training started as soon as possible. I tried to get in the car with Fred and Tanner, but I was outvoted.

We flew into Madison late Saturday. Mom had set up one of the guest rooms for Brooke down the hall from mine. A classic signal from Mom that Brooke should be treated as family for the duration. *Shiver.*

We dropped off Bevin and José before heading home. When we pulled up to the house, I saw Brooke's eyes widen and a gingery scent of shock filled the car. I knew Brooke wanted to look down on our bumpkin, backwater house, but the pack house looked large, modern, and impressive. Not even Brooke could find fault.

I made a beeline for my room. When I'd made it across the living room and to the hallway to my room, Mom's voice rang out. "Jade, before you disappear, can you and Owen give Brooke a tour, so she knows her way around the house?"

A scowl took over my face. Except for the car ride home, I had avoided Brooke all day. Our last-minute tickets meant we weren't near each other on the plane. "Yeah, let me throw my bags in my room first."

I dumped my stuff and returned to the main area. While in my room, I'd heard Owen describing to Brooke the living room as they moved to the kitchen. "This is your home? Like, where you grew up?"

Owen showed the rooms as if he were presenting prizes on a TV game show. *And here's the living room. And here's the dining room. And if you don't bid too high, we have the kitchen. And down these stairs, the basement.*

I caught up with them by the kitchen island. Seeing it through her eyes, I could understand why she was impressed. It was the size of a professional kitchen with an island that had a stove with six full-size burners and a sink on one side. It sat six people on the other. Across from the island was a huge counter with plenty of workspace, an industrial-sized refrigerator, a dishwasher, a microwave, and, though she probably couldn't see it, a walk-in pantry larger than a standard bedroom. Off the end of the island, an oval, solid cherry-wood table that sat an additional eight people. It had built-in seating against the wall. The three seats that faced in were rarely used.

I turned to her. "Yep. This is our home. It's also the pack house. Anyone in the pack is welcome here at any time. That's why it's so big." I pointed through the dining room to the sliding doors. "See the woods out there? That's where we run. It's safe."

Brooke's face transformed from interest to annoyance when I started talking. As always, her arms crossed over her chest and her foot started to tap. Her lip rose in a sneer by the end. Ah, full-on Brooke.

Mom walked in behind Brooke at the end of my explanation. Her brow shot up in disapproval. "Brooke, dear, I know you aren't being disrespectful to my daughter."

Brooke's eyes bugged out as she whipped around in to face my mom. "Oh, Mrs. Stone. I didn't see you there. Of course not. I wouldn't." *Was that respect? From Brooke?*

Mom's brow hadn't moved. "Good. Jade might be your best lifeline here and if you burn that bridge, you are *not* doing yourself a service. She got you out of that situation with the lone wolves in a way no other young wolf could.

She has abilities no one else has. Don't be an idiot, dear."

And with that she headed out. Before she was completely out of earshot, she added. "And no more tapping that foot of yours; you aren't a toddler."

Brooke huffed, and I clamped my jaw tight, trying to keep a straight face. She faced Owen. "God, she hates me."

"No, she's just protective of her pack. You've been invited into our den…try to be…well, I dunno, less… more…umm…Jade?" He shot me a hopeful expression.

Brooke's head snapped in my direction, eyes daring me to finish what Owen started. The thing was, she didn't scare me, and I definitely dared. "Try to be less you. In other words, be polite. We really are just trying to help."

"Help? Is that why you made me fall to my knees?"

I couldn't stop the snort this time. I tried, but it was just too much. "No, that was me trying to stay in character around a pack of lunatics, present company included."

"Jade!" Owen snapped.

"Sorry, she just brings out the worst in me. She's never polite no matter what I do. She goes out of her way to be nasty, and now I'm supposed to help her." I sighed. "I'm trying."

Owen assumed a Dad persona. I hated when he did that. "Are you?"

I sighed. "At times."

"Can you do more?"

"Probably."

His head tilted. "Then that is probably what you

should do.”

“Are you done being Dad?”

“What?”

“Nothing.”

His brows came together, and he gave me an odd look.

I smiled and hooked my arm in his. “So, Brooke. You’ve seen all the common areas. Has he shown you the basement yet? That is where the kiddos hang out.”

She frowned. “Kiddos?”

“When the parents are off running, their kids have to be somewhere. That’s the ‘where.’”

She nodded. “Got it. So, it’s for, what, like, babies?”

I closed my eyes. *Maybe counting would help....* I opened them and looked at her. “Nope, at other times it’s where we teens hang out. But you don’t have to go down there, I am *totally* okay with that. How about I show you the bathroom and your room.”

I started to pull away, but Owen held me in place. I stared at him. “What?”

“Basement, barn, grounds, meeting room, den, medical room, introduce her to Pebble; you seem to be short-cutting a lot of this.”

Her face scrunched in confusion. “What’s a Pebble?”

A tiny voice behind her said, “I am.”

Brooke jumped.

I finally won free of Owen and ran over to scoop the girl up in a big hug. “I missed you, squirt.”

Owen, who had followed on my heels, stole her away for his own warm welcome.

Brooke stared at us. "Since when do you have another sister? God, she looks just like you, too."

Joy flowed from Pebble. She loved that comparison. She was still in Owen's arms when she whispered in his ear, "Can I help show her around?"

She spoke so softly that Brooke didn't hear, she only saw that she said something. The tension rose in her. "What did she say about me?"

Oh, no, I wasn't going to let her vitriol touch Pebble. "She just wants to show you around."

Brooke glared at me. "How do you know? There is no way you could have heard that."

"Didn't we go over this in the compound? Werewolves have excellent hearing. Just because you didn't hear her doesn't mean I couldn't."

"Bull—"

"Brooke." Owen stepped between us, Pebble still in his arms. "That's what Pebble said. You've *got* to start listening to Jade. I don't know what you've had against her for all these years, but you've got to get over it, like, now. Mom was right, she's going to be your best trainer."

Brooke gave Owen her best puppy dog eyes. "What about you?"

"First of all, I'm not as good as she is at all of this. Second, I have a job this summer. Dad said now that I'm in college, I have to work. Dad has to work. Mom has to work. Jade doesn't. She doesn't have to help you, either, but she will…" Owen searched my face. "Probably."

I blew out a breath. "If I don't kill her first."

CHAPTER 31

The sun slanted through my window early Monday morning, and I wanted to get out and run to put the last week behind me. Between the lone wolves and Brooke, my body seized with stress.

I put on running shorts and a tight halter top and realized a lot of skin showed, but being out this early, it shouldn't be an issue. I added a belt with pockets for small water bottles that chilled in the fridge, so I headed there to fill up.

Bent over, digging in the fridge, I found the water bottles and stuffed them in the belt. Suddenly a voice slithered around me. "Damn, girl. Why do you hide behind all your hideous outfits?"

With my butt fully in the air, I stared at Brooke between my knees. "What are you doing up? It's five in the morning. It isn't even that late for you. It's what, three?" I slowly pushed myself up and finished filling my belt.

Her voice snapped out, commanding. "I'm running with you."

I stiffened for a moment with her declaration, then added the last bottle to my belt. I placed my hands on the counter behind me and dropped my chin to my chest. "No, you're not."

She clicked her tongue as a puff of air released. "And why not? I run almost every morning."

Leaning against the counter, I quirked a smile. "Look, Brooke. This has nothing to do with you. This is my time to stretch myself. It's early and there won't be many people out on the trail. My goal is fifteen miles in an hour. You can't keep up."

Her gaze narrowed. "You can't do it."

This wasn't the time for a fight. I closed my eyes and took a deep breath. I decided not to start my morning or my run clashing with Brooke. Trying to stay calm as I gazed at her, I explained, "I don't know. That's the question, isn't it? I'm close, though."

Folding her arms across her chest, her upper lip twitched. "I don't believe it."

"I don't care." I dropped my hands to my sides and just

stared at her. "How about this? I'll run with you at six-thirty."

She scoffed. "You'll run this magical run, come back, and run again? I don't buy it."

"Well, then, if I can't, Owen will run with you. I need to go. I can get you to the path and we can run separately if you want, but we're not running together."

She shook her head in disgust. I could taste how much she didn't like being in the kitchen with me. "Fine. Thirty minutes out, thirty minutes in. We'll see who goes farther, wolf girl." She stood and we headed through the dining room to the backyard.

We jogged to the path to warm up. When we got there, I set my watch up to track my time and distance. Thankfully, Mom had replaced the band over the weekend.

One last stretch and I was off. It took about three steps for me to forget all about my nemesis behind me. A few steps later, I found my zone as the path and trees flew by. As I ate up the miles, I passed a few other runners, but they didn't pay me much attention.

When my thirty-minute timer went off, I spun and headed back. Wanting to hold back any excitement or disappointment, I ignored my watch until the end. I didn't ignore the small thrill that surged through me when I noted that Brooke was nowhere to be seen. I knew she couldn't keep up, but something in the back of my mind worried she would be there with a sneer and a tapping foot.

My muscles tingled with fatigue, but my gait increased

as they stretched and warmed, and I sped through the space between me and home. Finally, my mind wandered over the last two weeks. How would being a werewolf change Brooke? We all took on aspects of our animal, and the pack tended to demand more. *Could* a submissive be a lone wolf?

Werewolves usually needed family and touch. They loved to congregate and spend time together, which was the reason the pack house was so big. People came over at all hours and knew they were welcome. Brooke made it clear since we'd known her that she shunned everything to do with family. Owen broke it off with her when she demanded he pick between her and family; it wasn't hard for him to choose. I believed this was the seed of her hatred of me. I was the family Owen had at school that he wouldn't turn his back on. At the time, he wouldn't choose her over me.

Soon, Brooke would be a submissive wolf. Traditionally, that meant the heart of the pack. I couldn't get my head around the prickly, independent, mean girl morphing into anything that would bring a pack together. Maybe she would be better with a different pack. She and I didn't like each other, we didn't mix—like oil and water, or vinegar and baking soda. I kept going back to the idea that a different pack would be a better fit for both of us.

I was so lost in my run; I didn't notice the runner I passed was the person I contemplated. She kicked it up and tried to pace me. I shot her a look and then checked out my watch. We'd run for fifty-eight minutes. I was at fourteen point eight miles. So close…. I sprinted.

Brooke tried to keep up, but I had a mission. When I got to the end of the path, I sucked air, a stitch threatening in my side. I stopped my watch and started large muscle stretches until Brooke caught up. It didn't take long.

She and I walked back. About halfway to the house her breathing evened out. "Did you do it?"

Focused on my body relaxing, I nodded.

"No way…I don't believe it. I mean, I'll admit you're fast. But that's impossible."

I sighed. Living with her would never be easy. I held out my wrist. The stats were still up so I could show Dad when I got home. She snatched my wrist and just froze in disbelief. "There's no way. You could go to the Olympics."

"Not really. They test blood and my blood isn't normal." I pulled my wrist out of her grasp, and we made our way back in silence.

When we got there, we found my parents up. They had to work and were in the kitchen waking up with coffee. I showed Dad my watch and he grunted. "Go record it in your book." And that was it. Sighing, I spun on my heel and made my way to the gym.

Mom watched me leave. "I'll get your breakfast started."

After breakfast and a shower, I flopped in the living room to read. My frustration was too high to start a new series despite the run, so I reread an old favorite, Wyldling Snare by A.R. Grimes.

Brooke followed me. "I thought you were supposed to be teaching me."

Putting down the book, I raised my eyes up to her. "Now you're interested in my help?"

She huffed. "Well, as long as I'm stuck in this backwater state, I may as well *do* something."

"Give me twenty minutes."

"Why?" The cayenne scent of disgust oozed from her.

I heard a car pull up to the house and used a bookmark to save my place. The book landed on the side table, and I smiled. I just continued to stare at her as the car came to a stop, doors opened and closed, and voices floated into the living room through the closed window. Finally, they got to the house.

Brooke turned to the front door as it opened, and a group of people entered the house. "Why are *they* here?"

Sarah came around the corner followed by Bevin and José, who stood a bit apart. I wondered if they'd figured anything out regarding their relationship.

Sarah's eyes sparkled. "As I live and breathe, it really is her."

The scent of cayenne intensified, exploding out from Brooke. Sarah's eyes began to dance as a smile spread across her face. "Oh, this is going to be fun."

Brooke whirled around to face me. "Why is *she* here?"

Unfolding myself from the couch, I stood. "The best way to train you is to both explain to you about werewolves and to show you. It's hard to do everything when I'm just one person." I pointed at the group who'd just entered. "They're here to help."

Brooke shook her head. "Everyone's a werewolf?"

I shrugged. "We'll go with that for now."

"What does that mean?" Well, at least she wasn't dumb.

"It means we need to start with the basics." I spun to Bevin. "Coffee? Cookies?"

He smiled and led the way to the kitchen.

We spent the morning teaching Brooke about being in a pack. We discussed the classifications and the hierarchy. Then, we ordered pizza for lunch. After lunch it was time to do some werewolf acclimation.

José faced me. "Okay chica, who's going furry?"

I surveyed the faces around me. "Brooke, who are you most likely to listen to, me or Bevin?"

"Whatever…probably Bev, she, er, he's always been the least obnoxious."

"Why do you do that?"

"Do what?"

"Why are you nasty to all of us?"

She rolled her eyes. "Well, as for him, what's underneath the clothes?"

I shrugged. "It really doesn't matter. Bodies don't equate to gender. He's a guy. He has had all his gender markers switched over for four years. And, as you just said, he is the least obnoxious. You're just being petty."

"Fine. Sorry. You're right. He's also the least offensive

of all of you."

Nodding, I stared at her pointedly. "Yeah. Okay. José, why don't we get furry? Let her see what werewolves look like. Give her more than the few minutes of exposure she's had in the past. Bevin can do the teaching with Sarah."

Brooke demanded, "I want to see Sarah's wolf. I've seen José's."

Snorting, I shook my head. "Too bad."

We moved to the backyard. José and I started to strip down. Brooke shrieked.

We whipped around to face her, both our heart rates up, eyes wide. "What?"

"Why are you getting naked?"

My head flopped back, eyes closed, exasperated. I did a count of five before straightening up. "Well, I happen to like these clothes and would like to be able to wear them again."

José smirked. "And I didn't bring a different set of clothes with me today."

We continued. I don't know about José, but my plan was to ignore any other sounds coming from the new girl.

I tuned out the conversation happening amongst Brooke, Bevin, and Sarah. Too much distraction would slow down the shift.

Dropping to my hands and knees, I focused on my wolf, and let her out. It took some time, and it hurt, but she came.

"Oh, my God! It's the devil-wolf! The child-killer!"

And then she shrieked.

When I surveyed the group, Sarah sat on her butt laughing, Bevin held onto Brooke's arm, restraining her from running off. Pebble stood at the screen door, eyes wide, searching the backyard. José continued to shift. I sat and waited.

Bevin spoke softly, trying to calm Brooke down; it wasn't working. He shot me a desperate look. "Jade, a little help."

I rolled my eyes, which set Sarah off again.

I shut my eyes and found my connection to Brooke. *Calm down and listen to Bevin!*

She clasped her head in both hands and screamed. "Voices in my head!"

Bevin turned to me with a raised eyebrow. I'd never made a connection that fast or easily. What about this… frustrating…woman got me to figure things out? Her screams grew louder. I released a burst of epsilon calm.

Brooke's legs gave out and she slumped. The only reason she didn't fall was because Bevin was there to catch her. Her eyes still wide, she watched me like I would attack at any second. I just sat there, watching her calmly.

Brooke's arm slowly raised, shaking, and a finger pointed at me. "Is she the devil?"

Bevin wrapped his arm around her, helping her fully to her feet. "No. That's Jade. She helped save the kids, she never harmed them."

"But the newspapers…"

Bevin's scent turned a cinnamony annoyed. He didn't look annoyed. He was a great actor. "The newspaper ran with a picture you and your friends took."

She stared at him. "How do you know I was there, that we were the ones?"

He waved his hand at me and José.

Her eyes widen in understanding. "Oh, my God. Who were the gray wolves, the baby and mom?"

I sniffed in laughter. José's tongue lolled out and Sarah leaned forward, trying to not laugh, a hand over her mouth. Bevin somehow kept his face blank. "They were Pebble and Owen."

Brooke pushed Bevin away, horrified. "Pebble is a wolf? That's awful."

Bevin nodded. "It is."

That finally broke her out of her fear and back into her normal mode. "What?"

"She's adopted. Her parents were lone wolves. We think they did it to her before they died. Jade and Owen's parents rescued her and are trying to raise her innocent despite what happened to her."

"So, she isn't related? But she looks just like Jade."

Bevin gave a small smile, one usually saved for Pebble. "True. It helped in the adoption process."

Brooke pointed at me. "What did she do to me?"

"When?"

"Don't play dumb. You asked her to help you and then

something happened. She talked to me." She touched her forehead. "In here…and then it felt like I took some really good drugs. It smelled like pine trees and water, and *bam*, all my muscles gave out."

"Oh, that. Those are some of Jade's special skills. She's the only one who can do them. We'll explain more when she can help; not my story to tell."

"She can talk in my head?"

Bevin nodded.

"And she didn't eat those kids?"

Bevin's scent started to darken, from cinnamon annoyance to spicy anger, though his poker face stayed in place. His ex-boyfriend ate those kids. Before we stopped him.

Sarah finally stood. "Can we get on with the lesson?"

After that, the lesson went smoothly. Brooke had a healthy fear of wolves and acted timid around me and José in our animal form, but as the afternoon went on, things smoothed out. It was almost like she forgot to be a brat.

Almost.

CHAPTER 32

As I slid on the black t-shirt, I remembered the last time I had worn it. A black t-shirt with a rainbow circle on the front and the word 'Pride' splashed across in white, the first time I'd let my school mates know my opinion on this topic. The back sported a purple heart and the words, 'I like grrls'. The only time I'd braved wearing was my second day as a werepanther and the first time as an "out" lesbian. I might have been biting off more of an emotional cookie than I could chew because it had turned out to be an utter catastrophe.

However, today was the pride parade in downtown

Madison. Today, the shirt would be perfect.

I lounged in the basement with Piper, José, and Bevin. We all sprawled on the couches, gossiping, waiting on Owen.

Brooke was out with her friends. We'd finally gotten through to her the importance of secrecy. It had taken most of the week, but it was Saturday, and we deserved the day off.

Bevin stood, mumbling something about caffeine, and went to the refrigerator, half-climbing in. "Anybody want anything?"

José, stretched out on a couch, nodded at Bevin for a soda and glanced at his watch. He sat up quickly, brows furrowed. "Where's your brother, Jade? He usually isn't late. Does he even want to go? He isn't gay."

I nodded to Bevin as well. "He seemed excited last night, really excited. I'm sure he's coming." I yelled up the stairs, "Owen! Where are you?!"

Bevin returned with the sodas for us and a slice of pizza for himself.

I heard Owen's door shut and then his and Sarah's footsteps on the stairs. Piper, sitting next to me, didn't react, but I smiled in anticipation of the day.

Owen sauntered down the stairs. I faced José and Bevin, my back to Owen. Their shocked faces and José's gasp clued me in something was different.

José leapt up. "What happened to you? You're not even gay."

"Do you like?" Owen purred.

I turned in time to see Owen dancing around in a circle to show off his new hairstyle. Sarah stood on the steps behind him, citrusy amusement coming from her.

He'd bleached his short, spiky brown hair white a few days ago. Today he had a red stripe down the center of his head. There were orange stripes to the left and right of the red stripe. Then yellow stripes, then green, blue, and he had ended with purple.

Bevin's jaw dropped, and he nearly spilled half-chewed pizza on the floor. Piper just clapped and cheered. She asked Sarah, "Did you do this?"

Sarah nodded. "He needed help with the details."

I laughed hard enough to fall and hit the floor rolling. Without a thought for how silly it might appear, Owen had dyed his brown hair into a rainbow gay pride flag.

That's my goofy, supportive brother for you.

José, waving his hands, sounding indignant, said, "But you're not even gay."

"So?" Owen threw his arms out to the sides wide, as if to embrace the entire world. His eyes shone, and his teeth flashed a bright grin. "It's a pride parade. I'm showing my support, bro."

"But...but...you're straight..." José stuttered.

"And?" Owen ran his fingers through his hair, fluffing up the bright, radiant colors. "I'm. Showing. My. Support." He gave another twirl. A few of the colors glowed under the lights. "The colors are UV reactive, so I'll shine under the sun." His eyes glowed as he spoke about his hair.

Owen stopped, looking at me lying on the floor. I stared up at him, smiling. "Is this so hard to understand?"

I shook my head. "It looks amazing." I hopped up, grabbing Piper's hand. "We should go."

"But he isn't gay," José insisted again, moving to follow.

Bevin went over to José and gave him a hug. He whispered something in José's ear. José took a deep breath and nodded.

I smiled brightly and ran up the stairs to get my stuff.

We were off to the parade.

We took one of the bigger pack SUVs that seated all six of us. José drove. On the way downtown, Owen spun to Bevin. "So, are you and José an official couple now?"

The tension in the car ratcheted up a few notches. Bevin's shoulders hunched and he clasped his hands. Staring down he said, "Not really. We haven't really figured things out. I don't want José to be with me simply because his wolf demands it." He looked up to gaze at the back of José's head. "I also don't want to lose my best friend."

Owen flopped back into his seat. "Well, hell. I thought for sure I'd found a safe topic."

José held himself rigidly. He focused solely on the road. I closed my eyes and found my connection to José. I had only done this a few times and it rarely worked. *You okay?*

Through the connection, I felt his whole-body jerk. It still irked me that Brooke had, indirectly, helped me figure out how to do this efficiently. I heard him let out a rush of air.

He screamed in my head, *Chica!*

You don't have to yell.

Am I yelling? he yelled.

Pushing my fingers into my temples, I responded, *Yes.*

He sighed. *Sorry. Yeah. I'm fine. I'll be fine. We'll be fine. Just don't worry.*

I dropped the connection. It was giving me a headache. I opened my eyes and saw José shake his head. He may have wanted to do more, but he was driving.

Owen sniffed the air then shifted his gaze back and forth between me and José. "What were you two just doing?"

I cocked my head to the side. "Really?"

He stared back at me. "Really what?"

"You can smell when I connect to someone?"

"Is that what that was? You two just smelled…?"

Bevin lifted his head. "The same."

I looked at him. "What?"

Bevin shrugged. "José started to have some of your river and pine tree smell. It's subtle. I don't know if I'd pick it up if we weren't in a small car together."

I slumped back and groaned.

Piper's brows furrowed as she turned to me. "What's wrong with you?"

Sarah up in the front seat started chuckling. "Your dad's going to have a field day setting up a new training and testing regime for this one."

I hit my head against the back of the seat a few times. "Can't we just forget about anything that just happened for the last ten minutes? I won't tell if you don't. Gods, sometimes I hate being epsilon."

José pulled into a parking lot as the others laughed at my embarrassment.

We walked the two blocks to the capital to enjoy the people and spectacle of the parade. Though Owen held Sarah's hand, his hair announced him as an ally.

Piper and I skipped along, hand in hand. My second time wearing this shirt was going much better than the first.

Bevin and José were a mixture of pleasure and stress. They walked together without being together. We found a food stand and bought hot dogs, fries, and shakes. Sitting in the grass, we lounged and enjoyed the day. The music blasted and occasionally, we danced.

A few hours later, Bevin, Piper, Sarah, and I were dancing when a smoking-hot guy with a rainbow painted on his pecks approached us. I liked girls and even I could appreciate how pretty he was. Just over six feet tall with dark hair and dark eyes, he appeared to be chiseled out of stone. I didn't think he was much older than us.

He began dancing in our area. He was a great dancer. Then a few others joined in. The attractive guy moved closer to Bevin. He leaned in and I heard say his name was Matthew. The two of them danced close enough to be considered dancing together.

A wave of annoyance and hate rolled over me. It was sharp enough to make me falter. I stopped and looked around. Owen stood at the snack stand getting more food and José leaned back on his elbows, legs out, and feet crossed on the grass a few feet away. His head rested back, and his eyes shut. I touched our connection; it felt like he attempted to center himself. I could see his chest rise and fall with deep breaths.

Deciding to ignore the situation, I went back to dancing with Piper. There wasn't much room, so we danced close, our bodies brushing together. The capital lawn was packed with people and our small dance floor had become popular. Another woman, almost as beautiful as Sarah, joined her. Sarah seemed to be taking it all in stride.

The guy with Bevin got close enough that they touched. There wasn't much choice in the area we had. The wave of hate morphed into jealousy, prickly and cold. I froze. José hadn't moved, he still lounged on the blanket, legs out, leaning on his arms, head back, as if he were enjoying the day, but I could feel his tension through our connection. It was more than I could block. It felt like tiny knives, so fierce I feared it may kill him.

It was more emotion than I could ignore. I grabbed Sarah's hand and dragged her towards the blanket. She'd stopped dancing with the latest onslaught from José. We both gulped in air, and not from the exercise. I leaned in close to Piper. "I'm sorry, I need to sit."

I made my way over to José, plopping down next to him. I stroked his arm; he nodded, but otherwise didn't react. Sarah sat down on his other side. Bevin continued to dance despite the ire emanating from José.

My motion turned to a squeeze. "Go to him."

He shook his head. "He doesn't want me to."

"Yes, he does."

"You heard him in the car. He doesn't trust me."

I pushed him. "Then tell him the truth. Tell him how you feel, not because of your wolf, but because of you, and him. Tell him how *long* you've felt this way. Just…be honest."

He rubbed his eyes with the base of his hands. Then he sat up. "Fine." He shot a glance to where Bevin danced with the hot guy. Not near, with.

José fell to his back again with a groan, jealousy pouring out of him. I could feel him struggling to clamp down on it again.

About three feet away, Bevin stopped moving. I could smell his confusion. He pushed the stranger away and shook his head. He spun to face José.

I stood and beckoned to Sarah. "Piper won't stop dancing until we leave. Let's get more food." I think she agreed there was too much emotion coming in from the dance area.

She headed down to the food stand with me. Owen, almost to the front of the line, laughed when we gave him our order and then stood off to the side to wait.

As Owen put in the order, I leaned against a tree. I watched the parade go by. I felt so free amongst people so open in who they were. Today I could be me.

I heard a clicking in my head and put my hands to my temples. It wasn't uncomfortable, but strange. I scanned the area. Owen and Sarah approached with food, Piper continued to dance, and Bevin and José…oh. José leaned over Bevin, kissing him. My heart skipped a beat. As I watched, he pulled back. Bevin lay on his back and José leaned on an arm staring down at him. They were finally talking. Bevin reached up to place his hand on José's shoulder as José smoothed Bevin's hair from his forehead, away from his eyes.

The moment soothed something in me with its tenderness, and through my connection to both of them I could feel the healing happening at last between them.

"Grab your grub, sis."

Broken out of my trance, my attention shifted to my stomach. Smiling, I took some of the food that Owen and Sarah carried.

Sarah, who obviously went on a bit of my roller-coaster ride of emotions with me, gave me a piercing gaze. "What just happened?"

I used my chin to point towards the boys. They both turned, but by then Bevin and José were getting up and moving toward the dance area.

Owen's face broke into a huge smile. "Finally. I didn't

think anyone could get José out of his funk!"

When we returned to our spot to eat, José, Bevin, and Piper were all out dancing together, and the tension was down to a breathable level.

A few hours later, we were in the car heading home. Piper was half-asleep in the back, sighing with happiness. I sat next to her with her head on my shoulder, a warm glow of contentment filling me. Sarah and Owen curled up in the middle seats. I thought I could hear a low purr coming from Owen. José sat in the front passenger seat, and Bevin drove us home.

José turned to Owen. "How long are you keeping the hair?"

Owen sat up and sighed. "I dunno. Considering how much it bothers you, I'm thinking a while."

"What will your job think of it?"

Owen shrugged. "I work at Hot Topic. I'm using this as my letter of request for a promotion."

CHAPTER 33

I woke up Sunday morning bright-eyed and bushy-tailed and crept down to the kitchen. No one else was up and I reveled in the calm emptiness. I made some coffee and sat to enjoy the peace.

However, soon Mom came out, poured a mug of coffee, and joined me. "We're having a pack meeting this morning."

"Did you and Dad hear about the latest?"

She raised an eyebrow.

"Yesterday in the car, I connected to José. Both Owen and Bevin could smell it."

Mom nodded. "The meeting starts at ten. We'll

introduce Brooke and talk about your new superpower."

"Do we have to?"

"Yep."

"Do we have to do it when Brooke is in the room?"

Mom put down her mug of coffee. "Jade, have you been holding things back from her in your training?"

I slumped. "Only the epsilon stuff. She needs to learn about werewolves first. Then we'll get to werepanthers and epsilons."

Mom sighed. "Oh, honey. I understand that you two don't get along, but I think you should've opened up a bit more. What did you tell her about Sarah?"

"Nothing. Only José and I shifted in front of her when anyone needed to shift. She only would listen to me or Bevin." I thought about it for a minute. "She may have listened to José as well, but we asked her, and she chose Bev."

Mom sipped her coffee. "Hmm."

"I really think we may want to find a different pack for her. She doesn't like Wisconsin. She doesn't like any of the pack members her age." I paused, taking a drink, trying to gather my thoughts. "I'm not trying to be spiteful, Mom."

"Let's take this one step at a time. You know the wolf changes us. I'm going to try to do for her what I did for Bevin. I want you to check her out this morning and make sure her wolf is ready, but then I want to pull her wolf out. I'll do it after the meeting so everyone can meet her in human form first. I'm hoping Allison, Chris, or Andy can help her acclimate. They understand the heart of the submissive wolf."

I let out a breath I didn't realize I was holding. "That's a good plan." I nodded. "Really good."

Mom grinned. "Okay, let's start making food."

The rest of the pack started arriving at nine. I sat in the kitchen eating pancakes and eggs with a side of bacon. Owen sat next to me. Brooke was on the other side of him. Sarah came in.

I bent to check things out around her. "Parents?"

"Nope, they're taking the day for a date day and night."

I snorted. "They got rid of you and are partying!"

She nodded as she went to fill a plate. She took the head of the table, sitting next to me. "Mornin', Brooke. I know we aren't the best of friends but, look…today's going to be weird."

"What's it to you?"

Sighing, she gave Brooke a serious look. "My first pack meeting was a trip. Sitting in front of a room full of werewolves…it's intense. A bit of advice, they all love Jade, so don't be a jerk. Oh, and they'll be able to hear everything you say, and they can smell your emotions."

She swiveled to me, pushing Owen back. "Smell emotions?"

"We did mention that."

"I thought you were joking."

"Why would we waste time on jokes? We've had a week. Everything we told you was real. After today, your life is going to be different. Next week's training is going to be much rougher."

She rolled her eyes. "If you all can do it, I'm sure I'll be fine."

Oh, she's such an egotistical…brat. My muscles tensed and my nails dug into my palms. I forced myself to relax. "You know what, you're probably right. How about this? We'll let you do it on your own. If you want our help, just ask."

I got up to refill my coffee mug.

I heard her mumble so low I knew she thought we couldn't hear, "About time."

I slowly turned. "I'll remember that."

Her eyes bugged out as I completed a full rotation to continue on my path to the coffee maker. I poured a cup, which emptied the pot. I took the time to set up a new pot to brew, trying to calm down by concentrating on the methodical actions.

While I worked at the counter, Clare, José and Estrella's mom, came up to me. "Hi, Jade, how have you been?"

Mid-sip of coffee, I put down my mug and gave her a quick hug. "Good. It's been a week, but you'll hear all about it at the meeting."

She nodded. "I was wondering if we could discuss other matters after the meeting as well."

There were so many things going on, I just wanted a break. "Sure, like what?"

"I was hoping we could talk about Estrella and her potential wolf."

Freezing, I knew the answer, but didn't know how to tell her. I knew it would break her heart and that of her daughter. Before I could respond, Alejandro, her husband, called for her. She rubbed my arm and headed off.

I picked up my mug and made my way back to the table.

At the table, I collected empty plates and brought them to the dishwasher. When I went to get more dishes, Brooke was behind me. She handed me a stack. I continued to fill the dishwasher before I could give away my shock. I knew the others in the room could smell it in their stillness. Brooke and I spent the next few minutes cleaning up together. As annoying as she was, at least she did chores without complaint.

I took my mug of coffee and headed to the meeting room. I could sense Brooke right behind me. When I got there, José and his family were camped out in the back, as were Bevin and his family. José and Bevin shared a couch. I waved. They smiled back.

With a sigh, I slid my hand into Brooke's. "We need to sit near the front. Sarah and I will take the front corner couch, you and Owen can sit behind us."

Brooke had seen the room during the tour on the first day, but now the room was full of werewolves. About half the pack had filed in, sitting, and talking. She held her head high as she sauntered across the room, but I could smell a thin thread of sickly-sweet fear.

Sarah snuck up behind me, sliding an arm around my

waist and whispered so low I barely heard, "She's bold."

I nodded in agreement.

We didn't have long to wait after we found our seats. Mom and Dad entered with Pebble hanging between them. Swinging. They let go of her hands and she ran to leap into Sarah's arms. I tweaked her cheeks. "What am I, chopped liver?"

She giggled and squeezed between us.

Brooke leaned forward. "Why is *she* here? She's just a baby."

I wanted to snap back, but her question was valid. "She's young, but she's a wolf. She has a right to be here. Today's meeting concerns her."

"How? She's already met me."

"Yeah. About that. You're second on the itinerary. Sorry about that. We've told you everything you need to know about you…just not everything about me."

Mom stood on the stage, listening to us talk. "Are you ready for us to start?"

Ducking down, I smiled sheepishly. "Sorry."

"Not a problem. Do you just want to come up here and start the meeting?"

Groaning, my top lip lifted. "Not really, but I can."

She smiled and waved her hand to present the stage.

I lumbered off the couch and walked up onto the stage. Several of the pack members laughed at my reluctance. I smiled and waved. "Hi, all, it's me…again…your friendly epsilon oddity."

This brought a fuller round of laughs.

Chris asked, "What is it this time? Can you float in mid-air yet?"

Andy, his partner, smiled brightly. "No, it must be better than that, maybe she can fly!"

I stood there staring at them as they had their fun.

Tyler, sitting in front of them, shook his head. "Nah, she can probably turn invisible."

At this, I swung my hands out to the side, palms up, in questioning exasperation. "Really, guys?"

They all gave me big smiles. I closed my eyes and found the connections. *How about this?* I'd never tried to talk to this many people, and it felt like a knife slicing my brain. The blast hurt but when I opened my eyes it had the desired effect. Everyone was stunned.

Well, not everyone. A few knew about my ability. The others started looking around. Then a buzz of discussion started. I just stood while they began to talk about what they'd heard. Then they started talking back. *Ouch!*

I held up my hands. "Wait! Please. Too much, too many. One at a time." I pointed to Andy. "You."

Can you hear me? came in my head through the connection.

Yes. I pointed at Chris. "You."

Is this for real?

Yes. I pointed at Clare. "Next."

Dad stood while Clare asked in my head. *Is José really okay?*

I think so. He's figuring things out. He and Bevin both.

Dad came up next to me. "This is all fun to watch, but no one hears anything. Explain."

I smiled at him. "Oh, Chris asked if I could hear him, I said yes. Andy asked if this was real; again, yes." Clare's started to tense; werewolves could hear lies. "I told Clare we'd talk about Estrella's werewolf status." As soon as I said it, I knew I'd said the wrong thing. It wasn't a lie, but the way she and José perked up I was in for another conversation.

Everyone sat back, stunned. "Dad, here's the real question." I focused on José. "José can you join me on the stage?" He shrugged and came up. "Dad, can you smell when we're connected?"

I smelled Dad's shock.

José, your mom is worried about you. You need to talk to her.

I know. I will later today…after the meeting. Bevin and I will make the parental rounds.

Good.

I glanced at Dad, raising my eyebrows questioningly.

He nodded. "It's weird. It's almost like José took on a bit of your epsilon scent."

"Okay…next test. This is going to be a nastier test. Chris, can I use you?"

Chris shrugged. "Sure. As long as it won't hurt."

"No, I just want to do a dominance test with you."

His head tilted. "But you're epsilon. You don't have dominance."

"Yeah. I know. But José does."

Chris eyed me. "You want me to do a dominance

test with José?"

"No, well, yes, but…just trust me."

José groaned. "Is there food close by? And something for the headache?"

Tanner snorted from across the room. "Better you than me."

Mom huffed. "Is that what happened while you were in the compound?"

I sighed. "Later. Please. I just want to know if Dad can smell this on José as well."

Chris paused. "You can borrow dominance as well as talk to us in our heads?"

I shrugged. "Apparently?"

He laughed and rubbed my arm affectionately. "Fly, I tell you. One day you will fly, and no one will be surprised. Knock me out with your borrowed dominance, dear one."

We faced each other, locking eyes. He smiled. I pulled on José and felt his dominance surge through me. Chris whispered, "Goodness." Before crashing to the floor. "José, I've never measured you. Are you really that dominant?"

I faced José. He kneaded his temples with a pained expression. "Chica, that sucks." He nodded at Chris. "I believe so."

Dad rubbed José's back. "Go, get something for your head and some food, enough for you and Jade, then get back here." Then he reached down to help Chris up. "As for the scent, your scent is all over José. It didn't linger, but as you pulled his dominance, I could tell you were doing it."

Chris had a huge smile. "That was trippy. I mean, it sucked, but wowza, you are a wonder to have in a pack. No one in the world is like you." He gave me a huge hug before returning to his seat.

I swiveled to Dad. "Am I done?"

Several in the room chuckled at the hope in my voice.

"Not even close. I want you to do the next part, too. You've been training her. You went to school with her. You know her. And, most importantly, you don't have rainbow hair."

"You've got to be kidding me."

Sarah snorted and Pebble giggled. When I looked over, Sarah was tickling the girl.

I turned to Mom. "Do I have to give the full back story?"

Mom nodded.

José returned with some food, and I quickly ate a banana while he told everyone about the road trip, getting to Vegas, and seeing me and Brooke getting kidnapped. It was nice having someone else tell part of the tale.

I gave him a grateful look for filling in that part. I continued as he hopped down to return to Bevin. "The kidnappers were lone wolves…like, the stupidest wolves ever. They beat the norm and bit her to make a werewolf. While they were in human form."

The room smelled appalled. I still felt disgusted. The whole idea was beyond unthinkable. "Well, when I checked her out, she had a wolf in her, so we brought her back here, somewhat against her will. She's from our high school."

I waved to indicate the lot of us who went to the same school. "Brooke, I think it's time you joined me."

Brooke stood like she was about to receive an award. She sashayed up to the stage and dramatically spun to face the room. She ended by striking a pose. I didn't roll my eyes. Really, I didn't.

"This is Brooke Winter. I believe she will be a submissive wolf. Mom plans on pulling her wolf out after lunch and wants the three submissives in the group to help. We—José, Bevin, Sarah, and I—have worked to get her caught up on everything werewolf this week. Next week, we hope to help with the actual sensory training. Questions?"

There were questions. Not a lot, but enough that we were there for about twenty more minutes. Afterwards, we were released to the…well, not to the wolves.

Before I got far, Clare reached for my arm to stop me. "Can we talk about Estrella?"

"Oh, sorry about bringing that up in front of everyone, I just had to say something that was true. Too many people in the room who could smell a lie."

"Do you know if she's a natural werewolf already?"

"I do."

Estrella came flying into the room like a Tasmanian devil. "Then why didn't you tell me?"

CHAPTER 34

Overcome with the inputs of so many people around me pulling me different directions, I clasped my head with my hands, shut my eyes, and tried to block out all the sensations. Standing frozen in place, Sarah and Mom flanked me, my alphas. They each put a hand on one of my shoulders and everything inside me quieted. My shoulders dropped and I lowered my hands. "Thanks," I mouthed.

Somehow, Sarah knew what I'd said. "My job," she said in a laughing voice.

I surveyed the faces expecting answers from me and pulled some energy from both my alphas. Not a lot, just enough to stay standing. They both shivered then squeezed my shoulders in understanding.

As I viewed the faces, I realized Bevin and José had joined the group. It seemed like they were there more as support than leeches of information, though José's eyes glinted with the anticipation of what I had to share. Estrella was his sister, after all.

I heard José's voice through the crowd. "Chica, put up a wall. You look ready to faint, and we're your family."

I shut my eyes for a second and took a breath. Slowly, I blocked everyone out until I stood alone in my head. When I opened up my eyes, I felt steadier. "I'm sorry. It was back in January when I figured it out. We were at school and there was a lot going on. It wasn't the time or place. It slipped my mind."

Estrella's perfect mouth pouted. "Well, tell me. Will I be a natural wolf like mi hermano?"

I shook my head in a small quick denial.

Her eyes grew to saucers of fire. "You're wrong." She snatched my hand in both of hers. "Check again."

"Estrella, it's done. I don't have to. You can be bitten. You can be a wolf one day. It just won't be natural."

She flew in a circle until she found her mom. "Then you'll do it, today." She glared at her mom as her hand flew out and a finger pointed at Brooke. "If she can be a wolf, so can I."

I pulled on some more of Mom's energy and dominance. "No." I wasn't going to let Estrella roll over her mom. She flew around to face me, practically spitting fire. "You're too young and you know it. Being a werebeast in high school sucks." I shook my head as I started to sag. I had done too much. "You know the rules as well as anyone in this room."

I started to see splotches of black in the sides of my vision, but I maintained my footing.

Her pointing finger punched me in the chest. "You're barely older than me. Who are you to decide anything for me, Jade?"

If Sarah and Mom weren't holding me up, I might have fallen over.

José came up behind her and wrapped his arms around his sister in a hug. "Hermana, she's right, and you know it. Don't vent that sassiness on her. She didn't take anything away from you." He pulled her down off the stage and away from me.

Taking a breath, I made my way to the dining room. I needed to sit and be away from the massive number of people who would be in the kitchen. Before I got too far, a hand reached out for my arm. I stopped and met Clare's gaze.

She tilted her head in apology. "We'll straighten her out. You did good." With that I headed out.

Sarah and Mom stayed with me until they delivered me into a chair. I worried about how bad I must look and feel for them to not be willing to leave me. Brooke stayed with us as well. I wasn't sure about that either. Dad brought plates of food—pasta with meatballs.

After we began to eat, others filled in the seats: Owen, Chris, Andy, and Aunt Allison.

Mom turned to me. "Can you check on Brooke's wolf?" At Brooke's questioning look, she explained, "Jade has a unique ability to talk to wolves while we're in human form."

Brooke sneered. "How many freaky things can she do?"

Mom smiled softly and shrugged. "We're still learning."

"Why does she need to talk to my wolf?"

"We have two options. We can wait for the wolf to come out naturally, or, as an alpha, I can bring it out early. It will take a bit longer for you to shift, but then we have the control of when you turn." Brooke looked bored but smelled interested. "Jade can find out if your wolf is actually ready or if it's too early."

"Fine. Whatever. What do I have to do?"

I reached my hand out towards her, palm up, and raised an eyebrow.

She surveyed the room, searching the faces. "Here? Now? I don't know half the people. What's going to happen?"

I sighed. "Mostly nothing. Owen?"

Owen gave his best smile and rubbed Brooke's back. "It will feel like a warm shower…but on the inside. Then it will be over. Unless your wolf gets excited. Then it will tickle."

"Really?" I asked. I had no idea about any of this.

He laughed. "Really."

Brooke relented and slipped her hand into mine. Panther leapt at the chance to play. I contemplated it and decided: why not? We moved over to Brooke, and her hand tensed. It didn't take long to find her gray wolf. It saw me and bounded at me, running in circles. If I didn't know better, I would think she was chasing her tail.

I held back a snort. I could smell Brooke's confusion. Sitting across from her instead of next to her made this harder.

Whoa, friend, slow down.

You look different, but it's you! You're back.

I am. Are you ready to come out and run under the sun?

Yes! Oh, can I?

Soon. I will see you soon.

I pulled out. Brooke trembled. She looked at me like I was a new creature she didn't know how to classify. *Whatever.*

I leveled a flat stare at Brooke before saying to Mom, "She's ready, more than ready."

Mom nodded and gazed at Brooke. She swept a hand around to indicate Aunt Allison, Andy, and Chris. "These three are our submissive wolves. I would like you to get to know them better over lunch. Once you've changed, one or more of them can change with you so you have someone to run with."

She reached out for Owen's hand. "What about Owen?"

I could feel the irritation from Sarah, though she hid it well.

Owen smiled. "I came home for the meeting, but I have to get back to work for a few hours. I'll be back for the run tonight, though." With that he checked his watch, stood, rounded the table to give Sarah a kiss, and left.

After lunch, Mom asked Brooke who she wanted with her in the back. She surprised me by selecting me, Sarah, and Bevin. After the change, the others would all come out to meet her one at a time.

Like Bevin's first transformation, Brooke's was slow and painful to watch. The three of us stayed by the house while Mom took Brooke to the center of the yard. The change took time, but eventually it happened. As with most submissive wolves, she didn't immediately attack, just gazed up at Mom before dropping down, cowering at her alpha's dominance. Mom tapped her nose and told her to explore. She gingerly circled the lawn, smelling everything, from grass to plants, trees to people. I could sense her cataloging what she smelled.

When she got to Sarah, she paused and looked up, confused.

I laughed. "Well, I guess the cat's out of the bag."

Sarah joined in my mirth. "I guess so." She knelt and gave Brooke some doggie pets. She never could resist. She knelt and looked Brooke in the eyes, and Brooke's snout dropped. "Sorry. I really didn't mean to do that. Damn. I'm really sorry. I forgot. I just wanted to explain, and I'm still used to looking people in the eye. Okay. I'm a werepanther, not a werewolf; that's why I smell weird, and that's what you're smelling."

Brooke paused and took a few more sniffs. She closed her eyes and nodded, as if remembering something she had forgotten, before approaching me. I plopped down on my butt cross-legged. She tapped my leg twice with her paw.

I nodded.

She snarled.

"No, I get it. You're asking if you smell two animals, right?"

She nodded again. The nod looked so weird on a wolf, but communication in animal form was hard.

"Yes, you do smell two animals."

She moved on to where Bevin sat, and froze. She looked to me then to Bevin and then back at me. She narrowed her eyes and I felt something almost like a knocking in my head.

I pressed a hand to my temple, but the knocking wouldn't stop. She tapped my leg again with a paw while glaring at me. The knocking continued.

I groaned. "Would you stop playing around with my abilities?" I mumbled.

I opened up the connection between us.

What?

Why does Bevin smell male and not female? I know I'm new and I may be wrong, but he doesn't smell like you and Sarah.

Because he's male. It's a really long story. Maybe if you're nice and ask him he'll tell you, but now is not the time.

But how?

Brooke, focus, not the time.

I closed down the connection, still massaging my temple.

Mom had been watching. "Did she really initiate the connection, dear?"

"More like she knocked on it, letting me know she

wanted me to open it up. I think I want to take a nap this afternoon…this sucks."

Mom nodded but said, "Let's wait until all the introductions are done."

I sat in a lawn chair while Brooke's wolf met the pack. Afterwards, Mom asked which of the three submissive wolves she would like to go running with. Tail tucked, she trotted over to me.

"Oh, no. I'm headed in to take a nap."

Brooke whined.

"Moreover, I was going to go as a panther tonight. It's been a while."

Brooke leaned against my shins and whined again.

I gave Mom a pitiful look. Mom shook her head. "Can Bevin come with?"

Brooke's wolf bounced in agreement.

Mom relented.

Bevin groaned.

I snickered.

The three of us ran through the forest. I showed Brooke how to find paths and run silently. Being a track star as a human, she was naturally good at this.

We found the stream, and all drank deeply before bounding off again. Eventually we found the scent trail for a rabbit. Brooke smelled it and we followed, but when we found the rabbits, Brooke froze and backed away. Bevin and I watched her. We each lurched forward, showing her how to track and hunt. Brooke, eyes wild, tucked her tail and started to whimper.

Finally, I sat. I turned to Bevin, and he sat as well. Brooke paced back and forth, unwilling to sit and refusing to hunt. Eventually she stood stock-still in front of me, and I felt the knocking on my brain.

My head pounded, only able to take so much abuse. Opening up the connection to both of them, though they wouldn't be able to hear each other, I decided I could relay their comments back and forth so everyone would know what was going on. Bevin's ears went back at first, aggravated.

What, Brooke?

I can't kill a furry bunny.

I sighed and Bevin lay down, putting his nose in his paws. *We're wolves, it's what we do.*

But they're cute and fuzzy.

And you're a wolf.

Not by choice.

You know what? None of us had a choice. Not about any of this. This run has been fun, but I'm ready to go home. Let's just call it a day. You can stay with Pebble when the pack goes out tonight. Or run with us and not partake in the kills.

Stay with Pebble?

Brooke, she's six. She doesn't want to hunt all night or kill cute fuzzy animals either.

With that, I dropped the connections and ran home.

Back at the house, I jumped into the treehouse and curled into a ball to rest. Pebble played with several of the kiddos, a version of monkey in the middle, and the delighted squeals were piercing but happy sounds I could ignore.

When Bevin and Brooke made it back, they joined in, helping Pebble catch the ball being thrown, rolled, and bounced across the lawn.

I realized a nap was never going to happen. Focusing, I found my connection to Dad.

I'm going to shift to panther.

Sounds good. I'll be out in a minute to time you.

He joined me and we headed out to a small field away from the play.

Still in wolf form, I shut my eyes and focused on Panther. I released her and she flowed over me. It hurt, but all the training had paid off. I remained on my feet, and once I shifted, I snapped my head to Dad.

"One minute, forty-one seconds. I think this will work. You're almost as fast as when going from human. Are you stable?"

I pranced in a circle.

He chuckled, nodding. "The shift wasn't even stomach-churning. I'm heading back in."

I trotted around the field to stretch out a bit.

My head began to pound. I groaned deep in my chest. The pounding got worse. I shook myself, realizing the pounding was Bevin reaching out to me.

What?

Front of house, run*!*

Bevin's demand shot through me like a spike. I ran.

I got to the front of the house. Cars littered the driveway. Full moon night. Owen and Piper stood next to a blue Subaru Impreza. It was Piper's dad's car. Piper leaned on the driver's door and Owen stood by the front corner. Piper had just gotten her license and had picked Owen up from work. Driving this close to the full moon wasn't fun.

Brooke cowered near the steps up to the house with her tail between her legs. Bevin stood behind her. I could smell her fear.

I smelled blood. I searched until I saw the blood on Piper. Was she bitten? Had Brooke attacked her? Did she get the taste of human?

Assuming the worse, I saw red.

I lowered my chest to the ground, aiming towards our newest wolf. No one who attacked norms was allowed to survive. I had laser focus on my prey.

The sound of footsteps drew my attention. Piper dropped down and hugged Brooke. *Hugging Brooke?* A growl low in my gut began to vibrate out of me. I inched forward.

My focus lasered in so completely I was taken aback when Owen's hand came down on my snout. He spoke to me as I tried to see around him, but he kept a tight hold on me. He kept talking.

What was Piper doing with Brooke? Did she know she was in danger? What was happening? I tried to pull back, but Owen held on tight.

My lip curled in a snarl.

Owen pinched my ear.

The pain caused me to jerk, and I pierced him with my death-stare.

He huffed. "Finally. Will you listen now?"

My growl continued.

"Brooke didn't hurt Piper." He had both hands on my head, framing my face. "Did you hear me? The blood, it wasn't Brooke. Jade, come back. It wasn't Brooke."

I shut my eyes. Could this be the truth? It smelled like truth. I started to shake.

"About damn time," Owen mumbled. Still holding my head, he forced me to gaze into his eyes. "Piper scraped her leg on the door when she was startled, that's it. Calm down, then go around the blue truck. You'll see what did it to her. I'm going to go help Bevin and Piper with Brooke. Can you control yourself, sis?"

I sat back and focused on slowing my system down. I searched for the unfamiliar truck and found it off to the side. I didn't recognize the driver, an older woman who sat there with an amused look on her face.

I stood and made my way over to the far side of the truck and froze. I stood nose to nose with a snarling brown bear. Our heights were almost the same, but he was thicker than me. He opened his maw and roared, and the fur on my face shifted in the resulting breeze.

I stared at Mr. Nelson. Who else would it be? That roar was probably bear language for "Stop messing around and hustle, Ms. Stone!" As always, he had some complaint to throw at me.

Too many things had happened today. Tired and fed up with it all, I lifted a paw and tapped his nose. Through my connection with Bevin—which I apparently hadn't shut down—I heard a faint, *Boop!*

Snorting and sending an amused chuff his way, I shut down our connection. I didn't need to use up any more of my energy.

Mr. Nelson snarled but I turned and made my way back to Brooke and plopped down next to her. I rested one of my large paws on hers. Wolf came forward.

You okay?

Her wild eyes settled on me. She was panting. *What the hell is that? How are you a panther? You were a wolf, like, a minute ago.*

A werebear. No one knew he was coming. Otherwise, I would have warned you. And I told you I wanted to run as my panther tonight.

My God, Jade! How many types of wereanimals are there? She sounded frantic.

At this point, you've seen as many as I have.

She sniffed Owen. *He's more than a wolf, too, isn't he?*

An amused purr started low in my gut. *Yep. He and I both have two animals. We are the only ones who do.*

Is it because you're siblings?

No, it's because I got attacked twice, and he wanted it, too.

So, could I be a panther?

The thought of someone biting Brooke and going through more training gave me the willies. *Let's figure out your wolf first.*

As we spoke, her shaking slowly stopped and her tail untucked. She began to breathe evenly and stood, which broke off our communication. She shot a glance at our paws and seemed to realize that was how I'd been communicating with her.

The front door opened, and Mom came out. "It's time for our run."

CHAPTER 35

Mr. Nelson left after the run, still in bear form. His wife stayed in human form. Brooke ended up coming on the run but avoided all the killing and eating.

When Sarah, Bevin, José, Owen, and I jumped up to join Pebble in the treehouse, Brooke followed. I froze for a minute, watching her, before sighing and curling around my adopted sister to sleep. I guess I didn't blame her; who else did she know?

When I woke, I slipped on one of the robes kept in the treehouse just for this reason. Then I made sure everyone was covered in blankets before trudging across the lawn to the house.

Inside, the rich aroma of coffee and cooking food permeated the air. Piper's mom had taken over the kitchen. I grunted in appreciation, pouring a mug of heaven, added sugar and milk, and trudged to shower and find clean clothes.

I was close to my room when I heard steps behind me. I spun. Brooke stood there. *Why?!*

"So," I said. "An early riser."

"Yeah. I've always been blessed." She started down the hall towards her room. "After the shower, can we talk?"

"Before food? Aren't you starving?"

Her stomach grumbled. "No, not really. I'm good."

I leaned against my bedroom door. "Brooke, you can't play games. You have a free card to eat whatever you want. If you don't, you'll become dangerous. You've been skipping meals. No more. We can talk—that's fine—but food first. There's no such thing as a girly wereanimal."

Her face took on the mean-girl sneer. She looked me up and down. "Really, and how much do *you* eat?"

I snorted. "Probably more than Owen." With that I spun and entered my room to get clean clothes and then headed off to shower. After washing, I put on clean jeans and a t-shirt. Today's top read, "There are two types of people: those who can extrapolate from missing data."

In the kitchen I reached for a plate and sat. Brooke eventually joined me. Her plate contained a quarter of the food I had on mine.

Mom, coming from the hallway, selected her own

offerings, and sat on Brooke's other side. She checked out our plates. "Brooke, dear, is that your second plate of food?"

Brooke looked scandalized. "Seconds? Never."

I rolled my eyes, realized my plate was empty, and went to fill it again. When I returned, Brooke gave me a scathing look of disgust. "Are you really going to stuff more food in?"

I gave her a bright smile as I dropped to the bench. "Hell, yeah. I may even get a third plate if no one stops me. You have one wolf, who you are apparently willing to starve. I have two animals, and a weird ability that sucks up lots of calories."

Mom gave me an appraising stare. "Start with two. You can graze throughout the day. Others have to go to work and don't have that option."

I slumped as I sat back. The rest of the pack came in, ate, gathered their things—which sometimes included kids—and left. If their "things" were older teens, they often left them sleeping.

It was just after eight and the adults had cleared out. Brooke and I were alone. "Did you get enough to eat?"

She slumped. "Your mom is obnoxious. She forced me to eat more than I normally eat in a day."

"And?"

She squirmed. "Yeah. Fine."

I knew she still needed to eat more, but realized we'd need to cross that bridge later, so I dropped the topic. "You wanted to talk?"

"Not here. After a week, I know this place. It won't take long to fill up again."

"Fact. Wanna hit the bike path? We can take a walk."

She nodded and we headed out. It took a few minutes to reach the path and then we walked for a few minutes. The day would've been too warm with the high sun but there was a cool breeze making it a perfect day for the walk. I finally broke the silence. "What's up?"

"Look, Jade…I don't like you." That was mostly true. After a week of working together, she also didn't hate me. I could hear the lie in her words…I wondered if she knew that.

This was going to be a long walk. "Yes, Brooke, I know."

"But you're the only one who doesn't hold back the truth. You tell it like it is, and I can respect that."

"Well, you don't seem the type who wants things sugar-coated."

We continued to walk, watching the path, neither of us looking at each other.

"Do you know why I ran with the pack last night?"

"I was wondering. I mean the run is fun, stretching our muscles and getting wrapped up in the pack 'oneness' is amazing. But there is always an element of a hunt, and I knew you didn't want to be involved in that. That's the reason Pebble stays back home."

I could see Brooke nodding from the periphery of my vision. "Right. The thing is, I could feel everyone in the pack's worry over me staying behind. It burned in here."

She tapped her chest. "I couldn't disappoint them. The idea of staying back was too painful. I just couldn't disappoint them, even if they were strangers." She stopped and stared at me, grabbing my arms. Confusion and pain shimmered in her eyes and a sweet minty scent filled the air. "Jade, what the hell is wrong with me?"

Frustration burned in my gut as I fought to keep a blank face. "I knew training you before the change was a joke. Did you listen to anything we said last week?"

She rolled her eyes. "Yes, but there was so much crap."

My head fell back. I searched the clouds. Nothing. With a big exhale, I faced her again. "You are a submissive wolf. You are the heart of the pack. That means your first instinct is to help the pack. That's what you felt last night."

A growl started low in her throat. She jumped back and stopped almost as quickly as it started. "What the hell was that?"

Snorting, I held out my hand before she stormed off in a huff. "Hi, Brooke, welcome to the world of being a werewolf. Though you only have to change with the moon, you will have the instincts and many of the aspects of a wolf all the time now. This is why we need to continue the training."

As we stood there, a runner passed us. Brooke recoiled. "Oh, my God, what was that smell?"

Sighing, I rubbed my forehead. "That was the runner. Breathe in again." She did. "Think about it: all you smell is male, sweat, and his interest in us. It was a bit vanilla, like a savory vanilla."

She shut her eyes as she cataloged the scents. She nodded. "Okay, that makes sense, but it was so intense. Wait, I can smell emotions?" She faced the receding runner and sniffed again.

"Yeah. Now, think about being back at your hotel and having to deal with this."

She shivered.

We continue our walk. Brooke's jaw worked. Finally, she asked, "So, this feeling of trying to keep the pack together and happy won't stop?"

"Not if you stay with a pack."

She perked up. "I don't have to?"

I fought my frustration and shook my head. "No, you can become a lone wolf, like those guys who snatched us up. But then you don't have the protection of the pack. You have to run alone and don't have connections."

Cinnamon filled the air as her annoyance with me grew. "Why does that matter?"

I reached over and touched her arm. She settled. Eyes wide, she gaped at me. "What did you just do? Was that part of your epsilon stuff?"

"No, I just touched you." I breathed deeply to keep myself calm. *We covered all this last week, and frustratingly, you ignored it all. You could've listened, but did you?* No. "Touching helps werewolves settle down and center themselves. That's why we stay in a pack."

We continued to walk. She had a far-off look and she bobbed her head slowly as if cataloging massive amounts of information. I could tell she processed everything. As runners and bikers passed us, she took in extra sniffs and nodded, determining scents. Sometimes asking about what she smelled. I couldn't deny how impressed I was with her methodical approach.

After a few more minutes, we headed back home. "So, Carrot-top. That's your girl?"

I cut a glance at her and then returned it to our path. "You mean Piper? Yeah."

"I could tell by the way you came after me last night."

I huffed out air. "Yeah, sorry about that. I didn't know about the bear."

"She's not right for you, you know."

I rolled my eyes. "Oh?"

"You need someone fierce, like Sarah."

"Well, if you didn't notice, Sarah's straight. And taken. By my brother. That's kinda gross."

"Straight and hot."

I raised an eyebrow at Brooke. "You don't say."

"First off, straight women can appreciate other hot women. But as it goes, I appreciate all the pretty people."

My feet kept moving, but my brain stopped working for a few steps. When it started again, Brooke was laughing at me. "Back with me yet? In high school I had to be careful. Now that I've graduated, I'm trying to be honest."

"But you've been flirting hard with Owen and Tanner."

She shrugged. "I thought I was here for a week. If I'm stuck here for any longer, I'm not going back into that box."

"Okay, good to know. So, you're planning on staying... at the pack house?"

"Could you sound more pitiful?"

"I just love living with a person who doesn't like me."

"Well, once I'm trained, maybe I can stay with Alyssa and Tiffany."

"Yeah, maybe."

Brooke stopped and stared at me. "About them...I may have told them I was a werewolf."

CHAPTER 36

At home, I found José and Bevin lounging in the basement. My heart was racing. From the pack connections, I could feel several others in the house. *How can I keep this from blowing up?*

My agitation rolled through me strongly enough they had to have tracked my approach. Standing in front of them, I reached for their hands and said softly, "Come."

They didn't budge. Neither of them. Not even Bevin, who usually was malleable enough to at least play along in my plans. Bodies relaxed and faces impassive, I could tell they were still tired.

My jaw tightened and my heart beat faster. I stared back and forth between them. "Please."

José grumbled. He slipped his hand out of mine but got to his feet. Bevin just looked up at me tiredly. Finally, he let me take his other hand and pull him up.

I led them and Brooke, who had waited in the kitchen, into the pack meeting room. The room was big but soundproof. José and Bevin immediately flopped down on a couch, leaning against each other. Brooke perched on the edge of one of the tables. I shut the door behind us, dragged a chair up to the stage so I could face the others, and plopped down.

"Chica, I'm barely awake. What's this about?" José followed this with a huge yawn.

Bevin rested his head on José's arm and said nothing.

"Last Saturday, while we were at the parade, Brooke headed out with Alyssa and Tiffany. She decided to tell them about being a werewolf."

Both boys sat up straight.

Bevin shook his head, his eyes snapping into focus. "Why come to us about it?"

I shrugged. "All the adults are at work. Even Mom is teaching a summer class. I hoped we could figure something out. And I dunno, it's you two…"

José nodded and rubbed his eyes. "Brooke, can you tell me—us—exactly what you told your friends?"

Brooke sighed. "Is this really that big a deal?"

"I don't know. That's why we need to hear your story."

She crossed her arms over her chest and rolled her eyes. "Fine. But I don't know what the big deal is." She crossed her legs and bounced the foot in the air. Like she was tapping it.

My hands fisted and I tried to remain calm. She just didn't understand how serious this was. If anything were to be resolved, I had to let the boys take the lead.

Bevin rose and leaned over Brooke. He slid his hand into hers. "I know this situation is hard for you. Everything about this has been messed up. I really get it. But telling people could endanger you, the pack, and our families. Please let us try to help."

I saw the moment Bevin got through to her. Her shoulders dropped and her breathing slowed. "Fine." This time the word wasn't sharp, but an acceptance. "The three of us were having dinner. We were discussing seeing the four wolves over winter break. The others were talking about the devil-wolf."

That moniker again! I sighed and lowered my head.

She snorted. "I know, I tried to tell them that title was dumb. I said the newspaper was being ridiculous to look at a pack of four wolves and decide that one of them was dangerous because it was black. They looked at me like I was nuts."

She looked down at her hand, still resting in Bevin's. She snatched it back and curled her fingers into a fist. Bevin just shrugged and moved back to the couch. Brooke's eyes followed him. She almost seemed sad to see him go, an earthy, oak scent emanated from her.

She shook herself out of her malaise, her face becoming hard. "We continued talking about wolves. I told them that werewolves were real. They scoffed and I got frustrated."

I barked out a laugh. I couldn't help it. I knew her flavor of getting frustrated. She just glared at me.

José gave me an alpha stare and I blanched at its intensity.

"Jade, if you can't control yourself, you should leave." He could've been Mom. *Did he learn that from her?*

I held up my hands. "Sorry. Please continue, Brooke."

She rotated on the table so she faced the boys instead of me. Apparently, I was no longer part of this conversation. "Anyway, they laughed at the idea."

I couldn't stop myself from snapping, "Of course, they did; you did the same thing to me."

All three just glared at me. My hands shot up again. "Sorry." I mimed zipping up my mouth and tossing a key.

Brooke very deliberately turned away from me again. "So, anyway, I got mad. I told them to just wait. After Sunday, I could prove it to them, and then I stormed out. They've been texting me all morning." She slumped, staring at her bouncing foot. "The thing is, they're my family. I don't really have other people in my life besides them. I know they can't know about this, but I don't know how I'm going to keep it from them."

Suddenly, something struck me. "Are they together?"

Brooke shot me a quick glance before focusing squarely on the boys again. "Yeah. Alyssa's parents kicked her out junior year. She's lived with Tiffany ever since. Tiffany's parents are great. Now they have an apartment together. They're planning on going to Madison for college this year."

My hands fell to my sides and my mouth dropped open. All the backstories I didn't know.... To think how much I didn't know about the people I went to school with…it was huge. "That's…I just…I had no idea."

Brooke lashed out. "Don't look so surprised, Jade. Why would you know anything? You're a nobody."

I just closed my eyes and took a few breaths. It just wasn't worth it.

"Enough," José boomed, freezing us all with a thread of alpha power. We all stared at him. "What?" he asked.

Bevin smiled and then shivered, seeming to release himself from some invisible hold. He gave José's hand a quick squeeze. "Brooke, what else did you tell them? Why do they think you're in Wisconsin? Who do they think you're staying with?"

Brooke shook, seeming to have to shake off whatever José had done as well. "I told them it was because some freaks had turned me into a werewolf. That a local pack was training me. And that I'm staying with Owen."

I groaned.

Bevin stood and started to pace the room. "Could you arrange for us to meet with them? Either at their apartment or somewhere public where we can talk privately?"

Brooke didn't take her eyes off Bevin. "How about the park by the school?"

I winced. The last time I went to that park, I ended up tied up in a cabin in the woods by a couple of rogue werewolves. To say it wasn't my favorite park was an understatement. However, it was secluded and there wasn't a playground, so parents didn't bring their kids. It also had a shelter so we could sit in the shade. I nodded, working out the logistics. It was a good spot.

Bevin and Brooke discussed details and then she texted her friends. They decided that Brooke and I would start off talking with the others. It would make sense that I would be around since I was Owen's sister and I'd been on the track team with Alyssa and Tiffany. They didn't completely hate me anymore. I would also be the one with the car.

Two hours later, we walked into the park. The shelter was deserted. José and Bevin sat across the shelter at another table in the shadows. They were around the corner and could only be seen if you really looked for them.

A few minutes later, Alyssa and Tiffany came in and joined me and Brooke. I sat while the three of them squealed and bounced, hugging each other, and, oh, my gods, my ears hurt. I used a finger to try to reactivate my right ear when the three joined me at the table.

Alyssa's eyes widened and she gave me a huge smile. "Oh, my God, Jade, it's great to see you. Have you been running this summer? Will you continue in track next year?" Eyes shining, she faced Brooke. "Have you seen her run? It's amazing. I had no idea how fast she could run before she joined track."

Brooke's eyebrow went up as she looked at me. "You have no idea."

I snorted.

Alyssa looked back and forth between us. Then she rolled her eyes. "Wait, don't tell me, Jade's a werewolf, too, and by the magic of her werewolf abilities, she can run like the wind…am I close?"Thick sarcasm dripped off each word.

It took everything I had to keep a straight face. I heard stifled laughter from across the shelter.

Brooke sighed dramatically. "Whatever. I was just, like, pulling your leg. What, you can't take a joke?"

Tiffany's eyes narrowed. "It was a weird joke, Brooke. You said you were kidnapped and beaten up. You said they bit you. It freaked us out. If that was a joke, don't do it again."

Brooke made a face. "Fine, whatever. I don't even have scars."

Tiffany shifted her gaze between the two of us. "Why are we meeting here, with her? I'm kinda confused. This is all really strange, Brooke."

Brooke sighed. "I just wanted to talk in private. Jade's here because Owen's at work and she has the car. It was too hot to leave the doggy in the car." I growled. She smiled. "I'm staying in Wisconsin for a bit. I'm thinking, maybe, if you have room, I could bunk with the two of you?"

They just looked at each other. I could smell their apprehension. Then they looked at Brooke. Alyssa took the lead. "Thing is, our place is tiny. We love you, you know that, but we'd need to get a bigger place. We signed a year lease, and I don't think we can get out of it. If we'd've known, we would've found a bigger place."

Tiffany, proving once again to be the shrewder of the two, leaned in. "Hold on. You love your job in Vegas. Why relocate?"

Brooke shrugged. "I miss you guys. I just want to be near friends."

Tiffany stared at me, really stared. I started to get uncomfortable under her penetrating gaze. She just wouldn't stop. Finally, after what felt like hours but was more likely seconds, she turned back to Brooke. "You broke up with Pat, didn't you?"

Brooke's blush was instant, and her curry scent of embarrassment rolled through the shelter.

Alyssa gazed at Tiffany. "Pat. You never showed me a picture of Pat. Why not? Who is Pat? What's so special about him?"

At the word *him*, the scent of embarrassment intensified on Brooke and Tiffany smelled like a lie. And then I knew. I could feel the shock coming from the boys as they figured out what was happening as well.

Brooke groaned; obviously she was learning how to translate all the undercurrents floating in the air around her.

Alyssa narrowed her eyes. "What's going on?"

Brooke looked at her. "Pat is short for Patricia. She is—*was*—my girlfriend."

Alyssa froze. She didn't move, she didn't breathe. Her jaw dropped as she just stared at Brooke.

Tiffany sighed and pulled out her phone. She found a picture and showed it to Alyssa. "Here is a picture of the two of them." Alyssa started to laugh.

I looked between them. "What?"

Brooke slammed Tiffany's hand down before I could look at the phone. "Nothing." She glared at Tiffany. "It's absolutely nothing."

Alyssa, who had been laughing hard enough to miss what Brooke said, snorted. "God, they could be twins!"

CHAPTER 37

During dinner, I filled Mom and Dad in on what had happened. We decided there wasn't any danger because Brooke's friends didn't believe her story. *Here's to being a mean girl.*

When we were done, Mom asked if all the teens could gather in the meeting room. I found José and Bevin sitting in the same spot they had been flopped in earlier that morning. I sat in front of Sarah and Owen in a seat on the far side of the room. When Mom and Dad came in, Brooke followed them.

Mom sat in the chair I had placed up front on the stage

that morning. Dad dragged another chair up to the front and joined her after shutting all the doors. Mom shrugged at seeing Brooke. I didn't think she had expected it.

She gazed at each of us. "You had a rough day today."

Sarah and Owen had already heard the story. We'd left out the part about Pat. That was Brooke's business, not ours.

"You came together as a pack and handled it. You're young, but you're old enough."

I looked over at José and Bevin. They sat together, not moving, eyes wide. It didn't look like they were even breathing.

Mom stared right at them. "José, Bevin, I don't know if you two want to start a pack and be leaders, but today when my daughter had a problem, she went to you. No one doubted that you were the people to go to. Even Brooke, who's your age, trusted your leadership. José Cortez, do you want to take up the mantle of alpha of your own pack?"

Shock and then acceptance wafted from Brooke's corner. Mom was right. I hadn't even hesitated. For some time, whenever something came up, I'd gone to these two for help.

Mom moved to kneel in front of José. She took his hands. "Is this something you want? Do you want to be an alpha to your own pack? Do you want to be an alpha-pair?"

José sat there like a statue, holding Mom's hands. He stared into her eyes. Then he looked deeply into Bevin's eyes. Bevin rested a hand on José's shoulder and smiled. Then he met Mom's gaze again. I smiled, too; I knew what that hand felt like and the support that came with it.

José slowly blinked and searched the faces of the people in the room. He spoke softly, but with authority. "I think I'm ready. It isn't something I want to do alone. But I won't be alone, will I?"

Mom released his hands. I could almost feel her smile. She moved to Bevin and took his hands. "Bevin Green, do you want to take up the mantle of alpha of your own pack?"

His heart rate jumped. José moved his hand over to Bevin's knee and squeezed. Bevin nodded. His voice came out smooth and confident. "Yes. I do."

Mom's pleasure and pride infused the room. I looked over at Dad. He, too, had a huge smile on his face.

Next, Mom came to me. "Jade, do you want to shift allegiance to a new pack? Do you want to join this newly formed pack and agree with the dictates of people who are your friends but now will also be your alphas?"

For a minute, I stopped breathing. I hadn't considered any of this. My friends becoming alphas seemed so obvious. Going to them with my problems was only logical. But did I want to leave my parents' pack? Did I want to leave the security and comfort of a pack that had been established for years? I swallowed hard and finally managed to get some air. My head bobbed up and down as I spoke. "Um… yeah. I mean, yes. I think having them as alphas would be…" One more breath. "…amazing."

Mom walked back over to José and knelt in front of him again. She faced him and the intensity between alphas infused the room. "This well be—" she flashed a smile at Sarah, "—intense." She put her hand on José's head and said, "Jade."

José jerked. "Mother of all that is sacred." Still shivering, he turned to Sarah. "This? This is what you live with?"

Sarah started to laugh with delight. "Oh, I am so happy to not be alone in this. She is a handful."

"Hey!" I said. "That's me you two are griping on about!"

"Chica, I can't even imagine how you get out of bed every day." José shook his head as if trying to settle all the extra information.

Standing again, she walked over to Owen and knelt. "What about you?"

He flashed her a grin. "Not having my mom know my every emotion? Yeah, I think I could get behind that. And like you said, we've been going to them anyway. I'm all in with these two as my alphas. Don't get me wrong, you and Dad are the best, but so are these guys."

Mom chuckled and headed back to José. "It will be nice being just 'Mom' again." She touched his head. "Owen."

José sighed. "That wasn't nearly as bad."

Owen snorted.

I rolled my eyes.

Brooke stood. "Me, too."

We all stared at her.

"I don't know anyone in this pack; everyone's a stranger." She gave me a challenging look. "Not to mention, your pack needs a submissive wolf. It will be hard to manage without one."

"Really?" I shot back. "That's the one lesson you paid attention to?"

Bevin snorted. "I don't know how this works, but does José have to take all the pack members? Can Brooke come to me?"

This was a concept I'd never even thought of. I whipped around to face Dad. He was silently laughing.

He shrugged. "I have Tanner, amongst others."

I flopped back in disbelief. Yet another thing I had no idea about. No wonder Dad and Tanner were so close.

Mom moved over to Bevin. She placed her hand on his forehead. "Brooke."

Mom and Dad moved to the door. Before opening it, Mom said, "Welcome. You are the sixth pack in the United States. River will sit you down and give you more info. You'll be introduced to the other packs. We'll train you before we send you off on your own."

I looked around the room. I couldn't believe it. I was no longer part of my parents' pack.

Eyes dancing, Owen turned to José. "Dude, you got your cats!"

**If you haven't read book 1 or 2 of the Jade Stone
Chronicles, find them here:**
Book 1: Wolf Healer: mybook.to/WolfHealer
Book 2: Epsilon: mybook.to/Epsilon

If you want to continue the story…
Book 4: Traitor: mybook.to/jade_traitor

Find back stories and updates on my website:
https://huckleberryauthor.wordpress.com

Find me on:
Facebook: https://www.facebook.com/Huckleberry-
Rahr-Author-1294822262301549
TikTok: https://www.tiktok.com/@huckleberryrahr
Instagram: https://www.instagram.com/huckleberryrahr/
Twitter: https://twitter.com/huckleberryrahr

Authors Note:

The following is a short story in Bevin's point of view. It takes place during the pride parade when he and José spend some time talking alone. Jade can't be privy to all the conversations her friends have, so in this instance, Bevin had to leap in to fill us in on what happened.

A DANCE – BEVIN'S POINT OF VIEW

"Bevin, are you ready to dance?"

Piper dragged me over to a small area that was clear.

I couldn't believe the whole group had made it to the gay pride parade. It was amazing. Right when we got here, Jade, Piper, and Sarah joined me dancing in an area we defined on the capital lawn as a dance floor. Though Jade tended to be clumsy and fall on her butt a lot, Sarah was glorious, and Piper could dance like a dream. She may not have always been confident, but she let loose when dancing.

After a few minutes Jade sashayed over to me. "Do you

know why José isn't dancing with us?"

I turned to our blanket and saw him lying on his back, propped on his elbows. Owen sat next to him, and they were talking. José tended to be the first out dancing. I shook my head. "No idea." He and I were best friends, but it had been weird ever since we returned from Las Vegas.

After I had become a werewolf, my wolf… healed me. There really wasn't a better word for it. I had been planning on surgery for my transition, but my wolf decided to take matters into his own magical paws, and suddenly I didn't have to worry about risking werewolf exposure with my desire to transition. It was the most magical spring break ever. I'd been pining over José for as long as I could remember, but he saw me as a younger sibling. When he finally met me as a werewolf, our wolves decided we should be mates.

I'd never heard of werewolf mates before. I guess they were pretty rare. Not unheard of, but rare. Jade's aunt and uncle were apparently a mated pair, but no one knew until this came up. You'd think I'd be thrilled, my dream come true. But I didn't want José because his wolf had decided it for him. I wanted him to want me, all of me. I wanted him to like me before the transition to werewolf and magical new body, not just the new me.

"Bevin, I've lost you and you smell sad." Jade looked up at me with concern as she grabbed my arms. "You okay?"

Her touch helped to center me. It was a thing with werewolves I was getting used to. Touch brought a bit of pack to you and, with it, comfort. I took a centering breath.

I forced a smile and nodded. "Yeah, let's dance!"

And we did. And shockingly, Jade stayed on her feet.

As the songs flowed, more people joined us. It was the powerful combination of Piper and Sarah. They were great dancers. Suddenly, this gorgeous man approached. He was carved from stone and taller than me, which was impressive as I was close to six feet tall. He had dark hair, dark eyes, and oozed confidence. He was the kind of guy who could have any girl he wanted.

I watched him approach, utterly entranced. It took me a few seconds to remember that we were at a gay pride parade, and to notice the rainbow painted on his pecks. He wasn't heading to Sarah, as was typical, but towards me. I gulped. Our dance area was small, and he started to dance inches from me. There was no way we wouldn't touch as we gyrated to the music.

After a few songs, I could smell his attraction. I was dumbfounded. I wasn't used to smelling emotions. I missed a beat and almost fell over. I reached out to steady myself and ended up with my hand on his six-pack abs. How much did this guy work out? He couldn't be that much older than me.

His mouth twitched and he placed his hands on my hips. My heart leapt into my throat as I gazed up into his eyes and shifted my hands up to his shoulders. My breathing was rough as we finished the song together.

An intense wave of jealously blanketed the area. My knees buckled. It was only this guy's hands on my hips that kept me from falling. He leaned down and asked softly, "You okay?"

I nodded as we danced one more song. After that, I knew it was too much. Finding his gaze I said, "I need water."

Backing up, I turned and realized only Piper from our group was left dancing. When I checked out where we had posted up, only José remained there. Taking a deep breath, I headed over and sat down next to him, hugging my knees.

"Why don't you dance?" I asked.

His eyes closed tighter. "Couldn't. Need to get control. Can't."

We sat there in silence for a few minutes. I hurt for him and didn't know what to do. We hadn't been talking since Las Vegas, not regularly. It had gotten weird, and it was hurting us both. Not knowing what to do and feeling strangely bold, I leaned over and gave him a kiss. It wasn't a peck, but it wasn't passionate. I felt him freeze. Then, I rolled over and settled on my side, back facing him.

My heart beat hard enough that I couldn't hear the music over it. My eyes were closed as I tried to slow my system down and focus on my surroundings.

I heard him move then I felt his hand on my arm. "Bevin, I don't know how to fix what is broken between us."

My heart was hurting. This was it. We were in public, but it was as private as we could make it. No one could hear us. I could say what I wanted, and only he would hear. Rolling to my back, I stared up into his sad brown eyes.

I lifted a hand to his cheek. "José, I think I've loved you my whole life, but I was always wrong." He flinched at that word as if I slapped him. "Now that I'm not, it hurts to think you only want me because I'm 'fixed' or because your wolf tells you to want me. It's tearing me up inside. I should be thrilled, but it's killing me."

He leaned down, touching his forehead to mine. "Dios mio, Bev. It isn't the wolf. I've been fighting my own instincts for a year now. Do you know what it's like to know you like guys, older guys, and to know you have this person who started off a younger close friend, and then you start to fantasize about them? I've been going out on dates since before becoming a wolf, and they have been not going well; why do you think I haven't had a steady boyfriend?"

I started to shake. I could smell his sincerity as well as his confusion in his own words. He was as messed up by this whole situation as I was.

He pulled away so that he could look me in the eyes. He slipped his hand on my shoulder near my neck. "Every time I go out with a guy, all I could think was, how soon can I get home to call you. And every time I kissed at the end of a date? I just wanted to be kissing *you*. It scared me. We're too young for what I was feeling, so I ignored it. But then the wolf entered the picture, and I couldn't ignore it any longer."

He groaned, as if trying to fight something that he

couldn't. Then he leaned down and kissed me… and it was good. My toes curled and I moaned. Oh, this was what it was supposed to feel like. He pulled back and brushed my bangs away with a small smile.

Closing his eyes, he sighed. Then he stared at me right to my soul. "Bevin, I know our wolves chose each other, but I think it was because we chose each other first. I have been trying to find a way to talk to you for months now. My heart chose you before any second nature did, and to me, that's more important. I was giving you space because I thought you just weren't interested. Now that I know you are…" He paused, clearly uncertain what to say. Finally, he looked up towards the dancers. "Can we go dance and let off some steam?"

My face broke into a huge smile. Scrambling up, we made our way over to Piper and let the music take us on a journey.

ACKNOWLEDGEMENTS

I want to thank the people who make me laugh every day and continue to encourage me to write despite the number of my words they are forced to read. Wes Imrisek and Angela Grimes take my stories and make them more. They see my vision, a bud of a story, and help me create the garden of words you see published today. My son, Gavin, brainstorms with me about every concept I need to work through. He grumbles as any good teen would, but his great mind has a whimsical way of turning my thoughts in new directions. The rest of my writers' group, Haydee Milner and Lawrence Henry, help to refine my thoughts and ideas, making me a better storyteller. And of course, my friends and family, as always, are rock stars who encourage me every step of the way. None of them seemed to think it weird that a dyslexic math teacher wanted to start writing about a wolf pack.

ABOUT THE AUTHOR

Huckleberry Rahr is a mathematics instructor at the University of Wisconsin-Whitewater. She spent many years teaching math around the Midwest and in Papua New Guinea with the Peace Corps. Her parents instilled a love of reading from a young age.

She grew up with lesbian moms who had a huge collection of women authors with heroines as the protagonist. Her favorite genre was fantasy and science fiction, that is, until she discovered urban fantasy. What her mom's library lacked were books with characters that looked like her family: diversity in background, gender identity, and sexuality. She decided if she couldn't find that series, then she would write it.